WHAT READER'S SAY...

Jerry Borrowman's skillful writing and attention to detail puts the reader front and center into one of man's greatest engineering accomplishments during the last one hundred years—the construction of the magnificent Hoover Dam. His masterful use of dialogue creates intriguing characters who bring the story to life.

—Mike Ramsdell – author of the best-selling book, *A Train to Potevka*

As an engineer at Hoover Dam I was asked to give a special guided tour to Jerry Borrowman, author of an upcoming book. I thought it would be like Gilligan's Island, "Just a three hour tour..." It ended up lasting six, and at the end of our time together I was surprised to find that a real friendship had developed, based on common interest. When a draft manuscript showed up with a request to proof-read for technical and historical facts I soon found that there was much more to the book than facts and figures, although Jerry certainly gets those right. The story was filled with the emotions of pride, stubbornness, determination, and the ugliness of prejudices that were prevalent during the Depression Era. It showed the character and dedication of the workers who lived and died constructing one of America's Seven Modern Civil Engineering Wonders--the incomparable Hoover Dam. Life and Death at Hoover Dam is a great book for readers of all ages.

—David Boyd, *Civil Engineer for the Bureau of Reclamation,*
** *Lower Colorado District, working onsite at Hoover Dam***

Being a student of history and growing up in Las Vegas since 1968, I thought I knew all about the building of Hoover Dam. I even had the chance to go scuba diving down to the old Concrete Plant, submerged in the waters of Lake Mead for the last 70 years. But Jerry Borrowman brings the construction of the dam to life in a way I did not think possible. His story of the drama in the everyday lives of the men who built the dam is a must read for anyone who has an interest in the growth of the southwestern United Sates. This is a fast paced story involving one of the greatest of American accomplishments. For all of us who have read Jerry's other books, you'll love this one. For those who are new to his writing, this is a great place to find a fascinating new author.

—Bill Gallagher

JERRY BORROWMAN'S PUBLISHED BOOKS:

NONFICTION

Three Against Hitler (coauthored with Rudi Wobbe)

A Distant Prayer (coauthored with Joseph Banks)

Beyond the Call of Duty (coauthored with Bernard Fisher)

Stories from the Life of Porter Rockwell (coauthored with John Rockwell)

FICTION

'Til the Boys Come Home

I'll Be Seeing You

As Time Goes By

Home Again at Last

One Last Chance

LIFE AND DEATH AT
HOOVER DAM

—a novel—

LIFE AND DEATH AT HOOVER DAM

Published by Black Canyon Press
Sandy, Utah

Cover design © 2010 by Jerry Borrowman
Copyright © 2010 by Jerry Borrowman

Cover Art: *Hoover Dam,* by Eden Borrowman
Photo Credits: The black-and-white photos inserted at various points in the text are in the public domain and are used with permission of the United States Department of the Interior, Bureau of Reclamation.

Printed in the United States of America
First Edition: August 2010

10 9 8 7 6 5 4 3 2 1

ISBN 978-0-9843836-0-3

LIFE AND DEATH AT

HOOVER DAM

—a novel—

JERRY BORROWMAN

Best-selling author of *'Til the Boys Come Home*

Black Canyon Press

Black Canyon on the Colorado River, twenty miles southeast of
Las Vegas, Nevada. Future site of Hoover Dam

Preface

Visionaries at the turn of the twentieth century dreamt of a monumental dam that would harness the flood and drought cycle of the great Colorado River. To do so would reclaim the vast desert lands of Southern California and Arizona by providing abundant water and electricity for agriculture, industry, and housing.

The question: where to build such a dam? An initial survey selected a site in an area known as Boulder Canyon, south of Las Vegas. Twenty-five years later, at the outset of the Great Depression, the proposed dam became a possibility with congressional authorization of the "Boulder Canyon Project." A more detailed analysis showed that Black Canyon, a few miles downstream from Boulder Canyon, had more stable bedrock to support the estimated 7 million tons of concrete that was to be the single largest structure in human history.

Since no single company in the world had the resources to complete such a massive undertaking, six Western state companies formed a consortium and won the bid at $50 million. Success would net the owners millions in profits. Failure would bankrupt them all.

Of all the resources needed to build the dam in 1931, men were the most abundant and expendable. Thousands of desperate laborers and craftsmen came from all across the United States to work on the Great Boulder Dam on the border of Nevada and Arizona. Among them were daredevil high scalers who dangled like spiders on slender threads from the rim of the one-thousand-foot-high canyon to prepare the walls of the canyon to receive the concrete of the dam. These men—indeed all who worked on the dam—engaged in a daily dance with death and disability. This story is written in their honor.

Acknowledgments

I received a lot of help from people who reviewed this story. First, I'd like to thank David Boyd, a civil engineer with the United States Bureau of Reclamation, who has worked for decades in the Lower Colorado Region at the Hoover Dam. The bureau was kind enough to allow David to spend an afternoon with me, taking me on a guided tour of the Hoover Dam, including the powerhouse and tunnels. He patiently answered all my questions about the dam and how it works. He is an interesting and enthusiastic teacher, and the tour was truly the experience of a lifetime. As we walked through the tunnels deep inside the dam, I could almost believe it was the 1930s when the dam was newly built. Later, David reviewed the manuscript for technical accuracy. His contribution and insights have been invaluable. I also appreciate Karen L. Cowen of the Bureau for her quick response to our request for copies of the high resolution photos used throughout the text, which are used with permission of the Department of the Interior.

I also employed a very dedicated panel of readers who took time to read multiple versions of the manuscript until I got it just right, including my wife, Marcella, as well as Mike Rodriguez, Norman Jenson, Bill Gallagher, David Borrowman, Evan Rowley, Eden Borrowman, and Mike Ramsdell—author of *A Train to Potevka*. Each made unique and important contributions.

Life and Death at Hoover Dam was professionally edited by two very capable and experienced editors, Val Johnson and Kirk Shaw, whose technical and substantive edits, respectively, were crucial to getting the manuscript in proper form for publishing. Mark Sorenson did a great job polishing off the cover and helping with typesetting and formatting. I had three proofreaders, including two professionals, Nan Rasmussen and Michele Preisendorf, as well as my 92-year-old mother, Geneva Borrowman, who was the last one to read the manuscript before it went to print.

I hope you enjoy the efforts of all who worked so hard to bring this story to life.

Cover Art, by Eden Borrowman

The dramatic colors and art deco sketch you see on the cover was selected after viewing hundreds of photos and sketches. Unfortunately, we never found one that was quite right—it's remarkably difficult to find a cover that captures the intense emotions of the Great Depression, the grandeur of the completed Hoover Dam, and the drama in the lives of the people who were involved in building the dam.. Fortunately, I had a terrific graphics artist to help me; my daughter-in-law, Eden Borrowman, who asked if she could try her hand at an original drawing. I believe her final design for this cover effectively captures the colors, the fonts, and the heroic conventions that are true to the period while creating a sense of mystery and intrigue. Of particular note is her original pencil drawing, based on a number of photos I took while visiting the dam during my research for the story,

I hope you enjoy Eden's meticulous attention to detail as much as I do and that her artwork adds to your appreciation of the story.

*"I give waters in the wilderness, and
rivers in the desert, to give drink to my people."*
Isaiah 43:20

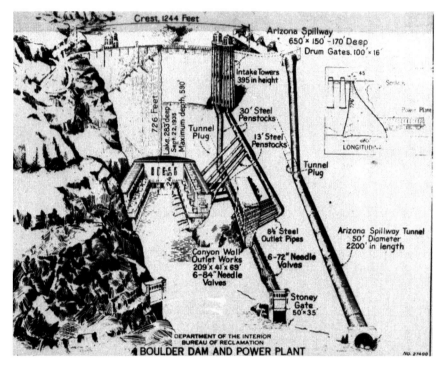

Original construction diagram of the massive Boulder Dam (later Hoover) Dam)

CHAPTER I
The Most Coveted Jobs in America

Black Canyon on the Colorado River—Site of Hoover Dam

That's all, gentlemen—let's get to it. David, can you stay and talk to me for a minute?"

David Conroy glanced up, surprised at the request. "Sure, Frank." He stepped to the side as the other engineers started to collect their things. David had been at the dam site for just a couple of months, having been selected as one of a dozen or so managing engineers by his old friend and associate Frank Crowe, superintendent of the Six Companies Consortium that had won the contract to build the Hoover Dam. At a bid of $50 million, it was the most expensive public works project in history, and Frank was the one who would build it. He was the most important figure in all of Nevada at that particular moment.

"Just let me settle this with Henry," said Frank.

David nodded and Frank was quickly lost in a set of blueprints. Left alone with his thoughts, David reflected on the phone call that had brought him to Nevada. It was easily the best day of his life, from a professional point of view, and he had made immediate plans to travel from his home in Boise, Idaho to Las Vegas to interview for a position.

Frank Crowe, 1931

In this year of 1931 when economic activity in the United States had slowed to a crawl, there were dozens if not hundreds of men applying for every position on the project. David recognized his good fortune in having worked with Frank on previous projects, including construction of the Arrowrock Dam east of Boise in 1912—the tallest concrete dam in the world at the time. The techniques they pioneered building Arrowrock made it a forerunner of the great Hoover Dam that was now to take form in the Arizona-Nevada desert. Since arriving, he'd been working on project plans, but he would shortly move to the high-scaling project that would prepare the canyon walls to accept the unprecedented weight of the gigantic concrete dam.

As the consulting engineer, Henry, started rolling up his plans, David moved to the front of the room where Frank had shifted his attention to another diagram, the features on his lean face drawn in such intense concentration that David decided not to bother him. Finally, though, he cleared his throat, which startled Frank.

"What? Oh, David. Sorry. You should have said something." David knew a reply wasn't necessary, so he just waited as Frank came around the table. He motioned to a chair. David sat down, not knowing whether to be excited or scared.

"So how do you like it down here in Hell's Furnace?"

"I knew it was going to be hot—I just had no idea it would turn into such an oven in March."

"It's terrible on the men. Do you know that it was over 120 degrees in the sun the other day? By July it's expected to reach that even in the shade, which means that working conditions could become intolerable once we start excavating the tunnels."

David knew how serious this was. It was almost unthinkable to ask men to work in that kind of heat, particularly when the new tunnels were started. Yet it was vital that they finish the four giant diversion tunnels before the 1932 spring runoff. Each tunnel was to be five stories high and capable of carrying most of the Colorado's flow by itself in the dry months of the year. It would take at least two tunnels to handle a normal spring runoff, three to handle the highest water flows on record. The fourth would be built to provide for an unimaginable deluge. That was the problem. They had to imagine the worst because if, after they started working on the new dam itself, the Colorado managed to swamp the huge cofferdam (a temporary dam used during construction) that would be built upstream from the construction site, it could wreck the whole project. If they fell behind schedule, the government would impose stiff financial penalties that could easily bankrupt the company. That was the kind of pressure Frank was working under.

Frank continued. "At any rate, we've got to do everything possible to manage the environment inside those tunnels. I've got to get water to the men, and I've got to get as much ventilation as possible. We've already had one death, although it isn't directly due to conditions in the work area."

David nodded, not really knowing how this applied to him. "We've been watching you, David, and have decided that you're the one to work on the problem. No one expects miracles—the environment is what it is. But I need somebody down there who is constantly monitoring the situation and coming up with ways to get air and cooling to those men."

"You're planning on evaporative coolers?"

"Already started." Frank looked away for a moment and then added, "There's also the problem of carbon monoxide."

David's stomach tightened. "What about converting to electric or diesel trucks? That would eliminate the problem."

"Not going to happen. We don't have time."

"But Nevada law . . ."

"Doesn't apply to us. The feds are in charge of the reservation, and they're backing us up. You got a problem with that?"

David bit his lower lip—a nervous tic of his. With unemployment approaching 30 percent, it wasn't smart to cross your boss, particularly since it was obvious that Frank's mind was made up. Still, he nodded. "If you want an honest answer—yes, I think we should convert. Until the two ends of each tunnel connect, it will be impossible to get a cross breeze, and the inside of the uncompleted tunnels will be blue with a carbon monoxide haze."

Frank's eyes were cold. "Like I said, David, it's not going to happen. So we need to do the best we can. That's why I'm talking to you."

"And if I don't want to do what you ask?"

Frank stood up. "It's not a democracy around here. There are jobs to be done, and I decide who does them."

David braced himself. It was time to decide. Or maybe it was too late. He could see Frank clenching his hands, and he fully expected to hear that he was fired. But after a deep breath, Frank demanded, "Well?"

David shook his head. "You're asking me to be in charge of ventilation, yet you're not willing to take my first piece of advice. Will I be second-guessed on everything, or will I have control?" It was risky to push back, but David also knew that Frank had little respect for "yes men." It was a calculated risk.

"Look, I don't like this any better than you. But right now I've got millions of dollars sitting on the sideline while we wait for those tunnels. It's not just the money it would take to convert the trucks, although that would probably run close to a quarter of a million dollars. It's the time. If we miss the construction deadline, I'll have people sitting on their rumps for a whole year. I just can't do it. I won't do it. The board of directors wouldn't tolerate it."

David nodded. It was certainly Frank's right to make the decision. He was the superintendent. The only question now was whether or not he'd be the one in charge of the tunnels. Did you take on a project even when you objected to it?

Frank sat down heavily. "I can't give you a pass on this, David—not and have any leadership authority left. I need someone to figure out how to ventilate the tunnels, and I think you're the best man for the job. But I'm not going to convert the trucks. So you've got to decide if you'll take this assignment or not. You know what it means if you decide not to."

David nodded. His heart was racing. After all of the piddly projects he'd worked on in Boise over the past three years, the thought of going back to that life was almost painful. Still, he knew there was only grief in front of him if he agreed.

"Come on, David—do you want me to assign some cold-blooded jerk who doesn't care about the men? If you do this, at least you'll do everything you can to make conditions better for them. Isn't that better than insisting on your principles and walking out of here?"

"What about control?" David asked. "I understand that we're not going to make a conversion, so that's just a fact to be dealt with now. But if I take on the job, do I have authority to demand requisitions and even to shut the job down temporarily if I believe things are getting too dangerous?"

Frank inhaled sharply. "It better not happen often. I can't stand the sight of idle men." David relaxed a little. Frank noticed. "So you'll do it?"

David nodded. "As long as we understand each other. And you need to explain it to Woody. He'll try to run right over the top of me, you know."

Frank smiled. "That'll be harder than he expects."

David relented and smiled. "I'm glad you thought of me, even if I have to deal with less than ideal conditions."

"Actually, it wasn't me. It was Walker Young who asked for you. I think he took your measure pretty accurately. He doesn't want people getting sick any more than I do. We all just want to get on with the job."

"Walker Young, the Bureau of Reclamation's on-site construction engineer? I had no idea he knew anything about me."

"Never underestimate 'Slow-Down Young.' He doesn't miss a thing." Young called Frank Crowe "Hurry-Up," making them the perfect pair.

David stood up. "Well, then, I've got some very hot men to take care of." He said this to end the conversation gracefully, but it wasn't necessary. Frank had already moved on to the next task, oblivious to the fact that David was still there.

The Los Angeles Highway South of Las Vegas—April 1931

"Hey, Nick. What are you doing? Pull over!"

Nick glanced in his rearview mirror at the stranded car with a steaming radiator. "I'm not pulling over for a stranger. His radiator's boiling over, and mine's about to overheat. The last thing we need is to get stuck on the side of the road trying to help him."

"Come on—you can see the guy's in trouble." Tony reached over and made a grab for the steering wheel.

"Knock it off, Tony. It's my car, and I'm not taking the chance."

"What chance? It's a brand new car. You never know—he might be grateful. Besides, you'd want help if it was you."

Nick stared straight ahead, trying to ignore his conscience.

"Ten to one says that anybody who can afford a brand-new Buick is some kind of big shot on the Hoover Dam project—who else would have that kind of money here in Las Vegas?" Tony waited, but all he got was silence. "Besides, I'm going to give you a good swift kick if you don't turn around . . ."

"Oh, for crying out loud; go ahead and kick me. I can't wait to get to Las Vegas to get rid of you."

With that Nick flipped the wheel, whipping the poor old '21 Ford pickup truck into such a sharp turn that its threadbare tires squealed on the sticky asphalt pavement. It also nearly threw Tony right out the passenger door.

"Hey, watch it! You're going to bruise me." Tony rubbed his right arm dramatically. "The last thing I need is to be banged up for my job interview tomorrow."

"Job interview. You still think they're going to talk to two Italians? After all the crap we've taken at every gas station and grocery store we've stopped at along this miserable trip?" Nick shook his head. "If you're lucky you'll get a job washing dishes at some Las Vegas dive, but you definitely won't get one of the high-paying jobs at the dam. You need to look in the mirror and wake up—your face is Latin, not white."

"We're Americans. No discrimination—that's what the flyer said. Open to American citizens, and that's us. I'm going to hold them to it."

They'd argued about this often enough that Nick didn't pursue it. As he made his way back to the stranded car, he flipped a gentler U-turn and pulled up next to the man standing by the car so Tony could talk to him.

"Hey, mister, want to trade cars? Ours is older, but it's got water in the radiator."

The guy laughed. "Maybe not yet, but as hot as it is out here you should come back in an hour just in case nobody else has stopped. I'll be so dehydrated by then I'll probably give you the car and my stock portfolio to boot."

"A stock portfolio! We've hit the big time, Nicholas." Tony laughed and jumped out of the car. "Permanent problem, or do you just need some water?" He looked for any sign of trouble, but the guy didn't so much as blink.

"Just low on water. I should have stopped miles ago but I thought I could make it. I really could use the help. I have a tab at Joey's, and I'd be happy to buy you a hamburger and a cold beer to make it up to you."

Tony cocked his head. "Joey's?"

"You must be new to Las Vegas. Otherwise you'd know that Joey's is the classiest bar in Nevada."

"Well, then, you've got a deal. About the only thing we do have is water." Tony made his way to the front of the Ford where they'd slung a canvas bag over the grill so that evaporation would keep the water inside the bag cool as they crossed the desert.

Nick moved close to him and whispered, "I told you we are running hot. Don't give it all to him." Tony ignored him and went over to the overheated car.

"My friend says this water has got to get both of us to town. How far is it, anyway?"

"Only about ten miles. I won't need a lot. You'd think a brand-new car like this would have a big enough radiator to handle this kind of heat, but it doesn't. I've had to stop twice. I simply underestimated how hot it would run." With that he reached through the open window of the car, pulled out a rag, and used it to gingerly remove the radiator cap. There was a huge sigh of steam as a small cloud of mist shot up into the air.

After making sure the radiator was fully vented, Tony stepped forward and poured in about half the contents of the water bag. He heard Nick grinding his teeth, but chose to ignore it.

The man replaced the radiator cap and turned to Tony. "I can't thank you enough," he said, and stuck out his hand. ·

It shocked Tony so much to have a white person offer him his hand that he hesitated, but even at that the guy didn't pull back. Finally, Tony reached out and took his hand. "You're welcome."

They stepped back from each other. Then the guy's face reddened, and he said, "What a jerk. I haven't even introduced myself. My name's Pete. Pete Conroy."

Tony nodded. "Tony Capelli. And my friend here is Nick Perry."

Pete returned the smile and stuck his hand out to Nick. "Well, you guys saved my butt. There's no question about that. I'd be glad to pay you."

Tony shook his head. "Nah. The water was free."

"I'm serious about Joey's. At least let me buy you a beer."

"Like they'd let us in the place . . ." Nick mumbled.

Pete turned and looked at Nick, by far the more serious of the two. "They actually would let you in as my guests. Not everybody might like it, but they would do it. Joey's a regular guy, and you're not the only Italian workers in Nevada."

"Any on the Hoover Dam project?" Tony asked quickly, his voice betraying a hint of anxiety for the first time in the conversation.

"Oh? So you're here to work on the dam?"

Tony nodded. Then his shoulders slumped as he saw the look on Pete's face. "So, there is a problem?"

Pete shook his head. "I don't know. It's supposed to be open recruiting. But I haven't seen any Italians—is it all right if I call you that? I don't mean any offense by it."

"It's fine—that's our race, after all, but we're Americans first. My family's lived in Southern California for nearly thirty years. It took us nearly ten years to become citizens. So we're American through and through."

Pete nodded and took a deep breath, letting it out slowly. "Well, the fact is I don't know if that will cause a problem or not. I heard that they weren't hiring any Negroes until the NAACP threw a fit. Now they've pretended to make up for it by hiring eight or nine black guys out of a couple thousand workers, but they treat them like crap." He frowned. "I doubt you'll be treated like they are, but you just don't see a lot of anyone but Smiths and Joneses around here. I don't want to discourage you, but that's what I've seen."

"I tried to tell him that," said Nick. "It's stupid that we're even up here, but you don't tell Tony much of anything."

Pete shrugged. "Listen. There's no harm in trying. There really are some great jobs that need to be filled. Just be prepared to stand up to for yourself."

Tony nodded. "Well, it's nothing I didn't expect. I hoped it might be different. I want a job real bad, and as Nick here can tell you, I often get what I want."

"That's the problem," said Nick. "Sometimes what he wants isn't what's good for him."

Las Vegas

MARVIN DENNEY LOOKED UP AND sneered. "Capelli? You're a *Wop*, aren't you? Just what are you doing here asking for a job? No foreigners allowed, and that includes Italians." He purposely used the long "I" sound when he pronounced Italian.

"I'm an American just like you. I've lived in California most of my life." He wanted to add, ". . . you ignorant jerk," but held his tongue. He needed the job. He pointed to his naturalization papers. "See—right there."

Marvin shook his head and turned to his companion, Charles "Chick" Flemming, and said in a loud voice, "His name is Capelli. There's another one right behind him. We don't need their type, do we, Chick?"

Flemming was the smoother of the two Six Company recruiters, and he realized that to blatantly turn away a bona fide citizen could cause some trouble. After all, the contract with the federal government specifically required no discrimination in hiring, except on the basis of U.S. citizenship. But in spite of that, nearly all of the Irish, Italians, Negroes, Mexicans, and Filipinos who had applied so far had found it impossible to gain employment—all for perfectly legal reasons—so, this situation called for finesse of a type that Marvin, Chick's oversized friend, was incapable of exhibiting.

"Let me see Mr. Capelli's paperwork."

Scowling, Marvin handed it to him.

Chick took the paper, studying it carefully for a few moments. "Anthony . . .

"You can call me Tony. That's what my friend's call me."

Flemming nodded. "All in good order, Tony. I assume your friend here has his papers as well?"

Nick nodded. Marvin started to interrupt with an indignant, "What? You can't be serious—they're Catholics!" but Chick cut him off and told him to shut up.

"Well, Mr. Capelli, you're eligible for work, but unfortunately there's nothing here that tells me you're qualified for any of the positions we have open."

"No one asked what I'm qualified for. Besides, you just hired ten men for general labor—those men, right over there. I know we're qualified for that."

"Ah, yes, we did, and that filled the quota for this morning. You can always come back tomorrow and try—"

"There are another fifty behind me—you're not going to turn all of them away, are you?" Tony's spoken English was perfect, with only the slightest hint of an Italian lilt to it.

"I told you there were no jobs," Chick said. "Now move along."

Nick tried to grab him, but Tony didn't budge. "I asked you if you are going to turn away everyone in the line behind me, because if you turn me away and hire them I'll file a complaint with the Bureau of Reclamation."

Marvin jumped up and doubled his fist. "How dare you—" but before he could do anything, Chick forced him back into his seat with a firm push against his massive shoulder.

"It's a perfectly fair question, Mr. Capelli," Chick said. "The fact is that I will not turn all these men away because most of them have the specialized skills we need."

"Which are?"

"Which are none of your business. Now step aside."

Tony needed this job. He needed it more than anything he'd ever needed in the world. Ever since the big flood some twenty years earlier had wiped out the canal that brought Colorado River water to his land in Imperial Valley, their crops had been infrequent and malnourished—getting only the water that occasional monsoon rains could produce. So he had been forced to eke out a living working for the railroad. Then came the Great Depression. With the onset of the depression, it was the Filipinos, Italians, Indians and Mexicans who had been fired first, and Tony had lost his relatively high-paying job on the railroad. After that, it was catch as catch can. Now, with this dam project opening up, he hoped to both earn a living for the next six or seven years and help build the infrastructure needed to finally bring water to his farm. The great Hoover Dam was central to providing a steady, controlled flow of water year round to the fertile fields of Southern California. Tony had other reasons for wanting to work on the dam, but he wasn't about to share them with Chick and Marvin.

Rather than argue, he leaned forward just a bit and said quietly, "I really need a job, Mr. Flemming. I've come all the way from California—it's our river—please help me."

Chick backed away. It was as disconcerting to him as it was galling to Tony to ask for a favor. Chick hated the feeling of having his emotions stirred even a little bit by Tony's sincerity. Even so, he had absolutely no intention of hiring an Italian. Not with so many white men out of work and waiting for a job. "Look, we need people experienced in mining and handling explosives, and we don't have time for fools to learn on the job. There's nothing in your application to show that you've done either. Right now, we're blasting the diversion tunnels, so you and your friend will have to move along and come back another time when we're hiring general labor.

Sorry, but that's the way it is. Now get out of the line so I can talk to the next man."

Tony clenched and unclenched his hands. He had to work really hard to avoid a fight when his Latin temper flared, and he was seconds away from it right now. "I can do the work, and you've no right—"

"What's the trouble here?"

The voice that came from behind Tony was firm and confident, but it was also quite soft, which was why he was so surprised by Marvin's and Chick's reactions.

"Nothing. There's nothing wrong here, Mr. Conroy," Chick stammered, only to be interrupted by Marvin, who added, "We was just explaining to this Dago that we don't have no job that's suitable for him or his friend."

If looks could kill, Marvin would have died on the spot, cut down by Chick's withering glance.

"Dago?" The voice was incredulous. Tony turned to see who was talking and was surprised to see a sharply dressed man, probably in his early forties, standing directly behind him. At 5' 10" the man was about his same height. He looked trim, fit, and well tanned. It was easy to see that he was someone important, even without the reaction of the two oafs.

Ignoring the two recruiters, Conroy asked Tony and Nick, "What kind of work are you looking for?"

"I told him we need experienced explosive men," Chick interrupted, "but he's just tying up the line . . ."

The man turned on Chick and said, "I'm talking, Mr. Flemming. I'll ask the questions, he'll answer, and you'll stay quiet. Do you understand?"

Chick's face turned beet red, but he nodded.

"Now, what are you looking for?" He glanced toward Nick. "I assume he's with you?"

Tony was so dumbstruck by the exchange that he stumbled in his reply. "Well?"

"Yes, sir." Tony felt like a child pleading his case to a sympathetic adult, which irritated him, but he needed help. "We need anything we can get. I'll work with explosives if that's where the jobs are. I'm a fast learner, believe me."

"You're small. That would be an advantage on high scaling, but those jobs aren't open yet. It looks like you're pretty athletic. Do you think you could take the strain of inspecting explosive charges and then running like the dickens when you've made sure everyone else is out of the tunnel?"

"Absolutely."

"You're not afraid of dark, enclosed places?"

Although Tony had no idea what this question implied, he quickly shook his head, even though he did get a bit frantic sometimes when he was in a tight place. He had already committed himself, so he didn't say anything.

He then asked Nick the same question, and Nick just nodded, though he looked absolutely miserable.

"Good." Then, turning to the recruiters he said, "I'll take both of these men on one of my crews. Do it on my authority."

"He's inexperienced, and he's a, he's—you know . . ."

"He's a what?"

Recognizing that he'd been bested, Chick replied curtly, "He's taking up too much of our time. He thrust some paperwork into Tony's hands. "Fill this out, assuming you can write, and give it back to me. Both of you should report here tomorrow morning for orientation."

Tony was relieved, but it took him a moment to regain his composure. "Okay . . . sure, I'll have this back to you in ten minutes."

"Fine, now get out of the way."

Tony grabbed a pencil and quickly stepped to the side.

By this time, the man who had hired him had already turned to walk away. "Hey, Mister… Mr. Conroy?"

"It's David. I'm a supervising engineer." He extended a hand, which Tony shook quickly.

"You don't have a brother, by chance?"

"Oh no. You haven't met Pete, have you?"

"Yes, we helped him out in the desert yesterday. His car had boiled over—"

"*His* car? Did he tell you it was his car?"

"He did," said Tony. Nick nodded.

"It's *my* car. He borrowed it and refused to take extra water. Said he'd be fine. I told him it doesn't matter how good a car you have, it gets hot in this place." David Conroy shook his head. "His car? Everything went fine? Oh, I'll have him for this."

"Listen, I didn't mean to cause trouble. He was really very nice to us, and I was just surprised that the only two guys who have been decent to us have the same last name."

David cracked a small smile. "It's all right. I'm on good terms with my brother. This is perfectly normal for Pete—vintage, in fact. I appreciate what you did for him."

Tony turned his head, gave Nick a knowing look, then turned back to David. "Anyway, "I want to thank you for helping us. We really do need the work."

David took a moment to size Tony up. "No problem, although I've got a feeling you really don't know what you're getting yourself into when it comes to explosives and tunnels." He saw Nick nod his head ever so slightly. Nick was apparently not as excited about all this as Tony was.

"I will learn," said Tony.

"So I figured. Try to get some sleep tonight since you'll have to meet the bus tomorrow morning at six a.m. for the ride out to the canyon."

"Yes, sir, I will."

David stared at him for a few more seconds. "Once those thugs give you your identification papers, go to the cafeteria and get some food. It looks to me like you two haven't eaten for a while."

Tony looked down at his slight frame in embarrassment. It was true. He hadn't had anything to eat today, and very little yesterday. It had taken almost all their money just to get to Las Vegas. "Do we need money to eat at this cafeteria?"

"Not now. There is a daily charge, but they'll put it on your bill and subtract it from your pay each week. The price is reasonable—$1.50 per day for three big meals of all you can eat. It's one of the best things about this job—unlimited food. Eat as much as you want for breakfast, take as many sandwiches as you like for lunch, and then at night you can come back and have a full dinner. Even better, the food tastes pretty good. The cafeteria is near the dormitories. These guys will see that you know where to go. They won't cross me."

"This just gets better all the time," said Tony as he slapped Nick on the arm.

David smiled. There was something infectious about Tony's energy. "All right, then, I've got to get going. It turns out that Pete is a crew foreman on the upcoming high-scaling project, and he has some problem he wants to talk over with me—something about how dynamite needs special handling when it gets hotter than 110 degrees out here, and those temperatures will probably be here next week."

Tony was impressed. Not only was this man an engineer, but his brother was a foreman. No wonder Marvin and Chick had been afraid of him.

"Perhaps I'm better prepared for the heat since I grew up near Los Angeles. I'm used to it."

"Well, you'll need to be. We expect that the heat will go above 130 degrees in the tunnels. We're doing our best to fix that, but it's pure torture, I won't kid you."

David left, and Tony and Nick went over to the makeshift table that had been set up for the new hires to complete their paperwork. When they sat down, Tony noticed that his hands were trembling. He really had been terrified of being turned down. Now after such a close call he found it hard to hold the pencil to the paper. Forcing himself to calm down, he smiled and whispered to Nick, "We've got a job—a high-paying job. And all the food we can eat."

"We've got a whole bunch of people who hate us . . ."

"Hate us? They just don't know us yet. When they do they're going to love us."

Nick nodded in the direction of Marvin and Chick. When Tony glanced in that direction, Marvin sneered at him. Well, maybe it wasn't a sneer, but whatever it was, it was unsettling. "Well, maybe not love us . . ."

Nick took a deep breath. He hated it here, already.

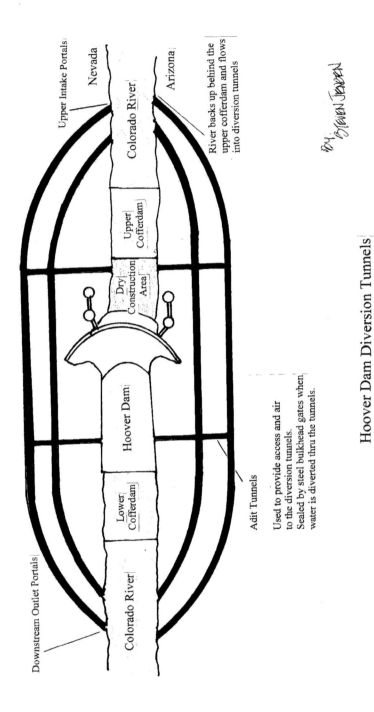

Upper Intake Portals

Nevada

Colorado River

Arizona

River backs up behind the upper cofferdam and flows into diversion tunnels

Upper Cofferdam

Dry Construction Area

Hoover Dam

Lower Cofferdam

Downstream Outlet Portals

Colorado River

Adit Tunnels

Used to provide access and air to the diversion tunnels. Sealed by steel bulkhead gates when water is diverted thru the tunnels.

Hoover Dam Diversion Tunnels

CHAPTER 2
Tunnels

Arizona Bank of the Colorado—May 16, 1931

Listen up!" Woody Williams spoke with such authority that all the men, including David Conroy, fell instantly silent. The group stood at the bottom of Black Canyon, next to the Colorado River, surrounded by jackhammers, diesel generators, and other construction equipment. Woody was at the front of the group next to a portable blackboard.

Woody scowled. "In just a few minutes some of you are gonna slam your jackhammers into that ugly red wall to place the first charges of dynamite to start the excavation of the first tunnel. When it goes off it's gonna sound like a blast right out of hell, because that's where we're all going to be working for the next eighteen months. If you get your minds settled to that fact, you'll be all right. If not, you'll either get yourself killed or you'll go home whimpering like a beaten puppy."

He smiled, pleased at the effect his words had. "In the meantime, we're in a race against the water. We have to get this river turned by late fall, or there won't be time to build the cofferdams that will bracket the construction site and keep it free of water and debris. A delay into 1933 will throw the whole project off schedule. So right now, you're in the single most important work area of this project. Everything depends on you. Any questions?"

"Why tunnels, sir? Won't the water leak through them when all this is done?"

Williams sighed. "David, why don't you take a few minutes to explain all this to them. It won't hurt for them to understand exactly what we're going after."

Woody Williams was the man in charge of building the tunnels, even though he was just twenty-nine years old. He'd been personally selected by Frank Crowe to be his number-two man, and the fact that he was in charge of this part of the project showed just how vital it was. David was to work with him on how to keep the air as clean as possible. It wasn't going to be easy working together, since William's personality was a lot more like Pete Conroy's than David's. He was a hard-drinking, often obnoxious fellow who pushed men past the breaking point. He did know tunneling, though, and that was all Frank Crowe was interested in.

David stepped forward and turned to the men. "Right. "Let me draw a simple sketch to show how it works," David continued. Using chalk and a slate blackboard, he drew a diagram of the project.

Here's what we're going to do. The goal is to divert the entire flow of the Colorado River away from the dam site for up to five years. In heavy flood years, the river can run up to 100,000 cubic feet per second, which is about 180 million gallons of water per minute. On a normal project a diversion canal could be dug with relative ease, but as you can see, we're sitting at the bottom of a 1,000-foot gorge, not much wider than the river itself, which leaves no place for the water to go. So we have to build four giant tunnels, each 56 feet in diameter and nearly three quarters of a mile long that will run parallel to the river through the canyon walls. Each tunnel will be five stories tall and capable of handling 50,000 cubic feet of water per second. So with all four tunnels open, we can handle double the worst the Colorado can throw at us."

"To isolate the construction area from Colorado River water, we'll build two temporary earthen dams, called cofferdams. The upper cofferdam will be fairly large and will back up the river in such a way that it forces the water into the diversion tunnels. The lower cofferdam will keep the water that exits the diversion tunnels at the downstream outlet portals from back-washing into the construction area. When the tunnels have been fully bored out and cleared of debris, we'll line the tunnels with three feet of concrete and then divert the river. It's going to be miserable, as Mr. Williams indicated, but it can be done. Any questions?"

Before anyone could respond, Williams stepped forward. "All right, that's enough of that. You'll all figure this out when the last of the tunnels is lined with concrete and water's flowing through all of them. In the meantime, let's get going. Take up your positions."

With that the miners picked up their tools and moved to their designated places. Immediately the ping of the jackhammers started chattering and reverberating off the canyon walls. David leaned over to Woody and said, "At least we have a landing to stand on here in Arizona. How are you going to do it on the Nevada side?"

Williams grinned. "That's gonna be real exciting. We'll have to float a barge down and tether it to the walls. Then we'll drive ringbolts into the sides of the canyon and string another cable bridge. The men will have to work from that until we get a landing carved out big enough to operate from."

"Impressive." In fact, it was absolutely amazing, although David didn't say so. Men blasting rock from barges and cable bridges. He could imagine that Frank Crowe had something to do with that particular piece of planning.

"Well, I'm off," Williams said. "We're working off limited power, you know, so do your best to keep the demands for electricity to the very minimum."

David nodded. What Williams meant, of course, was that David should use as little diesel fuel as possible to power the air circulators so that more was left for powering the drilling equipment. Williams, far more than Crowe, was interested in finishing the job regardless of its effect on the workers.

"I'll do what I can, but heat exhaustion carries its own price."

Williams bit his lower lip and his voice became strained. "I understand that, David, but resources are limited, so we all have to work together. Besides, manpower is the least of our worries. We have more than enough lining up at the recruiting office every day."

David took a moment to measure his response. "I hear you, Woody. But we can do the job fast *and* right. You worry about your part; I'll worry about mine."

Williams's hot temper flashed. "I get the point, David. Just don't slow me down."

"Of course." Then David added a bit superfluously, "I won't be the enemy of progress."

"Good." Woody tipped his head and took off toward the flimsy swinging bridge that would take him across the river and back to the Nevada side.

David turned to watch the men at work. He knew he was in for a constant fight for resources and wondered if he was up to it. In different times the men could threaten a work stoppage or strike if conditions became unbearable, but he had a suspicion those days were behind them. With the Herbert Hoover Administration unsympathetic to workers, they were on their own. And, for better or worse, Frank had placed him squarely in the middle of one of the most controversial decisions the consortium could have made.

Glancing toward the side of the rock cliff, David was pleased to see Tony Capelli working very carefully but quickly as he carried an explosive charge forward to his assigned miner. Tony was to be a nipper—one of the men who carried to the miner and his assigned chuck tender everything they needed to drill the holes, load the explosive charges, and then with-draw in time for the blast. It was a frantic sort of job that required Tony to pay constant attention to the chuck tender, usually communicating with hand signals so he could get the driller and the chuck tender whatever was needed. Any delay would stall the work and was sure to bring a reprimand. It was a crucial job, which meant the foreman must have seen talent in Tony to give it to him. It was also one of the most dangerous jobs since he would be hand carrying the explosive charges. That offered an alternative explana-tion as to why Tony was given the task. Either way, he was working, and that was what he wanted. His friend Nick was a general laborer, which paid less but wasn't nearly as dangerous. He'd be hauling out debris after a blast, in addition to other odd jobs. As David turned to leave, he caught Tony's eye for a moment, and Tony tipped his head at him.

A few minutes later David stood panting on the other side of the river, trying to calm the fear he always felt when he went across the swinging bridge. As he moved to one of the electric slings Crowe had designed to pull people straight up the side of the canyon wall, he felt the thud of a dynamite concussion across the channel. Glancing that way, he saw the puff of smoke and pile of debris that indicated that the first charge had gone off success-fully. The men were cheering even as some started hauling off the debris while the other skilled workers started preparing for the next round.

"And so it begins . . ." David looked at the river, wondering if it had any idea what was in store for it. Then he laughed at himself for personifying a river as the sling started its rapid ascent up the canyon wall.

Workers' Cafeteria

DAVID RAISED HIS ARM AND motioned for Tony and Nick to come over to his table. Although it looked like Nick was a bit disconcerted by the invita-tion, David being an engineer and all, Tony smiled widely and brought his tray and sat down.

"Hello, Mr. Conroy, both of you Mr. Conroys."

"Davy was kind of surprised to find out that we knew each other," said Pete.

"And Pete was kind of embarrassed to explain how you knew each other," David replied evenly.

Tony looked back and forth between them, not knowing what to say. Then Pete burst into a grin. "It's all right. Davy and I worked it all out." He stood up from behind the table and shook Tony's hand. "Good to see you again. I'm glad you got a job." While Pete was totally unaware of the stares this simple act precipitated, Tony, Nick, and David noticed.

Pete sat back down. "So my brother tells me you're a nipper. How's that going?"

"It's all right. I haven't had to run like this for twenty years or so, but I'm getting used to it. It's real motivating knowing there's a hole filled with dynamite in the rock wall behind you that 's getting ready to blow up." He laughed. "It'll be all right if I live through it."

"If you don't mind my asking, I'm curious what brought you here. Pete and I have both worked construction our whole adult lives, but it's new to you."

"I'm a farmer, actually. If our land is ever to be profitable we need Colorado River water, so it's crucial that this dam be built to prevent floods and to deliver water year round. With controlled river water, we can grow crops in any season. Without it, you can't depend on anything. We nearly lost our farm to a flood in 1907. Since then we haven't had water, except for rain. And there's not a lot of rain in the Imperial Valley."

"So how can you be a farmer if your farm doesn't have water? And how can one flood knock out your water supply for more than twenty years? It must have been some flood," said Pete.

"Yeah, it was," said Nick. "It was the flood to end all floods. It killed Tony's father, and it wiped my family out financially. That's what drove us up here. We need the money."

Pete started to ask another question, but David interrupted him. "Listen, if it's personal you don't need to talk about it."

"It's okay," said Tony. "It was a long time ago. But it's kind of a long story. Do you really want to hear it?"

"Sure," said Pete. "I love disaster stories. Besides, what else is there to do here in Eden since there are no nightclubs or bars? Let's talk about farming in Southern California."

"Well, it works like this. The Imperial Valley sits just north of the border between Mexico and California. It's part of a giant sink, some three hundred miles across. So most of the land is below sea level."

"A sink?"

"Like a big bowl," David filled in. "Geologists think it was once part of the Gulf of California, but sedimentation from the Colorado River just east of it eventually separated it from the rest of the gulf. All the water then evaporated, and now it's mostly sand. A great big hole in the desert. Do I have that right?"

Tony nodded. "Because the valley is lower than the Colorado, some land promoters at the end of the last century figured out that if they cut a canal from the river into the sink, they could use gravity to irrigate the area.

The land is fertile enough that we can grow about anything, particularly with a year-round growing season. They actually circulated advertisements in southern Italy where my father lived. It was a big reason he decided to immigrate to America."

"And the canal idea worked?"

"It did. They cut a canal mostly on American soil that opened the valley to settlement. Many people bought land, including my father. Our first few years were great, and it looked like we'd be able to make a go of it with no problem."

"So what happened?"

"The first canal silted over, making the canal worthless."

"And all of you who owned land were without water."

"Exactly. So to avoid lawsuits, the developer cut a new canal that started to the south of us in Mexico, and water started flowing again. The problem was that he didn't have enough money to build a reliable head gate, coupled with the fact that the slope from that direction into the valley is much steeper."

Colorado River water flowing unrestricted into the Imperial Valley of Southern California. At this point the cut is one hundred feet and growing. This water created the Salton Sea that still exists today, southeast of Palm Springs, California.

David shook his head. "So it was a disaster waiting to happen. An unusually high water flow could wash out the head gate and send water streaming into the valley—"

"And just who said this is your story?" Pete interjected.

"No, he's exactly right," said Nick. "The flood in 1907 was so severe that in a matter of weeks the opening to the canal was more than half a mile wide and growing with nearly the full flow of the Colorado River at flood stage ravaging its way down to the bottom of the sink. The force of the flow cut into the sandy soil and started to erode its way back toward the opening of the canal. At one point it formed a waterfall that was more than one hundred feet high—if it had kept going, it would have been three hundred feet by the time it reached the Arizona border. There would have been no stopping it then, and they figure the river would have continued to pour into the valley until the entire area was underwater and became part of the gulf again. It would have been a disaster for all of us. Believe me, it was an awesome, terrible thing."

Pete shook his head and whistled. "Wow. Now that's a great story. But how did that ruin your water supply?"

"They sealed the canal," said Tony, "although it took some incredible effort to do so. I worked on the railroad trestle they built out into the water. Sometimes we'd be dropping dirt into the mouth of the river with water up over the tracks. It was pretty frightening. But the death knell for our farm was that the 'New River,' as the remnant of the canal came to be called, cut a cleft so deep into the desert sand that it left our head gates and ditches high and dry with no way to get water to them. Now the only time we can get a crop is during the monsoon season when we get some rain." Tony had become quite agitated in the telling of this story.

"And the rest of the year?" Pete asked.

"I worked for the Southern Pacific Railroad until I got laid off last year. That's why I decided to come up here. Now nobody is hiring. I just need a job."

Nick spoke up. "Our land was completely covered in water, and there was nothing we could do about it. The flood created a huge lake, called the Salton Sea, and our property is at the bottom of it. So I've spent my life working for other people. Including, sometimes, Tony here. But now this great big dam you're going to build can solve the problem. Once it's completed, it will control the floods, letting the land developer dig a new canal that will open up the whole valley to farming again."

Pete rocked back on his chair. "There you go, David. You and your new dam are going to fix things."

The four of them were quiet for a time before David quietly said, "Nick said something about the flood killing your father, Tony. Do you mind if I ask how that happened?"

"He was working on one of our head gates when the main wave first came through. The water had been rising for a couple of days, and we knew that there might be trouble. By the time I reached him, he'd worked himself to the point of exhaustion. He could barely stand up. Then, an even bigger swell started toward us. We started to run, but my father . . ." Tony's voice tightened.

"Listen, I'm sorry," said David. "You don't need to tell us anymore."

"No, I think it's good for me to talk about it. Nobody up here understands why I want to work here, and they resent the fact that a couple of Italians are taking other people's jobs. The way I figure it is that the river has taken everything from me and my family. This is my chance to get even with it." He tapped his fingers on the table. "Does that make sense?" It wasn't really a question.

"So, what happened to your father?" David asked gently.

"He had a heart attack, right there in my arms. I was only seventeen years old, and he just lay there in my arms, the water rising and the sound of the river drowning out everything around us."

"He died in your arms?"

"No, I was able to carry him home. He lived for six months, but he was a broken man. In my culture, it's expected that the oldest male take care of the family, and my father chafed under the indignity of his health problems. Every other month or so he'd go out to work on the farm, only to suffer a relapse. It was humiliating for him. He finally died of a broken heart— literally and figuratively."

Tony looked up fiercely. "You want to know the real irony? I hate farming. I'm terrible at it. But because it was my father's dying wish, I have to keep the farm in the family. And my children after me."

"And that's where I come in," said Nick. "Tony is a lousy farmer. So he needs a partner. I'm good at farming. But since we can't do a lot of farming right now, I need to find another way to get by too. Unfortunately, I'm lousy at construction work. So I'm stuck here where I hate it—no one wants us here, apart from you two. At least in California where we live they treat us decently most of the time." There was more to this story, but this wasn't the time.

David glanced to the side and noticed a group of men quietly get up and leave the other end of the table. He hadn't noticed that they'd been listening in, and he wondered how they would react to what they'd heard— would they show Tony and Nick a little more tolerance, or would it make things even worse now that they knew their story?

Finally David said, "Well, I'm glad you told us about that. Somehow it makes it seem that what we're doing is even more important. For Pete and me, it's a job to build this dam, one that we love, to be sure—but for you guys, it's personal."

"You will control the river, won't you?" Tony's voice became animated again, as if he wanted to get past the melancholy his story had stirred.

Pete smiled. "Oh, we'll control the thing, all right. My little brother, David, here, has helped Frank Crowe bottle up a bunch of rivers. They design 'em, and I build 'em. Besides, Frank's the best in the world, and this is to be his masterpiece. So you can count on him coming through. I'm right about that, aren't I, Davy?"

David nodded. "He's obsessed with it, and he's also incredibly competent. By the time we're finished, the Colorado will be like a wild horse broken to the saddle. Downstream floods will be a thing of the past."

"Then it makes all this worthwhile."

"And you'll probably be a millionaire, won't you, once that farm of yours gets water?" said Pete.

"Like I said, it doesn't matter how much the farm is worth, since I can't sell it. It has to stay in the family. But it should produce a good, steady income. I think we'll do well if we can just hold on long enough."

High scalers working to clear the canyon walls of debris
prior to pouring the concrete of the dam

CHAPTER 3
High Scalers

Black Canyon, Men's Dormitory Bus Stop—June 1931

"Hey, Wop! You better be careful in those tunnels . . . you do know that grease melts when it gets hot, don't you?" Marvin laughed at his little joke.

It had been a bad week for Tony—not so much on the job, where the men on his crew had tolerated him since he had proved himself nimble enough at moving in and out of the tunnel—but it had been miserable here in the assembly area where they waited to be transported to the work site. This was just one of the locations where Chick and Marvin had been showing up to hassle him, performing to an often sympathetic crowd that barely suppressed its resentment of Tony and the handful of other "foreign" workers. On Monday Marvin had tried to trip him, pretending it was an accident. On Tuesday Chick had bumped him near the edge of the canyon, making him grab wildly to avoid losing his footing, and now it was Wednesday, which must be stupid-joke day.

He had to decide whether to ignore Marvin or respond. He decided to ignore him. A bad decision. "Hey, the man asked you a question, Capelli!" Chick said while swatting the back of Tony's head.

Instinctively Tony jumped up to take a swing at Chick, but as he started to bring his arm forward somebody grabbed it from behind, which infuriated him even more. Whirling around, he was startled to see the face of his foreman, Hank Toombs, who told him to sit down, emphasizing the point by moving his hands to Tony's shoulders and forcing him down into his seat. Tony didn't like it, but he didn't dare challenge Hank.

Just as quickly as he got Tony settled down, Hank turned to Chick and Marvin. "You two ever been in the tunnel? Are you talking about how hot it is from personal experience? Or maybe you're more of an expert on what it is to be greasy?"

Chick's face flushed. "This has nothing to do with you."

"And you'll have nothing to say to my men." Chick started to move toward Hank but stepped back when the entire group of miners and chuck tenders stood up behind Hank. That was a group you didn't want to mess with, since they had arms the size of most men's legs.

But Chick wasn't quite finished. "Maybe you don't know who you're talking to. We work for the chief of police."

"Oh, so you've left Six Companies and gone to work for Bud Bodell? Well, I'll be happy to chat with Bud if you keep harassing my man here."

"You know Mr. Bodell?"

"You might say that." Hank smiled coldly. "You're certainly welcome to talk to him about me, if you like."

Chick stared defiantly at Hank for a moment then eyed Tony with a look of pure hatred. After spitting a foul glob of tobacco on the ground next to Tony's feet, he said, "Come on, Marv, let's get out of here." The two of them strode out the open double doors toward their automobile, Chick kicking a rock hard enough to smack the wall of the paymaster's office with a noticeable thud.

As Hank sat down, Tony said, "Thanks."

"Look, Capelli. There are men here who don't like the idea of an Italian having one of the high-paying jobs, or any job for that matter. I'm not sure I like it myself with so many Americans out of work."

Tony struggled to stifle a response, but his face burned in anger. Hank took no notice. "The fact is you're a good worker, and for some reason you've been assigned to my crew. Once that happens, you're part of us, and we'll stand with you. You just can't let those jerks get to you. Their boss is one mean s.o.b. and now that he's got himself appointed sheriff he can override any one of us from Six Companies, so I don't want to have to mix it up with him. Do you understand?"

Tony swallowed hard to suppress the bile in his throat. "Yes, sir. I understand."

Without another word, Hank turned to the miner sitting next to him and started talking.

For once Tony was glad that his skin was olive, since it masked the flow of blood that had rushed to his face. He'd have killed Chick Flemming if he could, and that bothered him. And right now he wanted to manhandle Hank for his condescending attitude, even though he'd stood up for him.

He pulled out his canteen and took a long drink of water to help cool his anger. *What kind of man am I becoming?* he wondered. He wasn't at all sure he wanted to know the answer.

Black Canyon

"YOU SEE THIS?" PETE CONROY broke off a piece of loose rock from a small outcrop. "This insignificant piece of rock is fatal to the construction of the dam. The whole project could be a big waste of time because of a piece of loose rock. Here are the facts: Before we're done with this monster, we'll pour something like seven million tons of concrete. If you and I don't properly scale these walls to get rid of all the loose rock and seal off all fractures in the canyon walls, water from the lake will seep around the edges of the concrete, where it will freeze and fracture. Before you know it, the whole integrity of the structure will be compromised." Pete was pleased by the sober expressions on the faces of his new crew.

"Not only that, but unless the side walls where the dam will butt up against the rock are completely cleared of loose debris, it's very likely that men will be killed down in the canyon when the pouring begins a year from now."

"Killed? By what?"

Pete was glad to get this question.

Rather than respond, he simply reached inside the sack he'd brought to the site and pulled out a coconut, placing it very gently on the ledge next to him. It had cost him plenty, since coconuts were hard to come by in the middle of a desert, but this was the perfect way to make the point, and he wanted to make sure there was no mistaking what the point was.

"It's nearly a thousand feet from here to the riverbed. Once the river is diverted through the tunnels, they'll have to excavate even farther down to reach bedrock. Do you know what even a small piece of loose rock falling from a thousand feet can do to a man's skull if it hits him? It can do this." In a flash Pete lifted a heavy ball peen hammer and brought it crashing down on the hapless coconut with all his strength. Of course, the shell shattered with a sickening crunch while sending a spray of white goo in every direction, including on the faces of some of the men standing closest to him.

Instinctively, all the men stepped back and covered their faces, stunned by the violence of what they'd just seen. Pleased with the effect, Pete continued. "And pebbles are just a tiny problem. The sides of this canyon are lined with more than just loose gravel. If a boulder the size of the one I'm leaning on broke loose, it could smash a steam shovel to bits." Dramatic, but that's what Pete was famous for. "Now do you see why our job is so important?"

"So how do we do it, sir?"

"Before we get to that, let's take a minute and talk about what causes all this loose stuff in the first place. What is it, do you suppose, that causes all these cracks and loose rocks to form on the canyon walls, anyway?"

The men shrugged uncomfortably. They'd been hired to blast stuff, not to answer questions. One man, a short, wiry individual, raised his hand.

"What's your name?"

"O'Donnell, sir. Sean O'Donnell."

"Is that an Irish accent?"

"Yes, sir. But I'm from New York."

"Ah. Well, you probably have some stories to tell. But not now. Why don't you tell me what causes all this stuff."

"Three things: heat, wind, and water."

Pete nodded appreciatively. "That is correct, Mr. O'Donnell. Care to expand on how they do it?"

"Well, I'm no expert, but I understand that the winter and spring rains drench the top of the mesa with water that seeps down into the rock where it freezes and expands, fracturing the rock. In the summer the heat causes the rock to expand, which also cracks it. And the wind erodes the soft material first, which creates creases in the rock surface. In time these deepen until you have distinct boulders that are separated from one another."

"So did you study geology in New York?"

"No, sir. I was a structural steel worker. But I like to read up on things before I start a job."

"A structural steelworker? Any buildings we might recognize?"

"I worked on a lot that you have probably never heard of, but I did work on two you may have: the Chrysler Building and the Empire State Building." This caused a stir as the group of ten workers unconsciously straightened in respect.

"So you were one of those guys working out on the steel beams?" a rather stout young man asked.

"I was, and at one point I was working more than a thousand feet above the street."

"Well, then," said Pete dismissively. "This will be nothing to you, but for the rest of us it's going to take some getting used to."

Now O'Donnell was chagrinned. He didn't want to be seen as different from the rest of the men in the group, and his bragging had put that at risk. He'd been on too many jobs where someone got labeled as an outsider and life was pretty miserable for the guy after that.

"There is one big difference, sir."

"And that is?"

"On a building you start from the bottom up. There're never any rocks to fall on your head. It seems to me that this is a lot more dangerous since we have to go over the side and work down."

"Exactly. That's what each of you must understand." Pete said this with such ferocity that the group stepped back again. Pete continued undeterred. "In just a few minutes I'm going to train you on how to keep yourself safe when you go over the side. You'll learn how to check your ropes to make sure they're in perfect condition. You'll learn how to avoid having them hang up on some rocky point that frays them as you swing away from the hole you've drilled for dynamite. And you'll learn how to catch yourself by using the safety line, just in case something does go wrong. All this while managing a forty-five-pound jackhammer, handling live explosives, and working with shovels and picks while dangling with nothing more than a two-by-three-foot seat board under your butts." Pete paused for effect.

"I can teach you all of that stuff. What I can't teach you is how to protect yourself from some idiot who's above you and drops a tool or shuffles his feet in such a way that loose material comes crashing over the side. There's no way to learn how to make the other guy use his God-given common sense. So the only way to protect one another is to learn to do it right. If each of you learns how to do your work without sending anything down on the men below, then we'll be in the safest spot on the whole canyon wall. Do you get that?"

The silence that followed meant that the men were either so intimidated by Pete's intensity that they didn't dare make a comment, or they had been sufficiently impressed by his words that they would be careful. Pete hoped it was the latter.

"All right, then. You've got an hour to go to the quartermaster and get your tools. You'll carry some of them on your tool belt and keep them with you always. The really heavy stuff, like the jackhammer and drill bits, will be lowered to you by helpers up on the rim on a separate set of ropes. You'll each have an assigned helper who you'll learn to communicate with by signals on the ropes, so you want to take good care of that person. Once you're outfitted, report back here at nine a.m. for training. Then we're going to go out on a little field trip where I'll show you how to manage all this equipment while you blow things up and chisel the remnants away. My guess is that some of you will decide you're not really suited for high scaling. The rest of you will prove you're as big an idiot as I am. Once that's finished, we'll have you over the side right after lunch, and you can start hammering away—we'll give you some practice before you handle explosives. Any questions?"

The young fellow raised his hand.

"Your name?"

"Jeremy, sir. Jeremy Stephens."

"Well?"

"Yes, sir. Well, I was wondering how we manage the dynamite in this heat. I'm told it becomes quite unstable. I'm from the Pacific Northwest, where they use dynamite in logging operations."

Pete nodded. "You're absolutely right. We'll get to that on the field trip. Now anything else? No? Then get your sorry butts over to the quartermaster. Now." And with that, they all moved.

As the men headed for the quartermaster, Pete called out, "O'Donnell, wait up just a second."

Sean O'Donnell turned. "Yes, sir?" he replied defensively.

Pete cocked his head to the side, puzzled by the reaction. Maybe he'd come on too strong. "Relax, O'Donnell. I'm not mad or anything." The younger man shuffled his left foot in the sand but didn't say anything. Clearly he was scared of Pete, or at least mistrusting. Pete softened his voice. "That was impressive, O'Donnell. I like the fact that you studied the job before you got here. If you don't mind my asking, what is it that brought you this far? We don't have many Easterners on the job."

Sean shrugged. "Work. There isn't any, at least in New York. The building boom of the '20s just came crashing to a halt."

"Are you married? Do you have a family to support?"

"I'm not married, but I do have a family to support."

Pete raised an eyebrow, which drew an immediate reaction from O'Donnell.

"No, I'm not divorced or anything. I have a widowed sister, and her husband didn't leave her anything. I try to help her out, although she does make some money as a seamstress for some rich women on 5th Avenue. Still, if the kids are to have any kind of a chance in life, I need to send extra money."

Pete noticed that Sean seemed uncomfortable. "It's not that I'm being nosy about your private business. It's that I need to know how much I can ask of you."

Sean's eyes blazed. "You can ask me to do anything. You don't need to worry about me pulling my weight."

"Whoa, boy. Calm down. You've got a real chip on your shoulder . . ."

Sean dropped his gaze. "It's just that I've been busted from jobs for being a smart guy, and I wasn't doing that at all when you asked me those questions earlier. I'll keep my mouth shut from now on."

Pete laughed, even though he knew it would probably aggravate the situation. O'Donnell's suspicions were just so far different from what he had in mind. So, before Sean could get even hotter, he quickly replied, "It's nothing like that, O'Donnell. It's just that I'm going need an assistant to help me with the other men, and it's a dangerous job. I don't want to put you in a bad spot if you're a family man."

Sean's eyes widened. "An assistant? You mean, you're thinking of asking me to be your assistant?"

Pete nodded. "That's what I was thinking . . ."

Sean shook his head in wonder. "You're kidding." He shook his head. "So, what does it take to be your assistant? I've never done anything in management. Far from it, in fact."

"What it requires is that you learn how to rescue a man who gets into trouble. That can be pretty dicey because they don't get into trouble without also getting themselves into very hard-to-reach positions."

Sean nodded. "I can get into hard-to-get-out-of places—I think I just proved that." Pete was pleased at this attempt at a joke and didn't mind that Sean pressed his luck with the next question, "Does it pay better?"

"You mean $1.25 an hour isn't enough, already? High scaling is the highest paying work on the whole project, you know."

"Except for being a manager." Before Pete could reply, Sean hastened to add. "I'm kidding. A dollar twenty five is a great wage, and I'm glad to get it. If you really think I'm up to it, I'd be glad to be your assistant. It would be an honor." Sean's face colored after he added the last sentence, which made Pete suspect that it wasn't characteristic of him to talk like that to a manager.

Pete stared at him for just a moment, and Sean felt his eyes penetrate right through him. Then Pete relaxed. "Good. Something tells me you're just the right man. Now, before the others get back, let me tell you how I see the world. My job is to build the dam. My little brother is one of those pencil-pushing engineers who designs stuff. I know they're needed to plot every-thing out and make sure everything is in place to do the work, but that's just not for me. I'm the guy who builds things. So when this dam is done, it will have Pete Conroy's name written on it somewhere. Even if nobody else in the world ever finds that place, it doesn't matter because I'll know that it was me and my men who did the job. Just as important, my men always come first. I get a lot more work out of men by treating them like decent human beings. I don't treat them like slaves, as some of the foremen do."

"Well, that will be a change from what I'm used to."

Pete frowned. "A lot of foremen on this job will fire a man if it even looks like he's thinking about slowing down. After all, there are a thousand more guys waiting in line in Las Vegas for a chance to come out here."

Sean nodded. That's the way it was in New York.

"I don't see it that way." Pete continued. "If one of my men is slowing down, it probably means he's thirsty, or hungry, or over tired. If that's the case, it most likely means that all the men are in the same predicament and I need to give them a quick break—otherwise they'll make a mistake and kill themselves or somebody else."

"I could get used to that. It's not often you find a boss who stands up for his men."

"Of course, if there's a piker in the group, or an agitator, then he's gone. I don't have time for that crap." He turned his powerful eyes on Sean again. "Are you a union man?"

"I've worked as a union man. You have to if you want to work on some of the jobs in New York City. I like the wages they negotiate, but I'm not particularly a union man. I think they sometimes get in the way of the men, rather than helping them. Are you anti-union?"

"Not anti—I just don't have much experience with it. Unions aren't as big out here in the West. At any rate, you just need to know that Six Companies is anti-union. If you start to hear rumblings about union organizers, be careful. That's probably the one thing you could do that would get you fired so quickly that even I couldn't get you back on."

Sean nodded. "I understand." If he had other feelings on the subject, he didn't reveal them. Sean leaned down to pick up his lunch pail. "Thanks, Mr. Conroy. I won't let you down."

"It's Pete."

Sean nodded. "Pete, then." A smile flickered across his face as he turned to get outfitted.

As PETE CONROY SWUNG BACK to the spot he'd just blasted into oblivion on the side of a small outcrop, he glanced down at the men who had moved in closer after the blast. Just as expected, some of them were very pale. Pete considered this group the best of the men he had; it meant they understood the real danger they were getting themselves into. Chances were they would stay in the program and make good scalers. Another group had an excited look on their faces—they were the daredevils who would be the most dangerous until they realized just how hard and dangerous scaling was. At least in the beginning, this group would be responsible for most of the accidents. Finally, he noticed a couple of guys who appeared to be green. Not inexperienced green but physically green. Chances weren't very high that he'd be seeing them the next day.

"All right, then. Let's head back to the trucks. You four come up here and help drag the compressors down. Mr. O'Donnell is going to help me back up to the top, and we'll meet you at the lunch site. After that, it's over the side of the canyons." The group broke up nervously and started collecting the equipment they'd brought to the training site.

"So what did you think?" Pete asked Sean as they brought the last of the equipment down the narrow trail to the trucks.

"I wish I could have seen more of it, since I was helping out on top. But from what I did see, and from what you said, I think I can do it."

"Good man. Maybe you'll let me buy you a drink tonight, when we're done?"

"A drink? I didn't think they served liquor on the project reservation."

"And isn't that a crime against human nature? The idiots. But you're right—since the nearest real drink is twenty miles away, we'll have to settle for a Coca-Cola."

"Sure, that would be great."

Sean left Pete and went over to his truck, where young Jeremy Stephens was waiting with a big smile. "Should be exciting, don't you think?" Normally Sean couldn't stand the gung-ho type, but something about Jeremy was so completely sincere that it was almost impossible not to like him.

"Exciting it is. I can't wait to try it myself." Maybe if he said it loud enough, he'd believe it himself.

CHAPTER 4
Personal Lives

Coming out of the cafeteria after lunch, Tony heard Nick curse, "What the . . . ?"

"What is it? What's wrong?"

Nick pointed to his left, all the while shaking his head. Tony turned to follow his hand, and then he let out an involuntary Italian swear word he'd learned from his father, followed by "I'm so sorry, Nick." He started over to Nick's Ford pickup. "Come on, let's see what we can do." Nick didn't follow him. He just stood there shaking his head and muttering.

"Come on, so they let the air out of the tires." He squatted down in front of the truck. "At least they didn't cut them or anything." He stood up and motioned for Nick, but Nick still didn't move. So, even though a small crowd had gathered to watch him, some of the men in the group laughing, others shaking their heads as if they too were disgusted, Tony fumbled inside the truck until he found a hand pump. Leaning down he started pumping air into the driver's side front tire. He was enormously relieved when the tire started to inflate. He paused for a moment and listened for the sound of escaping air, but there was none. "See, they just let the air out. It's nothing we can't fix."

By this point Nick had come over to the truck. "How exactly are you going to fix that?" he said.

"What?" Tony stopped pumping and walked to the back of the truck. Again following Nick's pointing finger, he saw the enamel paint that had been splashed on the back fender of the truck. He also saw the words that had been scrawled in the paint, "Wops go home or die!"

The bile rose in Tony's throat. He turned at the crowd, flashing them a look that was enough to cause many of the men to move on. "Well!" he shouted. "Who's going to come make us? Who! You ever heard of the ancient Romans? They kicked ass wherever they went! You really want to mess it up with us?" But no one responded. He continued to glower until the group finally broke up. As the last ones shuffled off, he heard someone calling them a couple of crazy Italians.

Turning back to the truck, he said, "I'll take care of this, Nick. Let's get air in the tires, and we'll go see if there isn't some place safe to park it. Maybe they'll let us keep it with the company trucks."

Nick just shook his head. "Stop it, Tony. Just stop it. Can't you see it's over?"

"Over? What's over? We just got here. Things are going fine."

"Leave or die? You call that fine?"

"I call it imbecile. Some stupid dope doesn't like us, so he does this. It just shows he's a coward. A real man would have just done it. So this is nothing to worry about. It's an irritation, that's all."

Nick drew himself up, took a long deep breath, and then exhaled slowly. "Maybe it's just an irritation to you, but it's the end for me. I'm leaving. I'm going to the paymaster right now. I'm collecting the money they owe me, and then I'm going home. I know it's tough down there, but at least we know how to get along. Something bad is going to happen if we stay here. So I'm going home. I hope you'll come with me."

Tony turned around so that he could lean up against the truck. He folded his arms. Usually he'd try to come up with something sarcastic or profane to say at a time like this—anything to jar Nick out of his mood, but the look in Nick's eyes told him it wouldn't work this time.

"You should come with me, Tony. We don't belong here. Things will just get worse." There was fire in Nick's eyes.

"I'd like to go with you. I miss my wife and kids. I miss the valley. I'm not so stupid that I'm not aware that they don't like me here, but I have to stay. I need the money, plain and simple."

"You need the money to pay off that stupid farm. You don't even care about it. You're only keeping it because your father wanted it—you said so yourself!"

"You watch yourself, Nick! You're my best friend, but you watch yourself. Don't you ever say another word against my father. As for me paying off the farm—that's my business." Nick shrunk back a bit, but he didn't retreat, and he didn't withdraw his words.

Tony sighed. "Look, I'm sorry. I'm the one who took out the loan, not you. I have to make good on it. Even if I did walk away from the farm, which I won't, I'd want to sell it at the top of the market after the dam is built, not before. Besides, Paul seems to show some interest in keeping it."

"It's just that I don't want that farm to kill you, too. It's hard here . . ." Nick's voice trailed off. "I just don't like it here. I hate it."

"Then you should go. You should go." Tony's voice choked, which was intensely embarrassing, but he kept going. "I'll miss you. It's hard enough with you. Now there will only be one olive-skinned scapegoat for them to get mad at." He smiled at his own joke. "But now whose car can I borrow when I need to get out of this place?"

"I'll miss you too," said Nick.

Project Headquarters

"How's your brother doing?"

David Conroy looked up in surprise at the sound of Frank Crowe's voice. He hadn't seen the superintendent for a couple of months.

"I think he's doing fine. I haven't seen him for a couple of days, but last time I talked with him he seemed to like the high scaling. He says he's got this little madman of an Irishman who used to work on skyscrapers in New York City doing unbelievable things."

"I've heard about him—one of the real showmen on the job. The antics of the high scalers are getting us some interesting attention in the Eastern papers. I don't mind, as long as they get their work done."

"I'm sure Pete knows that, sir."

They were silent for a few moments as David struggled to find something to say.

Frank surrendered first. "How's the air in the tunnels?"

"Better since we got power. I've got ventilating fans in each construction tunnel, and I'm starting to figure out how to use the uneven temperatures in the tunnels to get some natural airflow going. It's largely manageable while the miners are in the mine but gets rather toxic when the trucks and shovels go in to clean the mess up after a blast."

"I'd prefer you didn't use the term *toxic.*"

"I'd prefer we used diesels and electrics instead of gasoline engines." David paused, but Frank didn't reply, so he continued. "Still, we're doing as well as possible, all things considered. I keep the miners out in the open air while the muckers are doing their jobs, then the muckers get a break when the mining crew goes back in."

"Good." Crowe was distracted now, and it was obvious that this line of conversation was over. "Do what you can. I was in the tunnel the other day, and it was over 120 degrees. It's awful hard to concentrate when it's that hot. The job still comes first, but make sure the men have water and as much circulation as possible."

"Yes, sir. Of course."

With that Crowe strode out the door so quickly that it seemed as though he'd never been there.

David turned his eyes back to the blueprint he'd been working on. It diagrammed the next phase of drilling that would start when the "attic shafts" were completed—twelve-by-twelve-foot square shafts that would extend the entire length of each of the four tunnels. Once a tunnel's attic was complete for the entire four-thousand-foot length, the crews could start blasting out the "wings" and the "bench," rounding out the tunnels. Blasting out the attic shafts, starting at both ends, would represent more than 80 percent of the work on the completed tunnels. Of greater importance to David was the knowledge that once the two ends of the shafts were connected, he could get a breeze from one end of the tunnel to the other. That would be a day to celebrate.

Westmoreland, California

"WHAT IS IT, MAMA? WHY are you crying?"

Louisa Capelli wiped a tear. "It's nothing. I just read a letter from your father."

"Is he all right?" The little girl's voice was shaky.

Louisa did her best to smile. "Yes, dear, he's all right. It's just that your papa sent us his check again. We're going to be fine for another month."

"Why are you crying, then?"

Louisa took a deep breath and exhaled slowly. She didn't really know why she was crying. Nothing in Tony's letter even hinted that things weren't going fine at his job. But the way he formed the letters was tight and constricted, as if he were under enormous stress. She realized he must be living on practically nothing, considering the size of the check. She knew something of what he was facing. Nick had told her just how cruel some of the men had been to him and Tony.

Adding to her concern was that Tony had written in three different places that she needed to be sure to make a payment on the mortgage he had taken out on their farm. Louisa had pleaded with him not to do that, but he'd insisted that it was the only way to keep food on the table during the long months when he was out of work. She knew how much he hated debt, and, with things the way they were, there were speculators who would love to have them default on the loan so they could get their hands on the farm. After all, when the great dam on the Colorado was finished, their land would go up in value.

But even all that wasn't what had made her cry. She looked back at the letter, and the words caused her to choke up again. At the very end he'd actually written that he missed her and the children. To Louisa's thinking,

Tony was one of those Italian men who tended to swagger in an overconfident way to show the world that he was tough. He often used sarcasm and wit to cover his emotions. It was part of how he'd been raised. "Something must be wrong," said Louisa quietly, "For him to admit to such a thing in a letter."

Cafeteria—September 1931

"WHAT'S WRONG, LITTLE BROTHER?"

David jumped at the sound of Pete's voice. Looking up, he deftly folded the letter and slipped it into his shirt pocket. "Nothing. Mind your own business."

"Yeah, right—you always scowl while having a cup of coffee."

"So, I've got my troubles in the tunnels. Nothing new. What about you?"

Pete sat down and surveyed David's face. David averted his eyes. "So, Crowe and the other bosses have taken to communicating with you by letter, have they?"

"Oh, for heaven's sake. Here, read it for yourself."

David took the letter out of his pocket and thrust it at Pete, who was smart enough not to act triumphant.

David,

> *Thanks for your letter. I'm sorry progress is so slow on building Boulder City. I had hoped to see you before bad weather sets in. Of course, it may be nice to come to Nevada in the middle of the winter when things get really cold here in Boise. I'll be all right. I do hope you get to come home for the holidays . . .*

The letter was from David's wife, Mary, and it was pretty routine stuff so far. Pete thought Mary was terrific and had always admired her dark eyes and short hair. He'd often said, with unusual sincerity, that she was probably the best-looking woman in all Idaho. He sometimes convinced himself that if he'd married her he might have succeeded in staying in a marriage. It was David, however, who had won her heart with his more even temperament.

> *The girls are doing well—Elizabeth won a math competition, which discomfited all the boys in her class and surprised the heck out of her teachers. Boys are supposed to be better, you know, although I don't believe it.*

Now even Pete could see that something bad was coming. Mary usually got right to the point, and the fact that something had irritated David in his earlier reading of the letter meant that Mary was having trouble getting to the point. He looked up at David and shrugged his shoulders.

> *I do need to tell you about something sad. My father says that with the slowdown, he has had to lay off all his workers, except for my brothers. They're not taking it very well since they're not used to actually having to lift the furniture into the moving vans. I keep telling them they should be happy to have a job at all, with so many people out of work, but they just growl at me.*

Bad, but still not enough to make David curse—unless they were coming to her for money, but Pete doubted that Mary would raise that issue in a letter or that she'd give in unless they were in the most dire of circumstances.

> *Then there's Jim. We had another fight. The principal called to say that he had been skipping class—mostly English—to go joyriding with friends. When I brought it up he threw a temper tantrum. I've grounded him, but I don't know if I can enforce it. Maybe you could talk to him. I know phone calls are expensive.*

Pete could almost hear the sigh that followed that line. Mary was no pushover, although she had a fairly even temper. She was the type to lower her voice when she was angry, so he imagined that Jim had been confronted with a barrage of logic and common sense at a time in his life when he was impetuous and impatient and often acted like a jerk. He'd better watch it, though, because when Mary was backed into a corner she could be tough.

> *Well, I know it's hard. I hope you can come home sometime soon. If we can come visit it will be a lot better. At any rate, we're okay. I'll get by, but I miss you.*

Pete handed the letter back to David. "So it's not really about the tunnels—gotta be tough being down here knowing what's going on up there. Mary's brothers are spoiled twelve year olds, even though they're both in their thirties, and now it sounds like Jim is turning into someone like me when I was his age. I wouldn't wish that on any mother."

David managed a smile. "I hope it isn't that bad. If it is, Mary's liable to just kill him and then I'll have to work to get her transferred to a prison here in Nevada so I can visit her."

"I know you love your job, Davy, but this is the bad side of the work we do—they never want to build anything that's convenient to home. Frankly I'm amazed how often Mary has traipsed along with you. Any chance she'd come to Nevada to live when they get the married housing built in Boulder City?"

"We decided against it. With two of the kids in high school and Katie in junior high, it just doesn't make sense to mess up their lives. I'll go home as often as I can, and we'll have them come down in the summers once I get a place for them to stay." He went silent for a few moments, and Pete chose not to interrupt his thoughts.

David finally picked up the conversation. "I don't know what's up with Jim. He's a good kid, you know that, and he's never been a problem. People used to remark on how we were so lucky to have such a sweet little boy. I don't get it why he's doing all this."

"I do," said Pete quietly.

David looked up and raised an eyebrow.

"He misses you."

"It's not like this is new."

"It's not like he's ever been a teenager before. Life's a lot tougher when you're changing from boy to man. It's easier if you have your father around."

David chewed his lower lip as he pondered this. "I suspect you're right, but I don't know what to do about it. I was out of work for six months in Boise. It nearly drained all our savings. If I hadn't paid off the house with the bonus on that California project, I don't know what we'd have done. I'm not down here because I want to be, but because I need a job."

Pete raised an eyebrow, and David caught the look.

"All right, so it's not like I don't want to be part of it—it is the biggest project to come along in the engineering world since the Panama Canal, after all, and it means I get to work with Frank Crowe again. So maybe I did make a selfish choice for my family because of my career."

Pete nodded. "And that's why you feel guilty—not that I think you should. A man should do well in his career. I know you well enough to know that if the only reason you were here was because you needed the money, you'd feel bad but tough it out. The thought that you might enjoy the work is enough to give you an ulcer. It makes it feel like you're betraying your family. You're really good at self guilt, you know."

David stared at his coffee. Then, without raising his head, he said, "I hate it when you're right. You know that, don't you?"

Pete nodded, but didn't smile.

The "Williams Jumbo," a moveable platform that allowed drillers and their support staff to prepare large sections of the tunnel for blasting simultaneously.

An early photo of one of the four diversion tunnels under construction.

CHAPTER 5
The Drilling Jumbo

The Diversion Tunnels—September 1931

L isten, David. I need to talk to you about something."

"Sure, Woody."

"After the strike last month we have to be especially tuned in to the worker's complaints, at least for a while. Even though the feds backed us up in facing down the Wobblies, it was embarrassing for them. Frank took the heat for Six Companies and made it clear there would be no compromises. The fact is that we've got to improve conditions, or we could face another slowdown."

David nodded. The Industrial Workers of the World, the IWW union, had sent one of their organizers into the project as a truck driver. Frank Anderson was a firebrand who had waited for just the right moment to strike the match to the discontent being felt by the men. August had proved the perfect moment. Not only was the work environment in the canyon unbearable because of the unseasonably hot summer, but the lack of decent living conditions had rubbed people's nerves raw. Then, when a crew of muckers reported to work in the tunnels on August 7, they were told they were being demoted to the lowest pay grade since some newly arrived machinery would start doing their jobs inside the tunnels and their services in the higher-paying job were no longer needed.

That proved to be the flashpoint Anderson was looking for, and he quickly set the workers' passions ablaze. Before the sun had set, crews all around the dam site had consented to forego work in favor of attending strike meetings. And with that, work on the project stopped.

Unfortunately for Anderson, Frank Crowe had a cool head. He simply shut down the whole project. When presented with the workers' demands, he and his team took a few hours to consider them and then rejected all of the demands out-of-hand. The next day he announced that every Six Companies employee was to report to the paymaster to pick up a three-day termination check, and to then clear the reservation. Those who were interested in getting rehired could get in line in Las Vegas, just like the thousands of others who wanted a job. In explaining the company's decision to the press, he indicated that Six Companies was a good six months ahead of schedule and that it would be much easier financially to wait out the strikers than to settle.

The agitators encouraged the men to stay on the site, hoping that the federal government would intervene, but instead of helping the strikers, the number-one government official on the site, Walker Young, made it known that he'd alerted the U.S. Army at Ft. Douglas in Salt Lake City to be ready to move in to protect the reservation in case anybody started to threaten project assets. Shortly after that, the State of Nevada made it clear that it would remain neutral in the conflict.

That was all it had taken to break the strike. The workers, appropriately terrified by the loss of their jobs, quickly made their way to the paymaster and then moved directly to Las Vegas so they could get a clean start at the front of the line. The strike was over in just eight days.

"I understand the tension," said David in reply to Woody's appeal. "My brother is a construction foreman, and he certainly was outraged by the 'change of assignment.'"

Williams nodded. "I know your brother. He makes a darn good drinking buddy. I can only imagine that he was ready to take on Frank Crowe and the whole board of directors."

David shook his head. Pete was one of those guys everybody knew somehow. They all liked him, even though he was a hothead. The very first thing David did when he heard of the strike was to drive down to the river, cross the flimsy cable bridge he hated, and find Pete to make sure he didn't do something stupid that would get him permanently fired.

"So what do you want me to do?" David asked Woody.

Williams shook his head. "It's the heat. I know you're doing everything you can. But are the men getting enough water? Is there anything more we can do about the heat in there?"

"You know as well as I do the real problem is the carbon monoxide. But it's too late to do anything about that." David said this with more emphasis than he intended, and it had an immediate effect on Woody.

"Give it a rest, will you? Everybody knows your position on that. But whether a good decision or bad, it was made, and you're right that we can't change it. What I want to know is about water. Is there anything we can do on that front?"

David nodded. "What we could do is give them refrigerated water to drink instead of filtered river water. Just having something cold going down the throat does a lot."

Woody paused for a moment. "Another thing we can do is to get their families up and out of the canyon. The new housing up in Boulder City should be finished soon. That will take a lot of pressure off the married men. In the meantime we still need to work on the tunnels." Woody looked up. "And I suspect as we make progress, your carbon monoxide problem will get even worse."

David had anticipated this conversation and had been working late into the night trying to work the problem out. "Let me show you what I've got in mind for the tunnels." The task would get harder as the shaft went deeper and deeper into the side of the mountain, making for longer drive times in the tunnel for the thousands of truckloads of debris that needed to be hauled out.

Williams stepped over to David's drafting table. "Show me what you've got." He smiled. "I figured you'd have something."

HANK TOOMBS STOOD IN FRONT of his crew, glowering. "Listen up, men. You're going to ride this ungainly monster for the next six months or so, and you're going to have to learn to work together like never before. If even one of you screws up, you'll throw off the timing of the whole operation. Put another way, if you slow down on the job you'll have to answer to the other eighty-nine guys on the crew. And me."

Tony stared, wide-eyed, at the huge Rube Goldberg contraption that stood before them. It looked very much like a four-story tree house built on the back of an ancient dinosaur. He was quite certain that no one in the world had ever seen anything like it.

"Let me brief you on a William's Jumbo, designed by none other than Mr. Frank Crowe and our very own Woody Williams to help us blast out the bench area—the upper portion of the tunnels where the initial cut is made—much faster than traditional drilling methods. With that, Hank moved closer to the truck, motioning for the men to follow.

"The jumbo is a four-story steel scaffold built on a ten-ton International chain-drive truck originally designed for the military. As you can see, each level has a wooden platform we work on—two for the miners and chuck tenders, the other two for the racks that hold the drill steel.

"The idea is that the jumbo will be backed into position against the face of the rock inside the tunnel, blocked into place by the nippers, and then connected to the pneumatic and water lines and to the electricity for lighting. Once it's in place, the miners will start drilling a standard pattern. You nippers will have to be on your toes to keep them supplied with the right lengths of steel. Once the holes are finished, the nippers will bring up the dynamite to be tamped into place.

"When the charges are set, we'll disconnect the electricity to avoid any sparks or short-circuits that could detonate the dynamite and then connect the blasting charges. Electricians will bring forward portable lights for that part of the operation. Then you nippers will disconnect all the hoses and connections so we can move the whole assembly into position for the next set of drilling."

One of the men raised his hand. "How many times will we need to move before the blast is ready?"

Hank expected this question. "That's the genius of this thing. It's big enough that we can drill half the circumference with each set. We'll drill once, unhook and move the jumbo, drill a second time, and then clear the canyon for the blast. Just as soon as the area is cleared of smoke after the blast, the mucker crews will go in with the electric shovel, the two-blade Caterpillar to push the debris into piles for the shovel, and trucks to haul it out. As quick as the floor is clear of debris, the jumbo will start to move back in for the next round, even as the electric shovel is exiting."

"You mean those two can pass each other inside the tunnel?" one of the men asked in astonishment. It seemed impossible, given their tremendous size.

"The tunnels are wide enough for a four-lane highway," Hank replied with more than a little contempt that the fellow would even ask.

"How long will the whole cycle take?" Tony asked. Apparently Hank didn't hear him.

Another worker spoke up. "Like Tony says, how long will the whole cycle take?"

This time Hank must have heard, even though the fellow had a soft voice, or he decided that it was worth an answer this time. "We don't know. Nothing like this has ever been used. Our best estimate is about five hours. So we may get two rounds off on each shift. At the very least, there will be a little overlap."

Hank glanced at each of the men. This was going to be mining on a scale never before seen, and he was excited by it. Yet he was also anxious, since he knew that the various crews would quickly start competing with each other, and he wanted to make sure his crew held its own in the contest.

"All right, then, I want the miners to be the first to come onboard so you can familiarize yourself with the setup, chuck tenders next, and then the nippers. We're going to practice here in the daylight until you know exactly what to do. I also want each of the miners to practice his hand signals with his assigned nipper so that we don't lose any time bringing the right length of steel or explosives forward. And you miners should feel free to use your nippers to bring water or whatever else you need. The nippers are the heart of the operation, and they're here to serve you. Any questions?"

Of course there were questions, but the men were way too anxious to wait around asking them. They couldn't wait to climb aboard the beast to see where they would be spending the greater part of their lives for the next half year.

"I DON'T CARE ABOUT YOUR inventory, Mr. McElroy. You will release enough fans to this crew that they can station them along the entire length of the tunnel. Do I make myself clear?"

Leonard McElroy looked at David Conroy with contempt. He hated wasting time on something so trivial. As the Stores manager he also hated losing control of the precious fans that were such a desirable commodity in Nevada, particularly on the black market. But Conroy was far enough up the company ladder that he could make trouble if he wanted to, so McElroy sniffed and said that he'd see to it.

As David stood watching him, doing his best to calm himself, he was startled at the sound of Hank Toombs's voice coming from behind him. "Thanks, Mr. Conroy. It's bad enough in there without having at least the minimum complement of fans."

David turned to look at Hank. "It's shameful the way McElroy and his ilk treat you guys. They think they own everything on the project and can't stand to see it get dirty, even though not one of them has ever set foot in the tunnel after a blast. If they did we wouldn't get this load of bull."

Toombs laughed. "I think that's why the men like you, sir. At least you go into the tunnels with us. Most don't, you know?"

"I don't understand that either. Either you're going to do a project, or you're going to watch it. You just can't make it happen without getting your shoes dirty. Frank Crowe knows that."

Toombs nodded. Crowe's unscheduled visits were legendary. Somehow he always showed up unannounced at the most inconvenient times, such as when a man slacked up a bit at the end of a shift. It didn't matter what time of day or night it was. He just had a sense about those things. Even though it scared the men to death when he snapped at them, at least they knew that the superintendent was willing to get his hands dirty along with the rest of them. It was part of what kept morale high.

"Well, at any rate, we appreciate it. The blasting is picking up as the men get familiar with the gear, and so the air inside is getting even worse than before."

"I know. It keeps me up nights worrying about it. I think I'd die myself if any of you got carbon monoxide poisoning."

"I wouldn't talk like that, Mr. Conroy. It's kind of inevitable that someone will get sick. We know the risks and we know that you're doing everything you can to help."

"Thanks, Hank." David shuffled uneasily. "Well, I've got another tunnel to look in on. Keep up the good work. I heard your crew broke a new record yesterday."

"Yes, sir. Two and a half blasts. The next crew was all set up when they got here."

David laughed. "At the rate you guys are going, we'll have to stop you before the tunnel reaches Mexico."

Toombs smiled and then took off for his tunnel. As David turned to leave, he almost collided with Tony Capelli. When he recognized who it was, he said, "How's it going, Tony? I haven't seen you for a while. I thought you were going to come over and play pinochle with Pete and me."

"Uh, right. I said I would, but I've been kind of busy on Sundays." He shuffled uneasily.

"You know you're welcome anytime." David continued. "I haven't even seen you at the cafeteria in a while, and we used to eat together with Pete and his work gang at least once or twice a week. Are you turning into a recluse?"

Tony looked away, and David regretted having said anything. But Tony replied, "No, sir. Most the time I eat a sandwich at my cot." Before David could respond, Tony added, "I like it that way." He said "that way" in such a tone that David knew he didn't want to talk about it. It had to be because of discrimination. Obviously his antagonists were making life miserable for him.

David wanted to share his insight with Tony, but he knew he had to let the impulse pass. Tony would be embarrassed. Still, David could be angry about it, and he found that it was easier for his blood to start boiling again after his encounter with the Stores manager just a few minutes earlier. He took a deep breath and said, "Well, from the reports I get, you're doing well on your crew. Do you like being a nipper?"

"I do my best." He'd heard that Tony was the type who went way beyond what was expected, but Tony wouldn't brag. David also knew that the men on the crew were cold to Tony, leaving him isolated. He wouldn't talk about that, either. David had experienced this attitude when he worked with some Italians on the Idaho dams. He knew that no matter what was going on in their lives, they would say all was going well. So it made no sense for him to probe any deeper.

"Well, I'm glad that you like the job and that you're doing well. Keep up the good work."

"I will," said Tony and started for the tunnel.

David shook his head as he watched him walk away. "It's hard in this canyon—and it takes hard men to survive it." He said this in a low enough voice that Tony wouldn't hear as he disappeared into the tunnel. "Even harder for you because of the social isolation. Hang in there, Tony." And with that he made his way to the infernal swinging bridge.

As he started out across the turgid red water, his heart sped up as the bridge swung lazily up and down in opposition to the motion of his walking. No matter how hard he tried, he could never clear his mind of the image of the cables snapping just as he reached the center of the bridge and him falling into the water and being swept downstream by the current. It was a persistent, irrational fear. Sometimes it was the source of nightmares, and in his more frantic moments he was convinced that one day the river would kill him. The fact that he was a poor swimmer added to the anxiety. Trying to calm himself, he said, "You've only got to stay with this long enough for the tunnels to be built so we can send the water around the dam site. That way you can walk to the other side." It didn't matter that he talked out loud. No one could hear him above the noise of the river and construction. "I can't wait for the day."

Swinging bridge across the Colorado, situated north of the diversion tunnels

High Scaler working to clear the canyon walls

CHAPTER 6
The Dance of Spiders

Canyon Walls—September 1931

"Did you hear about Salty Russell?" young Jeremy Stephens asked this of Assistant Crew Foreman Sean O'Donnell in a hushed voice, even though the sound of jackhammers pounding on the cliffs below would have drowned out a primal scream, had he been inclined to shout.

Sean simply adjusted his hard hat, an innovation in the construction world invented by the high scalers at this dam site by dipping their visored hats in hot tar so that when the hats cooled they would offer some protection from falling debris. There'd been a number of incidents where the tar-coated hats had saved a man, and Six Companies liked the idea so much that they had hard hats professionally manufactured for everyone working on the job site.

"Well?"

Sean turned and looked at him. "Yeah, I heard about Salty. It's a real shame. He was our best performer.

"The worst of it is that he wasn't doing any acrobatics—just down there minding his own business when a steel rod broke loose from a bundle and came straight down and through his head. Right through the hard hat! I hear that when his body hit the bottom it just kind of exploded." Jeremy shuddered.

Sean took a deep breath. The image made him nauseous.

"Everybody said he died instantly," Jeremy said.

"You know, for the life of me, I can't figure out how anybody knows such a thing. I mean, think about it, Jeremy. How long does it take a body to die, even when hit by a steel rod like that? Nobody knows because the dead man can't talk to you about it. Is it like, 'Wow, one second I was conscious and the next second it was pitch black,' or, 'It's true what they say—one second I was conscious and the next second I saw this incredible light,' or whatever else it is that happens when we die. For all we know it hurts like heck to have your head split apart, no matter how long it takes for your heart to stop beating."

Jeremy didn't reply; he realized he'd hit a nerve. Salty had become famous by doing acrobatic stunts for the people who were watching from the Nevada overlook. On some days, in those odd moments when everyone happened to be working on something quiet, you could hear people ooh and aah even from across the canyon when Salty swung gracefully out with his ropes, sometimes doing somersaults or other aerial maneuvers. Six Companies discouraged such behavior officially, both because it wasn't contributing to the work and because it was dangerous. Unofficially they loved it because it always got them good press and positive comments from the tourists who came to watch the progress of the dam. That was why Sean was so popular—he was as agile and graceful as the best of them. Some would say he was a showoff.

Jeremy shuddered again. "Well, I'm going to be careful. I can promise you that."

"You do that, Jeremy. Do you really think Salty died because he wasn't careful? A bar of steel falling from heaven wasn't his fault. The fact is that when your time is up, it's just up. At least that's how I see it." Sean spat on the ground, leaned down, rubbed some dirt onto the pads of his hands, and then rubbed them together vigorously. It was part of his superstitious ritual each day before he started work. "Well, time's a wasting, so we ought to be over the side."

Jeremy sighed and picked up his boson's chair. He'd already slung his tools over his shoulder, so he started to make his way to the canyon edge. "Well, you be careful all the same, Sean. I don't want you to get hurt." Before Sean could say anything smart, Jeremy lowered himself over the side.

"He's too sentimental, but he's a good kid," Sean said to no one in particular. He checked his knots, then attached his slipknot to the main rope and went over the side himself. They had made good progress on cleaning the rock face at the spot they were assigned, so Sean had to work his way approximately halfway down the face of the canyon wall. He did this by periodically releasing the slipknot on the short rope that tethered him to the stationary main rope. In this way he could rappel down the face of the cliff at his own pace, adjusting himself throughout the day without depending on anyone up above. He had his lunch with him since it would waste way too much time and energy to climb back up the rope. Instead, he'd signal a request that fresh water be lowered down to him when he was ready to eat the sandwiches he had picked up that morning in the mess hall after breakfast.

Once in place, he took a moment to spin around and take in the panorama before him. Just like in New York City, he loved this part of the job—being all alone in the air with a spectacular view all around him. Another thing he liked about this job even more than structural steel work was that once he was on the canyon face he was out of sight of all his supervisors, which meant he was totally in control of his own small section of the world. At least for a few hours. Once settled, he found that his assigned area for the day included a large outcrop of loose rock, which would have to be blasted completely away. The scaling job would be fairly complicated since the goal was to blast the outcrop from the face of the wall without leaving a crater. The first step was to chip away as much of the loose material as possible and then to drill a pattern of holes so that the explosive charge would create a directed blast that sheared off the outcrop. Once the big stuff was gone, Sean would go to work with his hand tools to smooth out what was left.

"First we'll whack that big fella right over there," he said to the air. "That means push off right about now." His leg muscles flexed and his body started to arc out into the canyon. "And come in for a landing right here." Not only did he talk to himself while doing a job, he also loved to see just how precisely he could position himself as he swung through the air. It was a challenge to land exactly where he wanted. "And now it's time to start breaking off all you vicious little shards that would blow a hole right through me if I didn't chip you away before the blast."

Perhaps the biggest difference between the scalers and those who worked inside the tunnels was that the scaler was a one-man crew who had to play the role of miner, chuck tender, nipper, and mucker all in one. On top of that, once the fuse was lit, he had to get out of the way by swinging out and to the side while the blast went off, rather than having the convenience of physically exiting the tunnel before it went up in smoke. That fact alone had a sobering effect on the work to be done, and all of that swinging was done while dangling four or five hundred feet above the river. Sean had started calling it the "dance of spiders," since that's what he and the others looked like as they moved about on their thin little web of ropes and tethers.

After perhaps half an hour of chipping, he felt he was ready to start drilling, so he signaled on the support rope to send down the drill bits. The jackhammer was already hanging by him. Once he felt the auxiliary rope take the strain, he spread his legs against the rock while waiting for the basket to arrive, daydreaming of his sister and her family back in New York City.

Perhaps that was why he didn't consciously register the explosion next to him, since it was inevitable that blasts would be going off periodically as the other men did their job. Yet, even against this background something sounded an alarm in his brain, a sense that something wasn't right. The sensation only lasted for a millisecond, however, until the suspicion was replaced by the soul jarring reality of an agonized human shriek.

Reacting out of pure instinct, he kicked away from the wall with all his strength to find out what was going on. At least that was what he tried to tell himself. The truth was that in his mind he knew exactly what was going on. The shriek had come from Jeremy Stephens, and he knew that Jeremy had somehow failed to swing away from the blast. He had no idea what to expect, so naturally his brain expected the worst. Just as he reached the zenith of his arc he heard the emergency whistle sound on the top of the rim, which meant that observers from the other side had witnessed what had happened and sounded the alarm.

Almost immediately all activity in the canyon stopped, and the silence that followed was disconcerting—nearly as unnerving as the sound of Jeremy's cry of pain.

"Okay, O'Donnell, you've got to stay calm," Sean said to himself as he craned his neck to see where Jeremy was, but he didn't feel calm. His legs were trembling. Still, he pushed off a second time and still didn't see anything on that arc except some dust below him arching out and down from the remnant of Jeremy's blast. Inevitably, gravity exerted itself and brought him back to the cliff face, where he pushed off a third time, but this time with a different angle and with even more force. As he reached the farthest point in the swing he saw something that chilled his blood. Perhaps twenty feet below him was the body of Jeremy Stephens dangling limply upside down, his lower arm swinging crazily below his head. "Oh, please, no. He's killed himself!" Sean jumped at the sound of his own voice, which had a very unnatural pitch to it. "I've got to get over there."

The question was how. He would have to reposition himself to get close enough, and he wasn't sure how to get that message communicated to the men up above. He knew that if he took time to pull himself all the way up the canyon and then reposition, he'd lose any meaningful chance he had to help Jeremy, assuming there was anything left to help.

"You've got to do something!" he screamed to the air. "You can't just let him hang there." Then, "But they'll pull him up. Surely they'll pull him up." This turned out to be one of those times when his mouth was saying one thing while his brain confidently asserted another. It took a few moments for his conscious mind to realize that Jeremy was not hanging by his main rope, but rather by the safety line. The safety line was a very frail thing to attach one's life to. It was also extremely dangerous to pull a man up the face of the cliff by his safety rope since the chance of friction rubbing through the rope was much greater when compared to the heft of the main rope.

"Okay, so this is more difficult than you thought. You're here, he's there . . . Do something!" After thinking for a moment, he gave a series of tugs on his rope to indicate that he was there and that something had to happen. He received a response but didn't know for sure what it meant. What he thought it meant was that he should come up.

"There's no time—they've got to realize that!" Shouting up to the rim he did his best to make himself heard. "You've got to think of something else." Just to make sure he understood what was happening, he swung out again. As he did so he looped around so that, for just a moment, he was staring straight at the observation post on the other rim of the canyon. That's when it dawned on him. "Of course! You've got to use the spotters there. They can signal to the people on the top of this side."

That seemed like a good idea, so, as he started to fall back against the side of the canyon, he purposely turned in his seat to face the Nevada side and started making exaggerated arm gestures to where Jeremy was. Without binoculars, he couldn't tell if they could see him, but he did his best to make gestures to indicate that they should move his ropes to bring him closer to Jeremy.

It was maddening as he hung there, waiting, while nothing seemed to happen. At last he decided he needed to climb up, regardless of how much time it took, because he couldn't stand just hanging there, taking no action. But just as he started to loosen his slipknot, he felt a series of tugs on his ropes that he was quite sure meant he should swing out. So he did. And as he did so he had the disconcerting feeling of having the rope slip on him, not at his level, but up above. As he started to swing back to the rock face he landed a bit higher than he had been, but more in line with Jeremy. As he realized what was happening he burst into a grin. "So you figured it out. Good for you, Pete."

What Pete, or whoever it was up there, had figured out was that on the outward arc of his swing they could slide his rope closer to the point where Jeremy's rope went down and then hold it there until the next swing. By doing it that way, they could move his rope until it was parallel with Jeremy's in just a few motions. It also meant they didn't have to try to move his rope to new eyebolts while he was still in the canyon.

Once he landed, he waited just a moment and then pushed off again. Sure enough, he felt the rope slip yet another time. In all it took four such maneuvers to bring him to the spot where Jeremy's blast had gone awry. Of course, at that point the folks on the top of the rim would know he was in position, since his rope would now be going over the edge at approximately the same spot where Jeremy's did.

"All right, now, you've got to get down to him." In the act of repositioning his rope, they'd shortened his distance to the top, which placed him even farther above Jeremy.

Even though he was eager to get to his friend, he acted deliberately, just as he had been trained to do, both to conserve his strength and to avoid putting undo pressure on his own rope. Eventually, he started to draw near Jeremy. That was when his superstition started to kick in, and he realized with dread that he may very well be coming face-to-face with a dead body. A mangled and bloody one at that. The thought made goose bumps of his skin. He'd never confessed to anyone just how frightened he was around dead people, nor how many funerals he'd avoided because of it.

"You can do this." His voice was strained, but talking seemed to help. So he continued to loosen the slipknot, slide down a bit, then loosen it again, reassuring himself each time. At the point where he knew he should turn and look at Jeremy, he felt his skin crawling so fiercely on the back of his neck he thought he might lose control of his arms if they went weak at the sight.

Taking a deep breath, he said, "It's your man, for crying out loud. Now do your duty!" Jeremy had always been a little irritating because of his relentlessly good nature. But he was also the glue that held the crew together. Everyone knew that Jeremy would do anything for them. "Which is why you have to do this for him now—even if it's to bring his corpse up for proper burial."

Gritting his teeth, he turned toward the body, knowing that if he stopped to think about it he might throw up. The shock was greater than his resolve. "Oh, Jeremy, what have you done to yourself?" There really weren't words for what he saw—the young man dangled crazily in the air, blood dripping from his forehead and disappearing into the bottomless pit of the canyon. It was clear that his arm had been broken, perhaps clean through so that only the muscle tissue was holding it to his body. The clothes on his upper body had been blown off, leaving a rash of torn and bleeding skin. Sean retched involuntarily, the contents of his stomach falling to the canyon floor below. The taste in his mouth was bitter, and he coughed to clear it, fearing for a moment that he might choke on his own vomit. But the retching helped him recover his wits, and he was able to force himself to turn again to Jeremy's body. As he looked at it carefully, he thought he could see Jeremy's chest rising and falling, if ever so slightly.

"Jeremy! Jeremy! Are you alive?" His voice sounded even more unnatural, but Jeremy didn't respond. Swinging over to him, he touched the body and was jolted when Jeremy twitched. The only thing worse than being next to a dead person was to be next to one who jerked.

"Jeremy? Jeremy, are you awake?'

"What . . . what . . ." Jeremy's voice was weak and confused.

"It's me—Sean! You've been hurt. Can you look at me?"

As he started to regain consciousness, Jeremy suddenly jerked as he opened his eyes. The rope he was dangling from slipped as a knotted loop tightened on itself. That made Sean gasp and Jeremy cry out in fear.

"Where am I? What's happened?" And with that Jeremy started struggling frantically.

"Jeremy! Stop moving—now!" Sean yelled at him. "Your main rope is severed, and you've only got your safety rope. You've got to stop moving."

"Sean, I can't see! And my head hurts. What's happening?" Jeremy started clawing at his face with his good arm.

As much as it frightened him, Sean realized he had to do something right now, or Jeremy's rope could separate. So he swung himself over to Jeremy, where he wrapped his arms around him. He could feel the warm blood of Jeremy's face drip onto his. "It's all right, Jeremy. I'm here, and we're going to get you up. You've got to trust me."

It was pathetic to hear Jeremy cry out as he tried to bring his injured arm to wrap it around Sean. "Oh, Sean, it hurts! Am I gonna die?"

Sean felt a lump grow in his throat. He really didn't know the answer. With more confidence than he felt, he said, "You're not going to do anything until I get you turned around and up to the top of the canyon. You will not die on us. Do you understand?"

It was heart wrenching to see a smile come to Jeremy's blood-stained face, but at least he stopped moving. "Tell me what to do," Jeremy said simply, and Sean knew the immediate crisis was over.

Now the problem was that Sean had to figure out what to do, and he really didn't have a clue. There had been no training for this, that was for sure.

"All right, I'm going to swing away so I can study it out. Don't panic. I'm right here. Okay?"

"Okay," Jeremy said weakly.

So Sean let go his grip and swung a foot or so away. And then it happened—something he'd heard Pete talk about but had never experienced himself. In an instant he felt his heart slow down, his breathing stabilize, and the fear evaporate. He felt totally in control—ice cold. This was a problem, and he was the one to solve it.

"Okay, I'm going to come back and tie us together. Once I know you're secured to me, then we'll try to untangle your ropes. If anything goes wrong, you'll simply fall against me and we'll both be supported by my rope."

"Is it strong enough?" Jeremy asked plaintively. "I don't want to put you at risk."

That got to Sean. "Listen, kid. If a rope can support that fat old George Roper, it can certainly hold both of us." Sean was pleased when Jeremy smiled again.

"Okay, here I come." With a gentle swing he reached Jeremy. "Now, try to hold to me with your good arm so I can work on the ropes. Jeremy tightened up on him, but not with as much strength as the first time they came together. And the color of his skin was now a pale gray. Sean knew he was running out of time. He reached into his knapsack and pulled out a length of rope. He quickly wrapped it under Jeremy's armpits, around his chest, and then over his own shoulders and around his chest. Once he'd completed a couple of loops, he felt secure enough to let Jeremy relax.

"Okay now, I'm going to work on your ropes." Jeremy muttered something incomprehensible. Sean's sense of urgency increased.

He started working with the tangle of hemp that held Jeremy in his unnatural position, but it was hard work since Jeremy was essentially dead weight and unable to assist him. As Sean struggled with the ropes, he finally concluded there was no hope of getting Jeremy turned while still connected to the safety rope. It was simply too tangled, and Sean just didn't have any leverage to manipulate Jeremy; they were both hanging free in space because of an outcrop above them. He took a deep breath and said, "Jeremy, I'm going to have to cut your rope. I can't get it untangled." There was no response. He reached for his knife. It was a dangerous maneuver, but he didn't know what else to do—Jeremy would bleed to death if he didn't get him turned.

Finally, hoping that his own main rope could take the strain, he started slicing through Jeremy's safety rope. Just like in cutting a tree branch, nothing happened for the longest time until suddenly, with a twang, the rope separated and Jeremy's body fell free with a powerful jerk. As Jeremy's legs dropped, Sean momentarily feared that both of them were going to fall. But as he had planned, the body flipped right side up as it slammed against Sean's body with a jarring thud. The weight was incredible, and he felt the tops of his shoulder blades burning from the strain.

"But it held," he said. At least it held. "Now we can get you up to help." Jeremy was completely unconscious. That was good in some ways since he wouldn't struggle. Sean just hoped he wasn't dead.

Taking a deep breath to steady himself, he tugged on his rope to signal that he needed to be pulled up. Of course, it would have been better if he could have pulled both of them up himself, hand over hand, which would leave his rope stationary and reduce any chance of it fraying, but he didn't have the strength for that. Instead, he would have to walk them up the side, being careful to keep his rope as far away from the rock face as possible to keep the rubbing to a minimum. The men on top would know how to protect the rope where it came over the rim.

A short time later but well documented by the cuts and scratches on Sean's legs from his stumbling as he attempted to walk up the canyon wall at the exceedingly fast pace at which the rope was being pulled, a group of hands reached out to pull Sean and Jeremy over the top. They landed in a pile with Jeremy still strapped to Sean.

"Is he alive?" Sean had never heard Pete Conroy sound anything but nonplussed and cool, at least when he was sober, which made the urgent sound in his voice startling.

"He was. I hope he still is." Sean's voice was surprisingly flat, given all he'd been through, but this wasn't really an ideal time for conversation. The members of his crew were quickly unstrapping Jeremy's body and gently lifting it onto a stretcher that had been jury-rigged from some wooden poles and several quickly donated shirts—one of them Pete's. Sean rolled to his side and then struggled to his feet, temporarily forgotten in the rush to get Jeremy taken care of.

After watching them lift Jeremy onto the back of a pickup truck, Sean watched as the truck started down the face of the hill toward the new wooden bridge. An ambulance was waiting. Feeling a bit overwhelmed, Sean asked quietly of anyone nearby, "Do you think he'll be all right? Is he still alive?"

"What the . . . ?" Pete was startled by Sean's voice. "Oh, for crying out loud—look at you. You're a mess."

Sean followed Pete's glance to the front of his own body, where he saw that his work shirt was covered in blood. Looking lower still, he saw that his pant legs had been shredded by the ascent up the mountain, with some of his own fresh blood dripping from wounds where he'd been scraped by the rocks. Still, as gruesome as that appeared, he looked up and said. "But what about Jeremy? Is he alive? I talked to him down there, but he went quiet . . ."

Pete softened. "He's alive. We know that. Will he get better? I don't know. He's totally unconscious, and his face is torn up pretty badly. The truth is that we have no idea what kind of injuries he's suffered. That will be up to the doctors to determine."

"I'm glad he's alive." Sean staggered a bit. Pete stepped forward to steady him and soon found that he was holding the bulk of Sean's weight.

"You better sit down." Sean nodded, and all Pete had to do was relax his arms for Sean to sag to the ground. Pete sat down next to him.

"Were you hit by the blast?"

Sean shook his head. "I just heard it—then I heard Jeremy scream." Sean shook his head at the recollection. Then, to his surprise, he felt himself start to tremble. The cold reserve that had helped him rescue Jeremy was starting to fade; perhaps it was shock wearing off.

Pete may have noticed, but he didn't say anything about it. "You did a good job down there. I was ready to go over the side when we got the signal from the other side. That was smart thinking."

"I figured time was important." At this point Sean was shivering.

"Listen, you should take the day off—with pay. I'll write you up a ticket indicating that you need to go to the infirmary to be checked out. You really should get looked at."

Sean shook his head. "I don't want to go. The last thing I need right now is to be alone. Just give me a minute to collect my wits and get a drink of water, and I'll go back down."

Pete laughed. "Does the irony of what you just said strike you at all?"

"No."

"You don't want to be alone, yet you're ready to go over the edge of the cliff for the rest of your shift where you'll be completely alone. At least at the infirmary there will be doctors—and maybe a nurse or two."

Sean shook his head again. "It's not the same thing, and you know it. I want to be here with the crew. If I go over there, I'll have to answer a thousand questions that I don't have answers to. I know from experience that if I don't get back over that cliff pretty quickly, I may never be able to do it again. I saw men on skyscrapers who had a close call who never came back. I like this job."

Pete nodded. "Okay. I'd want the same thing, but first we need to get you a new shirt and something hot to drink. After a sandwich I'll go down with you—"

"You don't need to go down with me! I can take care of myself. I just told you that."

"Steady, boy. You're my assistant, and we need to conduct an investigation. We've got to try to figure out what happened, like whether it was the fuse that malfunctioned or if it was Jeremy who made a mistake that caused him to be in the way. I don't know if we can figure that out, but we have to try. There's the accident report to fill out. Frankly, I need a second pair of eyes to judge that."

Sean was sullen. "I just don't want you to think that I need you to hold my hand . . ."

"Of course not."

Sean wasn't entirely convinced that Pete wasn't just making something up so he could be there with him. As much as the thought irritated him, it also reassured him. Particularly when he happened to glance down and see just how badly his hands were trembling.

Pete was thoughtful. "I had to memorize a bit of rhetoric years ago, written by Jonathon Edwards, a hell-and-damnation minister. Somehow it seems appropriate for what we've been through today.

"'The God that holds you over the pit of hell, much as one holds a spider or some other loathsome creature over the fire . . . you hang by a slender thread . . . yet it is nothing but his hand that holds you from falling into the fire every moment.' "

Sean laughed. "You don't know just how slender a thread it was. When I cut Jeremy's safety rope, I honestly had no idea if my rope could take the strain.

"Then you're a hero . . ."

Sean shook his head. "Don't talk like that. I don't need it, and it serves no purpose."

"Well, we're a lot like those spiders, aren't we? With only fate holding us," said Pete. He gazed off. "I hope he lives. He's a good kid."

Sean swallowed hard. "You said something about some coffee."

Pete smiled. "Stay here. I'll be back in a flash."

CHAPTER 7
On the Way to the Casino

Boulder City—October 1931

Is David all right?"

Woody Williams looked up from his desk to see a concerned Frank Crowe looking across the room. "Why do you ask?"

He didn't say a word at our briefing this morning, and usually he's pretty chatty."

Williams nodded. "I'm not sure. He's working harder than ever, but I've noticed a change as well. He never smiles anymore. I think it may have something to do with his family."

"Mary? I can't believe she'd give him trouble."

Williams shook his head. "His son. I was playing cards with Pete the other night—" Williams caught himself. "I mean, I was having a soda with him . . ."

Crowe shook his head. Gambling was strictly forbidden on the federal work site reservation, and he couldn't have his number-two man talking about the unofficial card games in public. "You were saying . . . ?"

"Yeah, well. Pete says that his son is being a little pain in the butt. He's sixteen or sixteen and giving his mom a hard time. Pete thinks he needs to be slapped around a little, but, of course, David isn't there to do it."

Crowe nodded. "It's tough. David's been on an awful lot of work sites throughout the years. Mary's as good as there is at supporting him, but without married housing she's on her own in Boise."

"I don't know that it's his kid for sure, but that's what I suspect. I don't get involved."

"Of course not." Crowe looked distracted. Then he abruptly took off across the room . At least it would have been abruptly if it were anyone else, but that was the way Frank Crowe always moved.

"Hey, David," Crowe said brightly.

David looked up. "Hi, Frank. Haven't seen you for a while."

"Listen, David, I hate to impose on you, but I've been having trouble with some of the engineers in Boise. They're second-guessing me on the plans for this concrete plant, and I can't waste any more time."

David got a puzzled look on his face. "So how can I help?"

Crowe leaned down and rested his hands on David's desk. "I need somebody up there who's been onsite. If I give you a thorough briefing, can you hand carry the plans and go through it with those morons? I've got to get it resolved right away. It would be a big favor."

David's eyes widened. "Go to Boise? Sure."

"You'd probably be stuck there for at least a week."

David smiled. "That's all right. It will give me a chance to see my family, and I can certainly argue your points for you."

"Good. Meet me tomorrow morning at nine, and we'll go over the drawings. Have my secretary order train tickets." As usual, that was it. Frank simply turned and strode out of the room.

"Well, I'll be." David sat back in his chair and smiled. He was going to Boise—maybe to save Jim's life, based on the frustration he heard in Mary's voice the last time they talked. He decided to go over and tell Woody about his good fortune and to make sure they could clear his calendar. But when he turned in that direction, Woody just gave him a little nod and waved him on.

Las Vegas—October 1931

"I'LL TAKE YOU TO THE HOTEL anytime you want to go," said Sean.

Jeremy shook his head. "No thanks. It's my going-away party, and I don't want to cut it short."

It wasn't so much of a party as a going-away dinner at a Las Vegas bar. Jeremy had been in the hospital for nearly six weeks recovering from the lacerations and burns over much of his body. The pain had been intense, and Jeremy's suffering made both Sean and Pete uncomfortable each time they went to see him.

Even Frank Crowe had called, particularly after it was confirmed that the accident was not a result of Jeremy's carelessness but rather a faulty fuse. Perhaps because of that, Six Companies had not protested about paying what they considered to be the exorbitant benefits provided under Arizona Workers' Compensation laws. They much preferred to 'have an employee injured on the Nevada side of the river where the law was less labor friendly.

"Can I buy you guys another beer?" Tony Capelli was a bit hesitant when he asked this since he'd been invited at the last minute and he hardly knew Jeremy. Pete had found him at the mess hall and talked him into coming into Vegas with them. Now Pete was off in some other corner of the bar, and Tony was left with Sean and Jeremy.

"I'm good for another pint—I mean glass," said Sean as cheerfully as he could. "I'm not sure Jeremy's up to it, though. He's been on a strict diet the last few weeks, and it might not sit so good on his stomach."

"I thought my mother didn't arrive until tomorrow," Jeremy said sardonically. As Sean started to apologize, Jeremy raised his hand. "Not to worry—you're absolutely right. I probably shouldn't have had the one that I already did. It already feels like it's churning into something unpleasant down there."

Tony raised his hand, only to be ignored by the waitress. Sensing the problem, Sean raised his hand. The waitress came over and took their order then quickly disappeared.

"Do you get that a lot?" Sean asked.

Tony shrugged. "Only everywhere I go."

"Kind of like being Irish in New York. If we get out of our neighborhood, things can get dicey real fast." He smiled. "That's why my right fist here and I are such good friends."

"I've heard that the Irish and the Italians don't get along so well in New York."

Sean nodded. "Not so much. It's kind of like the last one to arrive gets short shrift." He looked up at Tony. "But, the way I see it is we're not in New York. Plus, us Catholics have to stick together." He smiled.

Tony returned the smile. Sean's eyes twinkled when he talked. It was hard not to like him. "At least it isn't obvious from a distance that you're Irish. Try having olive skin and brown eyes, no matter how long you've lived in the 'neighborhood.'"

Sean grinned. "You don't think the hair gives it away?"

Tony was surprised. He had never thought of it, but Sean's red hair would certainly make him stand out.

"Nobody ever gave me trouble for what I look like," Jeremy said quietly. "At least until now."

That sobered both Tony and Sean. The severity of Jeremy's injuries would forever change his future—and not for the better. People were sure to treat him differently. The facial scars from his burns were the most obvious sign of his trauma and would put most people off, but it was the loss of his arm that was most likely to harm his future employment opportunities. As

Sean had feared while rescuing him, Jeremy's arm had been so badly severed that doctors couldn't save it. He had also lost the hearing in one of his ears, and Sean was still learning to sit next to his good ear so Jeremy could hear him more easily.

Going back as a partially deaf cripple would label Jeremy for life. He had come to Nevada as a handsome, blue-eyed blond with a medium build and cheerful temperament. He was returning home with red, blotchy skin, a missing arm, and a hearing loss that often forced him to ask a person to repeat himself. Even though his mind was the same as before the accident, it was the nature of some people that they would think of him as stupid from now on since he'd have trouble following conversations clearly or acting on his own when a task required two arms. So he was about to experience what Tony, and to a lesser degree Sean, had experienced all of their lives.

"So your mother's coming to help you get home?" Sean asked, attempting to change the subject.

"Yeah. My dad got some temporary work last week, after nearly a year out of work, so he can't leave. My oldest sister is going to take care of my little brothers and sisters, even though she's got a kid of her own."

Sean nodded, pretending this was a good thing.

"Pete's doing it again . . ." Tony interrupted.

"What?" Sean looked up in alarm, worried that Pete was picking a fight.

"He's egging that guy on."

Jeremy laughed. "He's a real firecracker, isn't he?"

"He's a firecracker who's on his own tonight. If he starts something, I've got to get you out of here. His fights tend to spill over to the whole bar, and I'm afraid it would kill you if somebody came crashing into you."

Jeremy sighed. The thought had crossed his mind as well. Which was just one more way that his short-lived job on the Boulder Canyon Project had changed his life forever. He'd no longer be one of the gang, ready to join in a brawl at a moment's notice.

"Maybe it's a good idea to go anyway. I don't want you to get too tired." Sean tried to smile. "Particularly since your mom will be here tomorrow. She'll have my hide if anything else happens to you."

Jeremy attempted a smile of his own, trying to keep the good feeling going. "Better your hide than mine—I don't have much hide left."

Sean was astonished how resilient human beings could be. As much as he ached for Jeremy, he knew right then that he would be okay. The fact that he could joke about himself meant that his native temperament would see him through.

"I should get up and help Pete," said Tony.

Sean turned his head. "I'm not sure that's a good idea. Pete's perfectly capable of starting a fight on his own, and in view of what we've been talking about, you could make it worse."

Tony wasn't happy, but he sat back down. Sean was right, but it still made his blood boil. The simple fact was that having an Italian come to your rescue would simply inflame things.

"Well, then, let's figure out how to maneuver past the combatants . . ." said Sean, but just as he started to stand up, Pete suddenly broke things off and came over to them.

"Guy's a real jerk," he said while casting a quick glance over his shoulder. "I don't want to start anything since it might end up hurting Jeremy." The three were pleasantly surprised. "I hope you won't mind if I take off a little early," Pete continued, "I have a date at the blackjack tables. I discovered that I've got a little too much money in my bank account. Furthermore, I need to teach Mr. Tightfist Capelli here how to lighten up a little bit."

Tony smiled but didn't say anything. Turning to Jeremy and Sean, he asked, "Do either of you want to come?"

Jeremy shook his head. "That's all right. I'm not really in the mood. Besides, I need to keep what money I've got. I've got a girl back home. I wrote her and told her everything, just so she wouldn't be shocked. I also told her she could get out of our understanding if she wants to, but she wrote back that she loved me before and she'll love me now. I hope she feels that way after she sees me."

Pete sighed. There was really nothing to say.

"What about you, Sean? You want to come along?"

"Nah—I'm going to stick with Jeremy. You guys go ahead. We'll be fine."

Pete looked at them, obviously feeling guilty for leaving, but he had a lot of nervous energy to burn through. "Well, we have to walk the same way for a couple of blocks. You two want to walk with me and Tony?"

Jeremy smiled. "Sure. I'd like that. It will give me a chance to say good-bye."

So they got up and allowed Pete to pay their tab, since he insisted, and then they made their way out onto Fremont Street. As they walked through the late fall air, Jeremy remarked that the cool air felt good on his face and that he was glad he got to go back to the cool, moist air of the Pacific Northwest.

"That'll be good for your skin," Pete acknowledged. "I always liked working in Seattle."

As they walked a little farther, Sean said rather casually, and in a way that he hoped wouldn't be offensive, that Pete seemed to spend a lot of his money on bar bills, barmaids, and gambling.

"You think so? I don't spend nearly as much now as I spent on my three wives. If you really want to burn through cash, just get married and divorced. You'll learn what poverty is pretty fast."

"Married three times?" Jeremy was incredulous.

"Afraid so. I've always liked women. I like the way they look, I like the way they smell, I like the way they feel. I just plain like them, but I'm no good at living with them. I used to marry them to stay respectable—it meant a lot to my mother—but after three I gave up. It's easier finding other ways to enjoy their company."

They continued walking down the street until they reached the intersection where Pete had to turn to go to the casino, while Sean and Jeremy would continue straight for a couple of blocks to their hotel.

Pete stopped walking and turned to Jeremy. "Well, I guess this is where we part company."

Jeremy smiled. "Thanks, Pete. You're a great boss. Wish I could have been here to the end, but I'll think of you."

Pete rather clumsily stepped forward and shook Jeremy's hand. He was more the type for a hug, but Jeremy's condition made that impossible. "I'll think of you too, kid. Good luck."

Before he got any more sentimental, Pete turned to Tony. "Your job tonight is to drag me out of the casino before I start borrowing money. It makes my brother crazy when I get stuck with gambling debt."

"Good luck with that one," Sean said to Tony. "By the time that point is reached, Pete isn't always as reasonable as he is right now. There's almost always a brawl for whoever it falls on to pull him away, and it's his friends who get the worst of it."

"I always say I'm sorry . . ."

Tony smiled. "I've had plenty of experience. They have tequila where I come from. I'll be all right."

Pete and Tony walked away and turned the corner of the block toward the casino. About halfway down the street they passed Judy's Place, a fairly seedy restaurant and bar. Pete suddenly looked up. "Do you hear that? What is it?"

Tony strained to hear. There was a muffled thud, followed by what sounded like a woman's sob.

"Come on," said Pete fiercely, "let's go." He was off before Tony could register what was happening.

"It's coming from down here," said Pete as he ducked into a narrow opening between two brick buildings. Tony felt his heart race as he followed Pete into the dark.

"What do you think you're doing?" Pete shouted as he tackled someone. It was way too dark to make out who it was, but the fellow was bigger than Pete—that much Tony could see. Fortunately, Pete had the advantage of surprise, and Tony watched as the larger man went tumbling to the ground, accompanied by a string of particularly foul curses. It wasn't the words that made the hair on Tony's neck stand up, though. It was the voice.

"Get the woman!" Pete shouted. "Help her!"

Tony looked at the two men wrestling in the muddy filth of the passage and debated whether he should first help Pete or find the woman he was talking about.

"NOW!"

That cleared that up.

Tony made his way forward in the dark until he found a young girl crumpled against the wall. He kneeled down a short distance from her and started to extend his arm, but she shrunk back in terror.

"It's all right. We're going to help you. How badly are you hurt?"

When the girl didn't make any reply, he strained to see her, but she had her face down on her knees. But the hair and color of her skin were clear enough. "Esta bien. Hablo Español. Cuan herida estas?" Having grown up in Southern California, Tony knew some key Spanish phrases.

The girl looked up and replied, "It's all right, I speak English."

Tony reached out his hand again and lifted her chin. What he saw made him angry, for her left eye had been hammered so hard that there was blood dripping down her face. There was also a drop of blood at the corner of her mouth. When he attempted to wipe it away, she winced in pain. Tony turned quickly to see how Pete was doing and, when he couldn't figure out who was winning, he said to the girl, "I'll be right back." He then leapt to his feet and, with a growl, dove into the pile, shouting "You filthy scum, I'll get you for this."

Tony lunged with such ferocity that he quickly displaced Pete—to the point that Pete ultimately had to intervene to save the life of the perpetrator. Tony sputtered as Pete pulled him away. "It's not worth killing him! It's Chick Flemming and you don't want to go to jail for murder, particularly for someone as worthless as he is. Now knock it off."

Tony allowed himself to be pulled away from Chick, stepped back, and struggled to bring his breathing under control. Pete reached down to constrain Flemming, who by now had started struggling to get up to go after Tony. "I'd stay down if I were you, Chick. Otherwise he's going to kill you, and I won't be able to stop him."

"This wop! I'll kill him!"

"Not now you won't." Pete was sitting on the ground, his arms firmly wrapped around Chick Flemming. When Chick finally shook his head and relaxed his shoulders, Pete loosened up just a bit. Tony stood there fuming, and Pete could tell that he could go off at any moment. To calm himself down, Tony moved over to the girl, who had managed to stand up. While her face was fairly battered, it didn't appear that she had any life-threatening injuries. Still, she cowered against the wall, afraid to run away but also terrified to be near Chick.

"So, Chick, before we take you to the police for assault and battery, care to tell us what's going on here? Just what did this girl do to deserve this?"

"She's a waitress . . ."

"A waitress? Just what were you going to do to her?"

"You really need to ask?" Tony asked bitterly.

"Tony, be quiet. You got your blows in. Now shut up and let me handle this." Pete flashed Tony a warning that at once silenced him but also let him know that Pete was firmly on his side.

"You two will pay for this," said Chick evenly. "Turn me into the police? I *am* the police."

"Yeah, well, unless she was pointing a gun at you, which she wasn't, this isn't exactly how police officers treat people. You were going to rape her, weren't you?"

"Rape! I wasn't going to rape her, I was going to . . ."

"You were going to kill her? We can testify to that, if you want."

Chick took a deep breath. "I was going to rough her up a bit—to let her know that she ought to get out of town."

"What did she do to you?"

"Do? She's a foreigner—a Mexican!" The disbelief in his voice was genuine. "I told Judy she ought to fire all her Mexicans since there are plenty of white girls willing to work. But it turns out she's a bleeding heart just like you and your brother. So I decided to do something about it myself."

"Why don't you come down to our neighborhood in Southern California," said Tony, "and we'll show you how we take care of guys like you who mess with girls like this. Our knives are very sharp . . . and for really bad guys we have friends." He didn't need to explain the Mafia, even to Chick.

Chick looked up with pure hatred in his eyes. It was obvious that some of the blows he'd absorbed had hurt him, because he was holding the left side of his ribs with his right arm. "Yeah, well they're not here, and you'll be going to jail for what you've done to me, you Dago! Assaulting a police officer . . ."

Tony started over toward them, but Pete waved him away. "Nobody's going to jail." Turning to Tony he said, "You know as well as I do that if either of us reports this you'll be in just as much trouble as he is—hitting a sheriff looks bad. Attacking a girl in an alley will look like rape, particularly when the three of us testify against you. So I say we all just calm down right now . . ."

Chick struggled to stand up. This time Pete helped him.

"So, here's what's going to happen, Chick. You're going to go in and apologize to Judy. You're going to promise her that you won't rough up her employees—no matter what their skin color. In exchange, we're going to act like this never happened."

"Never happened!" shouted Tony. "No way!"

"And you will promise not to take anything out on Tony. Otherwise, we're all off to the police station right now."

"I'm the deputy sheriff here!" Chick shouted. "You are not the one to give orders."

"You're the perpetrator here," said Pete evenly. "And even though the courts aren't favorably inclined to immigrants, the last thing the city wants is a scandal. There's already too much negative press about the corruption here, and you know it. They'll throw you over in a second to protect their reputation."

Chick growled, but his shoulders slumped. Finally he surrendered. "All right, Conroy. I'll lay off on Judy's girls, even though I don't like it. And I won't report the Wop over there." He turned to stare directly at Tony. "But you better stay clear of me. You understand? If you get in my way it'll be all over for you."

Tony bit his lip.

"Fine, then I think we have an agreement," said Pete. "By the way, I didn't recognize you without that parasite who usually walks three paces behind you."

"Marvin? He didn't feel like it tonight. Lucky for you, because if I'd have had backup . . ."

"If you'd have had backup there would have been two dead bodies here. Now get yourself around the corner to Judy and tell her what's happened. We'll bring the girl in a minute and she can tend to her."

Chick shrugged his way out of Pete's grip. "Have it your way, Conroy. Let the whole country get overrun with Italians and Mexicans and all the other foreigners. Just know that not everyone agrees with you—in fact, almost no one does. You and your brother are fools."

Pete inhaled deeply but decided it just wasn't worth the trouble. Chick feigned a small lunge toward Tony, who brought up his fists, but then Chick limped away down the street. It was satisfying to see him holding his ribs.

After he was gone, the three of them just stood there, trying to process what had happened. It was Pete who broke the silence. "So, is the girl all right?"

"I'm all right," she said. "Thank you for fighting for me. Thank you both."

Pete nodded then turned to Tony and said, "You've got to watch yourself, Tony. Now that you've mixed it up with this jerk, you've got to be on your best behavior. If he can provoke you on the construction reservation they'll fire you in a second."

"I knew it was a mistake to come into town tonight. I just can't go anywhere without it blowing up on me."

"Mistake? I don't think it was a mistake. Before you came barreling in like a British Mark IV tank I was having trouble with the guy. He's a lot bigger than me, you know. You probably saved my life."

"I doubt that, but I am glad I was here to help." He looked up and, in as controlled a voice as possible, added, "I will watch myself with him and with his friend, but I can only be pushed so far . . ."

"I understand. More than you know, I understand."

"Let's get her to Judy. She needs to rest."

CHAPTER 8
Caterpillars

Boise, Idaho—November 1931

He doesn't want to go."

"It's not his decision to make." David rolled over on his side to face Mary in their bed. A train whistle had awakened them in the dark and now, a happy half hour later, David basked in the contentment that came from making love to the most attractive woman in the world.

"It isn't always bad. There are days when he's civil." There was a desperate sound to her voice.

"Ah, Mary, you are a tender soul." He brushed her cheek gently with his hand, feeling the moisture there.

Slipping his arm under her neck, he added, "It really isn't punishment, even though that's what he thinks. He simply needs to be among men. He's a man himself."

"He's sixteen."

"And you were married at eighteen . . ."

Mary stiffened but then relaxed. "Perhaps I'm not ready to have a chick leave the nest." She smiled.

"But the chick has become a rooster, and it's time—"

She put her finger to his mouth. "I know. But don't I at least get to feel a little sorry for myself?"

David smiled and kissed her. "He'll be safe. I'll take good care of him. I promise. Besides, I think he'll like it when he gets there. It's an exciting place, after all."

"It always is," said Mary quietly. "No matter where 'it' is."

David took a deep breath and laid his head next to Mary's.

Black Canyon—December 27, 1931

"FIRE IN THE HOLE!"

Tony did his best to cover his ears while holding his elbow in front of his nose to keep out the smoke and dust that was about to come barreling out of the tunnel. With the passage of time he had found himself becoming ever more sensitive to the dust and smoke, and he sometimes started coughing uncontrollably when the main cloud formed after a blast. Hank Toombs had said something about it to him once, which meant he might use that against him if he ever wanted to fire Tony.

The concussion was extraordinary, even though the tunnel was deep now, nearly to the two-thousand-foot mark. The jumbo had proved to be one of the most remarkable mining machines ever created, and the average time required to clear the debris, set the jumbo, drill the holes, pack the explosives, and set the charge off had dropped by nearly half since they'd first gone in. Tens of thousands of tons of rock had been excavated, and they expected to connect with the crews working from the downstream portals within a month.

"Capelli!"

Two nippers sitting on a pile of dynamite crates

Tony jumped at the voice and dropped his arms to his side.

"Yes, sir." He quickly turned to face Hank.

"Come on, Capelli. You know the drill. Start getting your charges ready for the next entrance.

Tony sighed. It seemed like nothing he did lately was good enough for Hank.

"He's right, *paesano*. Let's go." Tony wished that his one friend on the job, Dean Farento, wouldn't call him paesano since it drew attention to his race, but Dean was the kind of person who just didn't care about such things. It helped that Dean was blond headed and that his mother came from a prosperous Anglo family that was tied into one of the owners of the Six Companies Consortium. Still, it was brave for Dean to use the paesano, which was an affectionate word in Italian meaning "fellow countryman." In this case Dean was a fellow nipper.

"Okay." And with that they started off at a jog to the supply dump where the charges were kept.

"I bet the government would have a heart attack if it saw how casually Six Companies handles this stuff. We carry enough explosive to blow the roof right out of the top of one of those tunnels if it went off accidentally."

Tony laughed. "If we did they'd just turn it into a temporary visitor center until they got enough entrance fees to pay for the cleanup." It was kind of a dangerous thing to say, but he said it quietly and with confidence that Dean would protect him. He liked to feel sorry for himself, but the truth was that some good people were on his side, including Dean, as well as the Conroys and their friend from New York.

After signing the appropriate log, they started back toward the tunnel entrance, being careful to stay out of the way of the steady stream of trucks that came roaring out of the tunnel, belching black exhaust from their vertical standpipes. As they drew near the jumbo, they saw Hank wave everyone in, so naturally they jogged over.

"Go ahead and stow your charges then come back. We have a problem." As was usual, Tony's stomach churned at the sound of that. No matter what it turned out to be, he had to deal with the anxiety that it might be related to him.

After mounting the jumbo and carefully placing their charges in the appropriate rack, they came back to where Hank was. Standing next to him was George Fisher, one of the foremen of the mucking crew. "Listen up. George has something to ask you." Tony glanced around and noticed that only the nippers and other support people had been invited to the impromptu meeting. The miners and chuck tenders were off getting some coffee.

"I'll get right to it. Do any of you have experience with a Caterpillar tractor? One of our men just got sick inside, and we need a replacement. If we wait for management to send somebody from above, it will throw off our whole schedule."

"What's wrong with him?" Dean asked. "Does he have pneumonia?"

Everybody laughed at that except Hank and George. The word *pneumonia* had become, it seemed, the diagnosis of every man who got sick on the job. It was never carbon monoxide poisoning, always pneumonia, even though it was still over a hundred degrees in the tunnel in January and the amount of gasoline burned was measured in the hundreds of gallons every shift. To call the sicknesses carbon monoxide poisoning would require Six Companies to buy electric trucks. Pneumonia was a lot cheaper.

"Knock it off, Farento."

"Yes, sir."

"Well, anybody? Anybody ever handle a regular tractor?"

Reluctantly, Tony raised his hand.

"Anybody?" Hank said.

Tony wasn't surprised. He's started thinking of himself as an invisible man where Hank was concerned.

"You, there. What experience do you have?" Apparently Foreman Fisher could see invisible objects and had detected his presence.

Tony cleared his throat. "I ran a Cat for the railroad in California. We used it to clear land and in construction projects I worked on."

"Perfect. Will you help us?"

Tony looked over to Hank. He didn't want to do anything to irritate him, but Hank refused to make eye contact.

"Yes, sir."

"Good. Then let's get going. I'll check you out on the equipment, and you can get to work."

Tony cleared his throat. "This will be temporary, sir?"

Now Hank looked up, catching Tony's eyes for just a second, and then he said to Fisher, "You can have him permanently. We'll get by until I can bring a replacement down tomorrow."

"Not so fast. We'll see how he does. If he's good, I'll keep him. Otherwise, he'll come back to your crew."

Now Hank talked directly at Tony. "You'll be good, won't you, Capelli." It wasn't a question. Tony turned his head just enough to see Dean flash him a warning sign. That confirmed it. Hank was going to use this to get him off his crew.

With nothing to lose, he turned back to Hank and said very evenly, "I'll be very good, Mr. Toombs. I'll be so good that you'll be proud of me. You'll probably even miss me."

Hank glowered but didn't say anything. For his part, George looked back and forth between the two of them and then said, "All right, then, let's get going. We're wasting time." And, just like that, Tony had a new job—at least for one shift.

Boulder City—December 29, 1932

"Hey, wait up you two. You're late."

David turned at the sound of Pete's voice. "Jim and I just got in. We stopped at the office on the way home from Boise, and the good news is that Jim was offered a job with Woody Williams. It's been two months, but we . . ." David stopped himself. "What brings you out so late to this part of town?"

"I was just out taking a walk. Decided to come by your house to see if you were home yet." Then, to turn the conversation, Pete congratulated Jim. "So, starting right at the top!"

Jim smiled. "Thanks. But I'm just a runner . . ."

"Which means you get to go all over the place on a motorcycle or in a truck, not tied down to one spot like the rest of us. Probably the best job on the project, except maybe for the money."

"I hadn't thought of it like that."

David was pleased with this exchange. When he had suggested that being a runner was a good starting point, Jim had simply shrugged. But when Pete spoke favorably about something, Jim was instantly in favor of it as well. Such was the dynamic of father and son versus a popular, hip uncle. David could have been jealous, but he realized that Pete had made Jim's adjustment to Nevada immeasurably easier. So much so that the boy was buckling down to his private high school lessons without complaining very much.

"Now, about you taking a walk," said David. "Do you really expect us to believe that? Such a thing borders on healthy."

Pete replied easily, "I know it's a shocker. I should have warned you. Every now and then I resist the urges of my worst nature. Besides, what's wrong with welcoming a brother and nephew home after Christmas?"

"You could have come with us. Woody cleared it, and Mary said she missed you. Besides, it was Christmas."

"I get motion sick on the trains," Pete deadpanned—this from a fellow who spent his days swinging wildly about on the face of cliffs. David shook his head but didn't say anything. Instead he went up to the door of his house and put the key in.

"So did you two play your music with anybody while you were in Boise?" Pete asked brightly. One thing that David and Jim had in common was that they played instruments—Jim the trumpet, David the piano. Jim had been in a jazz band in Boise, which was a big part of the problem there and the main reason he was grouchy about the move to Nevada.

In response to his uncle's question about playing in Boise, Jim shook his head. "Nah, everybody was too busy with Christmas. I didn't really have much time to spend with my friends." He sounded a little grumpy.

"You know perfectly well that getting four days off was a miracle, Jim, and something of a personal favor from Frank Crowe. Most of the men here would lose their job—"

Jim cut him short. "I know dad. I just wish I could have had more time with my friends."

"So, you get any good presents?" Pete asked, following him in.

"What is it with you?" David asked. "You're acting crazy."

"I just asked if everybody got a nice present. Sheesh, you'd think I was a criminal or something."

Turning to the left, David set his briefcase down on one of the chairs. "Yes, we got some nice presents, all things considered, and we even remembered you. Give me a minute to unpack—"

He was interrupted by Jim, who asked, "When did you get a piano, dad?"

"A what?" David started to say, but as he turned toward the living area, his eyes fairly bugged out at the sight of a massive old oaken piano sitting proudly against the inside wall. "What on earth?" Then he realized what was going on. Turning to Pete, he exclaimed, "You bought us a piano!"

His brother grinned. "Merry Christmas, little brother."

"I can't believe it. How did you get something like that out here?" The look of astonish-

Construction Bulldozer at the mouth of one of the diversion tunnels

ment on David's face was genuine.

"Money—that's pretty much all it ever takes to do anything."

David had moved across the room and was running his hand up and down the side. It was old, but the console was in remarkably good shape. "But you don't have that kind of money. Or at least you shouldn't spend it on . . ."

"What should I spend it on? My kids? A wife? My college fund?"

David sat down on the bench. "This is terrific, Pete."

Jim, who by now was leaning on the piano, smiled at his uncle.

"Well, for crying out loud, play something. That's why I bought it, so I could get some kind of entertainment in this hellhole of a place. Since I've gotten used to coming here on Sunday instead of spending it in Las Vegas I need something to make the time bearable."

David played a trill and then the opening bars of Gershwin's "I Got Rhythm." The music fairly swelled out of the instrument. As he played, he looked up and smiled at Pete. "This really is great, Pete. Thanks. Even if I think you shouldn't have."

"I'll decide what I should and shouldn't do." Turning to Jim, he added, "I don't think he should be telling me what to do, do you?" Before Jim could respond he tipped his head and asked David, "Does it play all right? They told me it would at the place I bought it in Las Vegas."

David nodded in time to the music and looked up and grinned.

"I bought it used, you know?"

"That just makes it even better—it's had time to mellow."

"So you like it?"

David stopped and looked directly at Pete. "I love it." He smiled. "And I like you."

"Pretty neat, Uncle Pete. We needed something to cheer us up."

"Well, are you going to get your trumpet?"

Jim looked down at his dad, who shrugged his shoulders and said, "Maybe a couple of songs. I'm pretty tired."

"Well, you need to practice," said Pete evenly. "Particularly since I've started inviting people here for New Year's Eve . . ."

David shook his head. But nothing could take away from the wonder of this surprise. In a matter of moments, the flimsy little house on Arizona Street had come to life.

Tunnel Number Three—January 29, 1932

"ALL RIGHT, TONY. LET'S GO!" Tony reached down and flipped the ignition switch then pushed on the starter with his foot while giving the big cat the fuel it needed to choke its way to life. The engine grumbled like an unhappy rhinoceros waking up from a nap, and a great cloud of smoke belched up and into the sky. Tony waited for the electric scoop shovel to start rumbling its way toward the mouth of the tunnel, and then he got in line behind it. He knew that he would be the second vehicle in a great caravan of muckers as truck after truck backed its way into the tunnel. In what had to be one of the most amazing displays of driving prowess, the huge dump trucks backed down the narrow canyon road and into the mine so that they wouldn't have to turn around inside the cave. That simple innovation by Frank Crowe had saved untold time in removing the muck and debris from the bottom of the tunnel floor after a blast, and it had undoubtedly shaved weeks off the job, even though it increased the risk to the drivers.

As Tony reached the mouth of the tunnel, he waved at George Fisher, who returned the gesture with a slight tip of his head. George was as fierce as any foreman on the job, but he was a decent man and treated Tony as just one of the crew. And because that was the foreman's attitude, the other men on the job treated him with respect as well, particularly since two of the men had grown up in Southern California and were comfortable around Italians. He had people to talk with at breakfast and on the way home at night. One fellow had even done some farming in the Imperial Valley, so he could carry on an informed discussion of what was coming. Before they were done they'd half convinced most of the men on the job to move there when the dam was completed. Of course, it was mostly just talk, since construction workers usually refused to settle down; they just kept moving from job to job.

As his Cat passed inside the tunnel, Tony was surprised to see the huge arc lights illuminate the figure of David Conroy, who turned and smiled at him. "Wonder what he's doing here?" Tony could talk all he wanted since no one could hear his voice above the sound of the steel links of his tread grinding against the tunnel floor. Pete Conroy had told him the sound reminded him of the British and German tanks he'd heard all too often in France during the Great War.

Their side of the tunnel was now almost a third of a mile deep, so it took a while to reach the mound of debris at the end. The job was called "mucking" because the natural condensation that took place in the tunnels due to the difference in temperature between the cool canyon walls and the putrid air turned the bottom of the excavation into a thick red mud that fouled everything it touched. Later, when they were scheduled to start excavating the riverbed to establish the foundation of the great dam, they would be moving thousands of tons of river sediment, which truly would be muck.

As his Caterpillar crawled its way to the end, he saw the muckers acting kind of strange, making wild gestures and jumping up and down. Even John, the electric shovel operator, had climbed down off his rig and was standing with his hands on his hips looking at the area that had been blasted out.

His stomach tensed as he wondered if they were looking at an unexploded charge or something just as dangerous. "But they'd be running, not jumping up and down." He pulled into position and idled the great machine. Then he hopped down and went over to John. "What is it?" he shouted. "What's going on?"

John turned and burst into a big grin. "Don't you feel that?"

"Feel what?"

"On your face. Pay attention to what you feel on your face."

"My face?" Tony didn't feel anything on his face except maybe a warm breeze.

A breeze! He turned to John. "You mean?"

"Yes. Look right up there. You can see the light shining through."

Tony turned and looked at what was supposed to be a solid wall of breccias rock, but instead he saw a small opening at the top of the heap that had light coming through it. "We've holed out. We've holed the thing out!"

It was the moment they'd all been driving toward for months now, and Tony shouted, "We did it!"

From behind him he heard, "Yes, you did. Congratulations to both of you."

Tony swung around to see David Conroy standing next to him. "Mr. Conroy, the hole—we're through!"

"And none too soon. I need this more than anything in the world to improve the ventilation through here. Now we can get you guys some good cross currents while you work."

Tony could see that David was smiling the same as everybody else. He also saw a relieved look on his face, a look that seemed to be backed by deep lines of worry. *So, paesano,* Tony thought to himself, *you have been worried all along. Everyone here thinks that Six Companies doesn't care about our health—that they lie to us about the carbon monoxide. But you've been worried, haven't you?* Of course, it wasn't his place to say any of this. But he did lean over to David and said quietly in his ear, "Thank you for keeping us alive, Mr. Conroy." He knew that David couldn't reply to that, since to imply that there had been any danger might cause problems later on, but Tony wanted David to know that he knew. In fact, all the men knew.

David didn't reply to the statement directly. Instead, he just said, "It's David. I keep telling you to call me David."

Tony smiled. "You bet, Mr. Conroy." And with that he jogged up to the rest of his crew and shared the moment with them.

Of course, the moment didn't last long. No one wanted to explain to Frank Crowe why the job had been slowed down just when they had made their breakthrough. But for a few unusual minutes, the group was one with each other. "And you're part of it, Tony," said David under his breath. As the drivers started their engines, David knew enough to get the blazes out of there before he started choking on the fumes. In one of the greatest ironies of the job, he found that he was particularly vulnerable to carbon monoxide, breaking out in a cold sweat and experiencing rapid breathing and weak legs nearly every time he went into the tunnels.

"You're a hypocrite," said David to himself. Pete would have smacked anybody who said that to David within his hearing. But David had said it to himself so many times he had nearly come to believe it. He had never quite wrapped his arms around whether he should have resigned before taking on the job without diesels and electrics, or if the men were better off for what he had done. That was a question he would probably never be able to answer.

CHAPTER 9
Smooth as a Clean-Shaven Face

Boulder City—Early February 1932

H ey, Uncle Pete, when are you going to let me try high scaling?"
"Well, certainly not on a Sunday when your father is cooking. This meal is too good to pass up for something as boring as rappelling off the side of a cliff. Anybody can do that."

David hadn't asked to become the cook for their weekly lunches, but he had become rather good at it. "Not a bad hidden talent, is it?" he asked.

"Not in a godforsaken place like this. No women, except every other week; no booze, except every other week; and no gambling, except every night after work." Pete looked up and smiled at how this discomfited David, who responded, "There's no gambling in Boulder City, Pete. His Eminence, the city manager, has so decreed. And his word is law."

Pete snorted. "There's the great irony. The same little government-sponsored dictator who throws families out into the desert if the husband ever slaps his wife or leaves his yard a mess is the same one who allows Bud Bodell to run a card game in the mess hall."

"He does not." David studied Pete's face to see if he was serious but found it to be inscrutable. "Does he?"

Jim responded for Pete. "He does, Dad. Everybody knows about it."

David looked at Pete, and then Jim, fearing the worst. "And just how do you know about it, may I ask?"

"It has nothing to do with Uncle Pete. Like I said, everybody knows. My tutor told me about it. Mr. Williams talks about it at work. Everybody knows." Everybody, apparently, except David.

"Woody Williams? But he's responsible for enforcing Six Companies' policies."

"Woody's one of the beneficiaries of the game," Pete replied. "Not many are willing to actually beat the number-two man in the company."

"I assume you are the exception to that rule?"

Pete smiled. "Let's just say that I'm willing to be the exception. Woody's harder to beat than you'd think. He was probably a card shark in a previous life."

"But why would they allow that? It goes against the charter. I can't believe Sims Ely hasn't shut it down." Ely was the puritanical city manager who ran Boulder City like his private kingdom.

"Because, brother, human beings are inclined to vice. They like it. It's natural, at least for the male segment of the species. Sometimes you have to indulge those inclinations or risk a riot. Even our exalted city tsar, His Lordship Ely Sims, can't change that. So he lets Bodell run his game on the Q.T. while successfully suppressing most of the other despicable habits that some of us are inclined to indulge in." Pete smiled. "He leaves those up to Las Vegas, which is outside the reach of either Six Companies or the federal government. In fact, I believe Las Vegas is even outside the reach of God—thank heavens."

"You are a reprobate."

"Not just a reprobate but an unrepentant one. I don't know how you got saddled with me for an older brother."

"Well, I hope Woody Williams beats you. That will leave you with less money for booze on the weekends and may actually save your liver from a slow, excruciating dissipation." David then turned to Jim. "I better not hear of you playing cards or going to Las Vegas—particularly with your uncle."

Jim dismissed this with a simple, "Dad!" and then promptly turned the conversation. "But you didn't answer my question, Uncle Pete."

"What question?"

"About high scaling. When can I try it? I've got the right build for it, and now that I'm eighteen I can get a job on the construction site."

"Nice try, but since you're still only seventeen you're still not eligible for the job, are you?" David's voice was quiet but unyielding.

"I wouldn't be the first to lie about my age." He knew this ploy wouldn't work, even as he said it. "Maybe I could work on the rim, at least for a while?"

"And just what is wrong with the job you've got? I thought you wanted to be an engineer."

"*You* want me to be an engineer. I'm not sure it's what I want."

Pete listened without comment. He knew David was disappointed. He hoped his brother wouldn't push it because he knew Jim well enough to know that pushing would only cause trouble without changing anything. He was relieved when David didn't say anything. That meant it was all right for him to join in.

"Tell you what, Jim. Give it some time, and I will let you work on a crew if you still want to. While I'm sure you'll like the excitement, you'll also have the chance to see what it's like to have your body wear out by forty-five as I hobble my way around the site with my arthritic knees, chapped hands, and eyes going blind from the dust that's always in the air." He gazed steadily at Jim, convinced that his next line would support his brother's position and motivate Jim to stick with school. "There are days when a drafting board sounds good to me."

Jim ignored the last comment. "Really, you'll let me have a job? High scaling?"

Pete shrugged his shoulders. "I tried, David. I tried."

David opened the oven, and a wave of heated air swept into the room. The heat felt good this time of the year since the temperature was quite cold on the rim of the canyon. As he pulled out a succulent pot roast surrounded by potatoes, carrots, and onions, the marvelous aroma filled the room. "Help me with the table?" This was something they could all agree on, and Jim and Pete had the table set in a flash.

"So how is the scaling coming?" David asked Pete. "I don't get over there as much as I should, although it's a lot easier since they built the trestle bridge."

"Still not up to the cable bridge?"

"Only when Frank Crowe threatens me with my job."

"You'd sooner risk your life than lose your job?"

"I'd sooner risk my life than stand up to Frank Crowe."

Pete laughed. "Yeah, I guess you're right. At any rate, a failure to appreciate the relative safety of the cable bridge suggests that Jim's father isn't really suited to high scaling. I hope you take after your mother, Jim."

Even though it was said in a lighthearted way, Jim's sullen reply left no doubt as to how he felt about that. "I don't take after my mother at all."

Pete glanced at David, who shook his head slightly. "Well, then, I hope you take after your irresponsible uncle, because you'll never make it as a high scaler if you have the same 'reckless behavior inhibitor' your father has."

David set the roast on the table. "This is quite a detour from my original question."

"Ah, yes. How is the scaling coming? Well, we're almost finished with the upstream face. You're welcome to view our handiwork from the rim of the Nevada side. That old rock face is as smooth as if we'd shaved it with a barber's razor. You could walk along the base of the canyon with nothing more than a parasol and never have to worry about a single pebble falling on you. Women and children could have a picnic down there."

"So you've just about put yourself out of a job?"

"Clever. But no, we have two things left to do after that. First, we have to scale above the downstream outlet portals of the tunnels so that debris won't fall on the workers lining the tunnels with concrete, and then we have to cut the wedges that will transfer some of the weight of the water behind the dam to the canyon walls. That's the project I've been looking forward to the most."

"Why?" Jim asked.

"Because we finally get to blow the heck out of something! No piddly charges like we use on the small outcrops and loose rock we've been working on so far."

"Of course," David broke in. "A much better chance to get yourself blown up and scattered out over the river . . ."

"Well, it may be a little dangerous, David. Let's say that I wouldn't start Jim on that particular part of the project."

Jim reached for a dinner roll while saying, "But it sounds like it's the most interesting of the jobs, although I'm not sure I understand exactly what you're going to do."

Pete took a drink to clear his mouth. "What we intend to do is slice a great wedge out of the canyon walls that will then be replaced with poured concrete. It will be the piece of work that gives the dam its flair."

"I don't understand."

David answered. "The front of the dam will be crescent-shaped to form an arch. That adds to the structural strength of the dam, as well as giving it a rakish appearance. The wedges Pete is talking about are where the sides of the dam will curve forward and abut into the canyon walls."

"I think it's easier to understand if you see it . . ." said Pete impatiently. "If you could spare a piece of paper I'll draw it for you." Jim got up and went over to his father's desk, returning with paper and pencil. Pete took them and started his sketch, drawn with such great exaggeration that even David laughed.

"I think maybe you should stick to construction, Uncle Pete. Dad's a better draftsman." Pete feigned a wounded look, but it was clear that he was pleased that Jim had acknowledged his father's skill. That's what brothers were for.

CHAPTER 10
Cloudburst on the Virgin

Black Canyon—February 9, 1932 at 4:00 p.m.

"Clear the tunnel! Clear the tunnel!"

Tony's heart started racing as he jumped up on his Cat and slammed it into gear. Unfortunately, a Caterpillar tractor wasn't something you could hurry along, so he watched in dismay as the trucks raced past him out of the tunnel. Only the electric shovel moved as slowly as his Cat.

He wished he had someone to talk to, to find out what was wrong. It might be an unexploded charge, which meant that every second he was in the tunnel exposed him to the risk of an explosion that could blow out his eardrums or bug out his eyes. Or kill him. *But they usually just tell us to run—not to bring out the equipment.*

So the truth was that he had no idea why they were beating a retreat to the upstream portal. Nothing like this had happened since they started on the job. As the bulldozer clanked its way out of the entrance of the tunnel, George Fisher motioned for him to stop but made signs for the steam shovel to start crawling its way up the road that would take it to the ledge that had been carved out for the supply buildings. Tony watched as his friend rumbled up the side of the canyon, and then he glanced down at the river.

Suddenly he was struck by the fact that the surface of the water was roiling and turgid. Usually the river was calm and placid with hardly anything to indicate even so much as a current. Yet right now it had an ominous look to it that made the hair on the back of his neck stand up. "It's just like the opening to the old Mexican canal when we were trying to plug it," he said to himself. That was when he realized that a flash flood was on its way. Not knowing how fast or how far it would rise, Tony stood up in the tractor, as if that would give him a little extra protection from the inevitable rise in the water. Now he wished he could goose the ponderous old thing and get it up to safety. But Fisher had been very specific, so Tony just had to sit there and wait, wondering why they were leaving the Cat in harm's way.

That was when he saw Frank Crowe himself and a number of engineers pull up in a dusty Chevrolet. As they piled out of the car, David Conroy turned and, spying Tony on his tractor, waved at him. Tony put his hand up to his helmet in a mock salute, pleased at the recognition yet very much aware that some of the men on his crew were critical of him for being friendly with one of the bosses.

Crowe was not a man to waste time, and he quickly had some large blueprints laid out on the hood of the coupe where all the assembled men pored over it. One of the unexpected things Tony had learned as a Cat operator was just how much time he had to spend idling while awaiting new orders on how to proceed. The company was effective in keeping him busy for routine processes, but when something went wrong, he could sit for an hour or more waiting for a new assignment.

Glancing up, he saw the engineers piling back into their car, apparently planning to drive across the trestle bridge to the Arizona side of the river. Meanwhile, Fisher was waving for all the men on his crew to come forward for an impromptu meeting. Tony climbed down and jogged over to the spot. When all the men were assembled, George got right to the point.

"There have been severe thunderstorms in Utah, and the Virgin River is experiencing flash floods. The water's already started to enter the Colorado, and the prediction is that the river is going to rise for at least the next twelve hours. Mr. Crowe says it's critical that we reinforce the dikes to protect the tunnels from getting inundated. With as much silt as the river will be carrying, it would be a disaster to have all of that stuff find its way inside the tunnel. So for the next twelve hours we need all hands to work with sandbags and hand shovels to keep the river at bay. Tony, it will be your job to move as much material forward to the dikes as possible."

Tony nodded. He also felt his stomach react to the raw fear that he had experienced nearly two decades earlier when he'd last seen the Colorado at flood stage. He doubted that any of the men on this crew had any idea how different this canyon would look and sound as the water level started to rise. What was now a dull rumble would soon become a terrifying roar, particularly since the canyon was so narrow at this point and since there was absolutely no place for the water to go except through. It was an axiom of physics that as the volume increased and the area remained the same, the velocity and depth had to increase. That was why it had been so easy for the river to cut the new channel through the soft desert sand, creating the Salton Sea.

"All right, I know it will be an extra long shift, but you're all in it until the river crests or until the dikes fail and we have to run like demons to get out of here." Fisher deliberately turned his head to make eye contact with each of the men. "That's the bad news, I suppose. The good news is that you'll get overtime, as well as seeing the Red Bull when it gets angry." Red bull was an enduring nickname for the Colorado. "That's something we haven't had to experience so far on this job. It could turn out to be pretty exciting. Any questions?"

There were a few, but Tony didn't pay much attention since his mind was racing, calculating the logistics of the task in front of him.

"Okay, let's get going. Tony, let me talk to you for a minute."

The others started off toward the dike that formed a crescent around the entrances to the four tunnels, and Tony moved toward Fisher. George didn't waste any time. "Here's the deal, Tony. You can do more with that Cat than the other ninety men on the crew put together. It's a different type of operation than you've had before. Can you do it, or should I send for a more experienced operator? Be honest with me."

Tony didn't detect any rancor in his boss's voice. "I can handle it, sir. I've fought this river before during a flood, and I know what's coming."

Fisher pondered for a moment, looking intently into Tony's eyes. Finally, he nodded his head. "Well, then, let's get to work."

As Tony jogged back to his rig, Fisher called out, "By the way, you're a good man, Capelli." Trembling slightly, Tony climbed aboard. He wanted to stop and savor that remark for a moment, but there was no time. The first thing he had to do right now was to shove a large pile of heavy rock up against the back of the dike on the upstream side. The dike itself was waterproof, but it needed more weight behind it to stand up to the increased pressure it would have to bear.

As he pulled back on the throttle, the powerful diesel engine coughed a great cloud of black soot into the air. "A good man . . ." He pondered the comment for a few moments, repeating it several times to make sure he'd heard it correctly. "Not a good worker—a good man." As he used the brake to pivot sharply to the left where his front blade would meet the heavy rock, Tony Capelli smiled.

February 10, 1932 at 3:00 a.m.

"Get that thing out of here, Capelli!"

Tony didn't waste any time executing Fisher's command. Even with his prior experience, he had been unprepared for just how ferocious the river had become. Rising more than eleven feet from its pre-flood stage; the volume of water surging through Black Canyon had increased more than five times, and the noise was deafening. Tony had never thought anything could drown out the sound of his diesel engine, but at this point he couldn't really detect the increase in the pitch of the engine as he started clanking his way up the escape road. The dikes were still holding, but the metal equipment shed on the upstream face had been swamped by the river.

What made this flood so spectacular was that the powerful electric lights that kept the canyon aglow twenty-four hours a day were still shining down on the river. The entire spectacle was playing itself out in full view of the crews working by the river. The most hair-raising sight had been to watch as the river swelled and swallowed up the trestle bridge. At first it seemed it would survive, even though underwater. But then, with a fearful groan and tearing sound, the timber was ripped apart like a child shredding a piece of paper. With the peak flow approaching fifty thousand cubic feet per second, it seemed impossible that any man-made structure could stand up to the force of the river. Which was why Tony had been ordered out. There was no sense losing a Caterpillar tractor on top of all the other damage the company would have to repair.

As Tony pulled up to the rim, he shut down the engine and climbed wearily off the tractor. Then he made his way over to the edge of the cliff to watch the river with all the other men who were assembling at the spot.

"Just how much water do you think that river can hold?"

Tony turned to John Ralston. "More than this, I'm afraid. This flood is the result of a single rainstorm. Just imagine what happens in the spring when all the snowmelt comes down."

Ralston shook his head. "But that comes in fairly steady, doesn't it? Not all at once, like this."

Tony thought back on the years he'd spent trying to outguess this river. They could go years with steady, predictable flows, and then word would come that a flood was on its way. At that point, all bets were off.

"It all depends on the spring. If the snowmelt in Colorado and Utah starts in late April, the river will be pretty tame. But if it stays cold until May, followed by a sudden warming, you can get floods that dwarf this one."

John shook his head. "Well, I don't see how those dikes can hold—in spite of the terrific job you did."

Tony was surprised. "You watched?"

"Of course. Everybody did. You and your counterpart on the Arizona side were the men of the hour."

Tony didn't respond. He was too pleased to come up with anything that would sound appropriately modest.

"Another ten feet and the dikes will be swamped. What a mess we'll have then." It was very much like watching cars on a collision course. You want to shout at them to stop, all the while knowing that they couldn't possibly hear you and that a wreck was inevitable.

As the minutes passed, the water climbed slowly up the face of the dikes, the sound increasing proportionately as it did. And then there was something odd.

"Do you hear that?"

"Hear what?" John replied.

"The sound of the river?"

"Of course I hear the river—"

"No. I mean, it sounds different than it did a few minutes ago. Or is it just my imagination?"

John strained to listen and was surprised that Tony's observation seemed correct.

"It does seem quieter. What do you suppose that means?"

Tony smiled. "It means the river has crested. The great wave from the storm has peaked and will now start to recede."

John peered over the edge and looked at the thousands of ripples and waves on the surface as they shimmered under the great carbon arc lights, the color of the water refracting the light into a dazzling display of color. "It looks as deep as ever."

Tony looked as well. He knew that it would take some time for the water to recede. The diminished noise simply meant there was less volume upstream.

"Look! It's one of the bosses. What's he waving?"

Tony laughed. "He's signaling that the level has started to subside. We've won!"

As word spread through the crowd, the men started to cheer, some even hugging each other. The huggers were most likely those who had been on the top of the dikes, with the water just inches below them as they placed the sandbags while the river was doing its levelheaded best to rip the earth right out from under their feet.

"Good job, Tony."

Tony turned to see David Conroy and Mr. Crowe coming up behind him. Of course, Tony blanched at the sight of Frank Crowe.

"Thank you . . ."

"You were the Cat operator?" Crowe asked.

"Yes, sir."

Crowe nodded. "Then David's right. A good job. I watched you, and you handled it just right."

Tony felt his face flush. He wanted to say something profound, but he didn't have time to say anything since Frank Crowe simply stepped around him and moved over to another group of men to congratulate them.

"Wow. Frank Crowe himself. It's not every day you're going to hear something like that." Somehow it even felt natural when John put his arm on Tony's shoulder. "Congratulations!"

Not wanting to let the moment end but realizing that such moments were best when short-lived, he responded to John. "I don't know about you, but I'm hungry and tired."

Ralston laughed. "Now that you mention it, so am I. Let's find a bus to the dormitory."

CHAPTER 11

Report from the Little Colorado

Boulder City—February 10, 1932

Frank Crowe shook his head as he read the telegram. "There's more coming, Woody. A lot more, if this is correct."

Young Jim Conroy looked up from his desk, where he'd been hired as a runner, bracing himself for the flurry of activity this news was likely to provoke.

"More?" Woody asked incredulously.

"The same storm that clobbered Utah has moved over to Arizona and decided to take another shot at us. Stations on the Little Colorado River are reporting an all-out downpour that is quickly inundating the canyons and flooding the tributary. It should hit the main channel in a matter of minutes."

"So we have a lot more water and a lot less time?"

Crowe nodded. "And a lot more sediment. It's going to be like a river of mud, which means a lot more weight and pressure against the dikes. So get the word out right now. I want every available hand working on those dikes until we sound the alarm. Then tell the men to get out of there as fast as they can. In the meantime, evacuate all the equipment you can, except for the Cats. Leave them to the river if you have to. I want them working to the last second."

"Got it, boss."

Jim paid special attention to "boss," since Mr. Williams usually called Mr. Crowe by his first name.

"Jim. Bill." The two young men jumped from their chairs at the sound of Woody's voice. "I assume you both heard Mr. Crowe?"

The boys nodded. "Then get your butts out to the motorcycles and down the canyon! Go straight to the managing supervisors and tell them to evacuate all equipment. Tell them to increase the height of the dikes as much as possible. The main thing is to keep the water out. Don't leave until you are absolutely certain they understand."

"Yes, sir!" The boys started for the door.

In a disgusted voice, Woody Williams shouted, "And just which one of you is going to Arizona and which one to Nevada?" The two messengers whirled, embarrassed. Woody shook his head.

"I'll go to Arizona, sir. My uncle's over there . . ." Jim's embarrassment was compounded by that unnecessary and stupid addition. For one thing, the high scalers weren't going to have to worry about the river unless it rose more than nine hundred feet, in which case all of Southern California was likely to be washed out. But somehow he had hoped that he would see Pete because he would appreciate just how exciting this was.

"You're not afraid of the cable bridge?" Woody asked this with a perfectly straight face, the unspoken part of the phrase, "like your father." Somehow it pleased him to no end that David didn't like the bridge, which was why Woody found so many occasions to send him across it.

"No, sir!" Jim smiled. "Not afraid at all."

"Well, then, get out of here." The two young men bolted for the door and their waiting motorcycles.

"Watch for my signal," Fisher said. "If you see me waving like this, just get off and run. Don't even take time to shut it off. Just run. I'll have a car waiting. Do you understand?"

"Yes, sir." Tony's heart was racing. The river had already risen some five feet in the past thirty minutes, far faster than it had the previous day.

Fisher held Tony's gaze, reluctant to release him. From the gossip that was going around, this flood was going to easily surpass the one yesterday, and they'd barely survived that. To send Tony on top of the dikes in his bull-dozer was to risk his very life. But that was the order. "All right then, go. But if you don't watch me I'll—"

"Don't worry, Mr. Fisher. I'll watch. I know what's at stake."

"It's George. I've told you to call me George. Now get out of here, Capelli."

Tony bolted for his machine, his mind racing. They'd done so much work the day before reinforcing the dikes that he couldn't imagine what else they expected him to do. The available fill material had nearly all been moved into place. "But we've got to try."

In this particular emergency, Tony was just one of many players. Up on the rim the high scalers had all stopped their work since so many of the men were moving around at the base of the canyon walls that they couldn't risk dislodging any material to rain down on them. Of course, Pete wanted to go down and help with the dikes, but there were a maximum number of men that could crowd into a work area which, once exceeded, would slow things down rather than move the project along. Pete knew he would just get in the way.

"It's exciting, don't you think?" Jim asked his uncle.

Pete turned to Jim. "And how is it, again, that you happen to be up here?"

"It was Mr. Williams. He sent me across the cable bridge to confirm his orders to the men down there. Then, when it became obvious that the water was going to come up a lot faster than expected, he called over and said that I should come up here rather than risk crossing the river again."

Pete nodded. "Well, you're in for a once-in-a-lifetime show. To watch the Colorado at full flood in the middle of a bright, sunny afternoon is something few people ever get to see."

Jim smiled, pleased to be sharing this with his uncle. Not that his dad wouldn't be excited; it was just that he'd be worried about the men and fussing about the work, whereas Pete had settled down right on the edge of the cliff with his feet dangling over the side.

"They look like ants, don't they?" Pete said philosophically.

Jim nodded. The sight of the men and the machines in the canyon was fascinating from this height. He found it impossible to make out individual features without binoculars. He could still see the people scurrying around, moving rocks and material from one place to another.

"That's Mr. Capelli, isn't it? I mean, he's the only one on this shift to run a Cat?"

Pete nodded. "He's one brave man, I can tell you that. Do you see how high the water is? And it's still climbing. If this keeps up for another hour, he'll be swimming his way back to his house in Southern California."

"I hope not. My dad likes him."

Pete caught his breath, realizing how his flippant comment could be misinterpreted. "Sorry about that. It was a stupid thing to say. He'll be fine. George Fisher is an excellent foreman, and he'll watch out for him." He paused. "The only risk is that if the water undercuts a portion of the dike where Tony's working, it could give way under the weight of his machine."

When Jim turned to question him, Pete said, "Look, Jim, I'll try to soft-pedal things when I can, but I won't underplay a real risk. The fact is that he's in a dangerous spot right now. That much water can wreak havoc on mounds of dirt even a big as that one, and a Cat on the top is in a very vulnerable position."

"It's okay. I understand." Jim turned thoughtful, which was okay with Pete. He liked the chance to just sit and ponder the scene.

A moment later Jim spoke up. "Can I ask you a question?"

"Sure."

"It's about Mr. Capelli." He hesitated. "It's just that . . ."

"Just what?"

"It's just that I don't understand . . ."

"You don't understand what?" Pete puzzled for a moment, and then it dawned on him. "You don't understand why people treat him the way they do?"

Jim shook his head. "No. I think I get that. What I don't get is why you and my dad treat him the way you do. You're nice to him. From what I hear, nobody likes the fact that an Italian has such a good job. They think it should go to an American."

Shock registered on Pete's face, and he spluttered as he struggled to find words. "Is that how you feel, Jim? Do you think he shouldn't have the chance to work here because he came from Italy? You do know that he's an American citizen since he was a kid? He's been an American longer than you have."

"No, I don't mean—"

"Look, Jim. People are people, in my book. Chick and Marvin are the ones who don't deserve a job. A man should be judged by what he can do, not by where he's from or how his name is spelled. If you take it far enough, none of us are Americans except for the Indians. And even they have a hard time getting a job on this project, even though they've lived here for thousands of years."

More than anything, Jim regretted having brought the subject up. "It's okay, I was just asking . . ."

"Well, you should . . ." Pete's voice trailed off. "Listen, Jim. You were born with every advantage in the world. You've got a great father who is absolutely devoted to your future. He makes good money, so you grew up in a nice house. You can go to school as long as you want to, which means you can become a professional. And you're white, which means that you'll always be judged on your personal qualifications for a job, not on the color of your skin. Not everyone has what you have, and it's not because they're inferior. I've got a Negro on my team, and he outworks all of us. He's one of only about ten who have a job on the work site, and that's because the NAACP made a huge issue of our hiring practices. So they hired ten men. Ten out of how many thousand?"

"It's okay, Uncle Pete. I didn't mean anything by it." But Pete was not to be deterred.

"And that's not all. I've got an Irishman who can do magic on his cables, the smartest worker on my crew, yet there are plenty who think that all the Irish should go back to Europe. No matter how smart he is, I get to be the foreman because I have a good old English name. It stinks, but that's the way it is."

Jim knew his uncle was hot, but he still didn't have an answer. So he decided to press his luck. "But aside from the Indians, we got here first, didn't we? So shouldn't that mean something?"

Pete sighed. "I'm not getting through to you, am I?"

"It's not that I'm prejudiced or anything."

Pete shook his head in frustration. "Maybe you are." At this point Pete didn't care if Jim was angry. He was angry, so why should Jim get off scot-free? "It's like this, Jim. It's not as easy as you'd like to think. When your dad and I were teenagers, your grandfather owned a dry-goods business."

"I remember. I used to go into the store. It was great."

"Yeah, it was a lot of work, is what it was. Dad wasn't much of a businessman, and our family was always getting into financial trouble because he'd help people out by giving them merchandise on credit, even when they didn't stand a chance of paying us back."

"I don't understand what that's got to do with this?"

"There was one group who always paid their bills. Late, sometimes, but they always paid. That was the Mexicans who came up to work in the fields. Others would take advantage of my dad; they never did."

"So, what's that got to do Tony?"

"People hate Tony just because he's foreign—and Catholic. Most of the Mexican people were itinerant, meaning they came to Idaho only during the harvest season, so they got the same kind of crap that Tony gets. Yet, they were some of our very best workers and most reliable customers.

"So that's why you respect them."

"It's more than that." Pete's voice had grown serious in a way that Jim had never heard. He looked over at his uncle expectantly, but Pete was brooding. So he waited.

"There was this time when Dad got into real trouble. He couldn't pay his bills, and the bank was threatening to close him down. Davy and I were teenagers, and we gave him everything we could earn, but he had this one big bill that he just couldn't pay. It was humiliating."

"So what happened?"

"What happened was that Juan Martinez gave Dad his entire life's savings. That's what happened."

"Who's Juan Martinez?"

"One of Dad's employees. He'd been saving for a house. He was a perma-nent resident who'd gone to the trouble to become a U.S. citizen. He was the hardest working man I ever knew, and, unlike my dad, he was a saver. When he saw how bad the business was doing he just gave everything to Dad."

"So what happened? Did it save the business?"

Pete shook his head. "Nope. The business still failed, and we lost every-thing. Juan's money, too. It was just gone."

"So what did Grandpa do?"

"He just walked away from it. He left Juan on his own, all his money gone."

"No! Grandpa wouldn't do that. When I knew him he had a nice house and plenty of money. He wouldn't do something like that."

Pete turned to him, his eyes cold. "That's what you'd like to think, isn't it? That's how the story should end, but it didn't."

"But that wouldn't be right . . ."

"I told you earlier that I put all my cards on the table. I'm doing that now. The fact is that after declaring bankruptcy, my dad went to work for a competitor. While your grandfather wasn't much of a businessman, he was a marvelous salesman, and he soon attracted all of his old customers to the new business. So his boss made him a partner. In time they both did very well—well enough to send your dad to college."

"But he certainly must have paid Mr. Martinez back then?"

"He pretended to try." Pete paused. "Maybe he did try, but he didn't try very hard. Juan had moved out of the area, and my dad never made any effort to find him. So how can you pay somebody back if you don't know where he is?"

"Grandpa would have paid him back if he could, right? He just wasn't there . . ."

"No, Jim. What we found out is that he wouldn't. In spite of all his positive experience with Mexicans, it turned out that he was just as preju-diced as all those men who tell you that Tony Capelli or the handful of Mexicans who work on this project don't have a right to work here. Because he felt guilty for the way he treated Juan, my dad started to tell himself that it was all right that Martinez lost his money because he wasn't equal to a white person anyway. The more he told himself that, the more he believed it. That's the way a prejudice works; you come to despise the people you've taken advantage of so your conscience doesn't hurt."

Jim was stunned into silence by both the anger in his uncle's voice and the shame he felt for his grandfather. "So what did Mr. Martinez say to Grandpa when he first learned that the money was gone? Was he mad?"

"He didn't say anything, just that he knew the risk when he took it. He didn't ask for any repayment, and he didn't accuse my father of taking his money. He just accepted it. Fortunately, he didn't stay around long enough to know that Dad made it all back and betrayed him. He had to leave before that. He never said a bad word about my father to anybody."

Jim had felt indignant before, but never like this. When it finally dawned on him what he was feeling, he realized it was much worse than indignation. It was humiliation. He felt humiliated for his own family. "But you and Dad . . . have you tried to find him?"

"The year after Dad died. By talking to some of the other Mexicans in the Boise area, we learned that he'd moved back to California. It was just that easy. We also found out that Juan had died three years earlier. We took part of our inheritance and repaid his widow. She tried to refuse, insisting that we needed it, but we made her take it. We never told her the whole story."

Jim shook his head. "So is that why you and Dad didn't turn out prejudiced like Grandpa?"

"Your dad and I knew the truth. We knew that it was a Mexican—an American—who had tried to save us, and we knew that as a family we had done nothing in return. That's a lot to live with. It helps you figure out what makes a man good and what makes a man bad, and it has nothing to do with his skin. I personally don't care where a man comes from, what his religion is, or what kind of an accent he has. It's all about the kind of man he is that matters. "

"That's a pretty hard story. Part of me wishes you hadn't told me."

Pete pointed to the Nevada bank of the river. "You see the man on that Cat moving material around? Right now he's the most important guy in the whole canyon. Tens of thousands of dollars, maybe hundreds of thousands, ride on the work he does. Yet when it's over he'll get the blame if the dike fails. If it holds together, he'll get a small pat on the back from management, and then people will be talking behind his back faster than you can cross the river on that swinging bridge. That's not a very easy story, either. Now do you understand?"

Jim nodded. "I won't say anything bad about the Italians again."

"Well, that's something. It doesn't fix society, but at least it may fix you." Pete was restless, swinging his legs with more energy than usual. Finally, after surveying the flood control efforts again, he turned and looked at Jim with a piercing glance. "Listen, Jim, I need to go for a walk. I don't like thinking about this stuff."

Jim nodded. "I'll be fine."

Pete got up and dusted himself off, and then he took off on a walk along the rim. Jim felt bad that he had upset his uncle. He also felt bad that he'd never get the chance to ask a hundred more questions this conversation had raised in his mind—like if Pete and his dad still loved their father, and if they'd ever heard from the Martinez family. Most of all he wanted to know if it had been things like this that had caused such bad blood between his uncle and his grandfather. But he knew that he'd never get to ask him again. Getting Pete to open up this much was the most unusual thing he'd ever experienced with his uncle. "Maybe I can talk to Dad sometime, but the timing will have to be right." At least he'd know what to ask.

"Run for it!"

Tony couldn't hear what George Fisher shouted, of course, but he did recognize the arm signal and could even make out the words on his face. He'd been waiting, and now was the time to act. As fast as lightning he hit the "kill" switch on his tractor, even though Fisher had told him to leave it. Just in case the machine survived, he didn't want the carburetor fouled by having it run out of fuel while idling. It took just a moment, and then he leapt from the tractor.

"Jump in!" As he climbed into the passenger seat, George let his foot out on the clutch and the little truck lurched forward so hard that it killed the engine. "Oh, for Pete's sake! We don't have time for this."

No one knew that better than Tony. He'd watched as the water had risen an astonishing fifteen feet in less than three hours, and it was still coming up. Although they wouldn't know the exact number until later, the volume of the flow must have been incredible because the roar of the water echoing in the canyon walls was deafening.

The truck growled its way back to life, and George revved it to maximum while letting out on the clutch. This time it grabbed, snapping Tony's head back as they lurched forward and up the canyon road.

"I've never seen anything like it in all my years in construction, and I've worked on some pretty big dams prior to this."

Tony stared ahead, willing the truck to move faster. "I've never worked on dams, and I haven't seen anything like it either. Even the big floods down on the Baja are nothing like this—it's open down there, so the water spreads out. All this water concentrated in the canyon is spooky."

George laughed. "Spooky—now there's a word I didn't expect. But you're right. It is spooky." He cast a quick glance at Tony. "Particularly, I'd think, while sitting on top of a hundred thousand pounds of steel bulldozer. You're lucky the bank didn't collapse."

Upper intake portals on the Arizona side being flooded by the Colorado River before they were finished.

"Ah," said Tony. "Luck has nothing to do with it. It's all in the handling. Not that I'm trying to brag."

George swerved to miss a boulder that had tumbled onto the road. With all the equipment they'd been moving up and out of the canyon, the whole place was shaken and battered. "I don't take it as bragging. The fact is that you are good at what you do."

Tony was pleased at the recognition.

"Well, here we are. Let's join the rest of the whole Six Companies workforce and see what else the river plans to do to us."

As they got out of the truck, they heard a huge groan from the crowd. That prompted them to rush over to the edge. "What is it?" George yelled.

David Conroy, standing at the edge of the canyon, turned at the sound of George's voice. "The river just overtopped the Arizona side. The dike is melting like frosting on a birthday cake in the rain."

George had never seen a birthday cake left out in the rain, but he decided that it was an apt description. Shaking his head he said, "So it got us, then. The Colorado has taken its revenge. For ten months it's slept down there with hardly a ripple. And now, just as we're ready to start lining the tunnels, it breaks through in a season that's usually safe."

It was an awesome sight to watch as the water seeped slowly over the top of the earthen dike on the Arizona bank. At first it was a trickle, then a stream, and then a flood. In what seemed a matter of moments the whole mound turned liquid, and an ocean of red mud started pouring into the Arizona tunnels.

"Frank Crowe is going to be mad about this." David and Tony laughed at George Fisher's understatement.

"Our dike is still holding," said Tony tentatively.

George reached down and picked up a stray piece of wood and knocked on it. "Don't go saying stuff like that, Tony. It's bad luck. You don't want the river to think we're arrogant."

"No, sir."

"Just look at those tunnels. There's going to be a real mess to clean up. Do you see the force of the river as it smashes into the tunnel openings?" David asked.

"Well, we'll see what effect water has on the rough edges. There wasn't supposed to be a drop of water hit the tunnel walls until they were lined. There's so much sediment in that water that it's going to coat everything." George shook his head in disgust as he said this. "And then how do you get the concrete to bond and set up?"

David nodded. "Like the man said, Crowe is going to be angry."

"There goes a supply shed!" Tony called out. Sure enough, a small structure outside tunnels three and four collapsed and was swept into tunnel three. The blacksmith shops and air-compressor plant had water flowing through them but were still standing up to the flow.

"Has it crested?" George asked. "I don't see how any more water can be coming. What kind of a rainstorm is this, anyway?"

David was about to say something he hoped would be clever, but Tony said very quietly, "The worst may be over . . ."

"What do you mean?"

"Look at the surface of the water. It is a little smoother upstream. And the sound hasn't exactly diminished, but it isn't getting any louder."

"What's that got to do with it?" George asked.

"The sound tells you the volume of water," David replied, impressed at Tony's common sense. "The surface turbulence upstream indicates what's coming. I think you're right, Tony. Let's hope so." Then, turning to George, he said, "If he is, then it may be that you and your crew's dikes have held the river out on this side of the river. That would be something, wouldn't it?"

George nodded. "My boys worked hard. Real hard. It would be terrific if we managed to avoid the mess they're in over on the Arizona side."

"Well," George added. "We still have plenty of a mess to clean up. With the bridge out, we'll all have to pitch in to help the folks on the Arizona side. I'd say the Colorado has had its way with us." He looked up and furrowed his brow. "I hope that dam you plan to build is mighty big and strong, David. It looks to me like it has its work cut out for it, trying to tame this monster."

David nodded. He knew the math was solid. They were overbuilding the dam by an impressive factor. Still, this flood made it clear that nature was not to be trifled with. They'd have to do their very best work. And yet, in an odd way, the thought of the river fighting them made him feel good. Their victory would have even more meaning. He glanced up and looked at the other side of the canyon. Without knowing why, he searched among the faces of the men he could see over there, even though he didn't have binoculars in hand. He was surprised when he saw one of the figures waving, and he asked to borrow George Fisher's binoculars. What he saw was Jim looking back at him through another pair of binoculars. He couldn't help but smile as he waved back at his son.

The smile quickly vanished when he heard someone shout, "Would you look at that! The water is up and over the Cat. That's going to cost a pretty penny!"

The Caterpillar? He got a sick feeling that maybe the Nevada bank dikes had collapsed as well. He breathed a sigh of relief when he learned it was the Cat on the Arizona side. For now, at least, the dikes on the Nevada side were holding.

Cleaning up the mess after the spring floods in 1932.

A worker's house in Boulder City, circa 1932

CHAPTER 12
Concrete Linings

Why is it, again, that we're down here scrubbing river ooze off these tools? We're high scalers, not janitors," Sean O'Donnell said.

"Can it, Sean," Pete replied. "You're getting paid the highest wage in the canyon, so if Six Companies wants you to wash out latrines, you'll shut up and start cleaning. You got that?"

Sean O'Donnell burst into a grin. "Got it, chief. The Irishman is to mind his own business."

Pete growled. It was despicable work. The simple fact was that no one except those who had stuck their hands into the Colorado River or one of its upstream tributaries could possibly understand just how muddy and mucky and filthy the water was. The red soil and sandstone that made the canyon lands of the Southwest so spectacularly beautiful was the very same stuff that became silt when suspended in water. The silt was so pervasively red and penetrating it permanently stained every piece of fabric it touched. And the mud that accumulated in spots where the water receded was roughly the consistency of wallpaper paste, with the same gooey feeling when it got on your hands and clothes. When it dried, it was like red concrete. And now this very muck had coated everything inside the perimeter of the failed dikes that should have protected tunnels three and four on the Arizona side of the river.

"I'm surprised there's anything left of the Colorado plateau," said Sean. "I figure at least half of it has attached itself to this shed and all the tools inside it."

"You just can't stop talking, can you Sean?"

"Oh, sorry, boss. I know I'm not supposed to make the miners feel bad. Just because they don't know how to build a dike that works, we shouldn't hurt their feelings."

Pete shook his head. The problem with Sean was his cleverness. It had caused more than one fight when they were liberated to Las Vegas. He had taken the "pride in the outfit" concept way past its logical conclusion, managing to insult nearly everybody who wasn't a high scaler. Even Pete could see any number of the regulars in the tunnel crews glowering at them. So he resorted to his ultimate weapon. "You're gonna love your vacation time, O'Donnell. Too bad it's without pay. They should have all this cleaned up in another week or so, and then, if you haven't been replaced, maybe you can go back to work on the canyon walls. We'll all miss you in the meantime, won't we boys?"

The other members of the group chimed in to support their boss, an outcome Pete expected. "Yeah, it just won't be the same without you, Sean," and "Write to us from New York; no mud there, that's for sure."

Most guys would have been provoked, but Sean knew he had it coming, so he just grinned and dipped the trowel he was cleaning into the bucket of water. He found he had to use a small chisel to pry the mud off it.

"So do you really think it will take two weeks?" he asked plaintively.

"I hope not," said Pete. "At least not out here. You can see that every tool, every hose, every electrical line that was caught in the flood has to be cleaned off by hand. That's the easy part. The bad stuff, as far as I'm concerned, is inside the tunnels, where the force of the water scoured the canyon walls and left them coated in this muck. We have to get as much of that crap off as possible before they can start lining the tunnels with concrete, or it will never form a permanent bond with the rock walls. The task of cleaning the surface of rocks is called 'scaling,' as in removing the scale!"

Sean got a horrified look on his face. "You don't mean . . ." He coughed and cleared his throat. "You don't mean . . . I mean, they couldn't . . ." He coughed again. "They have to know that we're outside guys. I mean, the tunnels are big, but they're . . . they're . . ."

"They're what?" Pete asked. "Enclosed?"

"Did I mention that I get claustrophobic when I'm in enclosed places?" Sean tried to sound light about it, but Pete could sense the real terror in his voice.

"Oh, for crying out loud. The tunnels are six stories high. They're wide enough for a four-lane highway. There's light at the other end, with a nice breeze inside that's supplied by my very own brother David. It's a real stretch to call them an enclosed place, don't you think?"

"Have you ever heard of the Holland Tunnel?"

"Sure," Jake Windham replied, another member of Pete's crew. "It's in Holland, right?"

"No, idiot, it's a tunnel under the Hudson River between downtown Manhattan and New Jersey."

"Well, what about it?" Pete replied.

"A man could die in there; I almost did, until I managed to stop traffic in both directions while my cab driver turned the car around so we could go back out. It was a little embarrassing given the fact that each of the two tunnels is one-way and we had to go back the wrong way." He shrugged. "But who needs to go to New Jersey, anyway?"

"How far did you make it in?" Pete asked.

"About a hundred feet."

"Isn't that tunnel more than a mile long?"

"Who knows? I never made it all the way through."

"You are pathetic." Then, turning to the whole crew, Pete said, "The answer is yes, by the way. We are going into the tunnels to do scaling work. Probably on Monday. It's what we're trained for, and it's what the job requires. So get used to it."

No one said anything, not even Sean, but he wasn't the only one who had a concerned look on his face.

"High scalers! Those 'daredevils of the canyons,' the 'acrobats of the desert,' the 'trapeze artists of the Colorado!' If only the newspaper writers could see you all now." Pete spat on the ground, where the muck turned a deeper red. "If any of you want to be transferred to latrine duty before we march in there, just let me know. I'm sure something can be worked out."

For the moment, no one raised a hand.

Boulder City—March 1932

"TONY? COME IN. I HAVEN'T seen you for a while." David stepped back into the living room. Once Tony was inside, David said, "Congratulations. Your dikes held. I've wanted to tell you that ever since the flood, but I haven't seen you. Meanwhile, your counterpart on the other bank lost everything, including his Cat, while yours stayed up there safe and sound. I know that everyone is pleased with your work."

"Thank you, Mr. Conroy." David wished that he'd call him by his first name. He had invited him to do that a dozen times, but it just wasn't in Tony's nature. He put great stock in hierarchy.

"Well, you saved people much backbreaking work. My brother is in the Arizona tunnels right now trying to blast and chip all that sediment off the walls. He hates it."

"Yes, sir."

David gave up on light conversation. "So what brings you by?"

Tony shifted uncomfortably.

"Is there something we can do for you?"

Tony dropped his head, not wanting to make eye contact, which was disconcerting given how friendly he was usually. "Perhaps. I do need something, and I haven't been able to come up with any other way. So maybe you can think of something."

"Okay . . . what is it?"

Jim put down the math book he was reading. Tony's evasiveness made him just as curious as his father.

"It's my wife, Louisa." He paused as if he couldn't start up again.

"Is she ill? Do you need time off?"

Tony looked up. "No, it's not that." He looked down again. "It's that she wants to come visit me here and to bring our oldest son. She thinks he's been going around with the wrong crowd, and she wants me to talk to him."

David could certainly empathize. "I think it's a good idea. She should come here and see where you work. I've been trying to get my wife and daughters to come down for a visit, but so far things haven't worked out for them to make the trip."

"Yes, sir."

David waited, but they'd reached an impasse again.

"So is there a problem with her coming?"

When Tony hesitated yet again, it was Jim who stepped in. "You don't have any place for them to stay, do you?"

David turned to Jim, surprised by this insight, and then back to Tony. "Is that the problem? You don't have a place for them to stay?"

Jim let out an exasperated sigh. "He lives in the men's dormitory, Dad. They can't stay there, and the hotel isn't finished yet."

"And Las Vegas is so far away," Tony interjected. "Besides, I don't think Louisa would like Las Vegas."

"No. I'm sure she wouldn't," said David. "It probably wouldn't be good for your son, either. How old is he?"

"Seventeen." Tony looked up. "He's a good boy. A good man, really. He could work here, if he was old enough. Right now he does whatever he can to earn money, including keeping up our farm. Not that we can grow much, except maybe a single crop in the monsoon season when the rains come, but he has to keep working the soil so we don't lose title to it. But a boy needs his father . . ." Tony stopped, embarrassed that he'd shared so much.

"Your wife and son should stay here with us. We can move Jim into my room, and they can have the other bedroom."

Tony looked up quickly. "No, that's not what I meant by coming here. I thought perhaps you would have an idea."

"I do have an idea, and that's it. Your family is welcome. And since Jim and I are at work so much of the time, we wouldn't be underfoot at all."

"It's too much to ask."

David looked at Jim, who mouthed the words, "Uncle Pete."

David crinkled his brow until it dawned on him what Jim was suggesting. "Ah. Even better. Jim and I will move in with my brother while your family is here. That way you can stay with your wife, and your son can have his own room."

"Oh, no. I can't move you out of your house!"

"Well, Jim and I are leaving, so the house will stand empty. It's up to you."

Tony looked at the two of them, and his lip trembled ever so slightly. "Thank you. I am indebted to you. Again. A debt I don't know how to repay."

David just put his hand up and smiled. "When will they get here?"

"In two weeks, if that's all right. I will send a telegram tomorrow. That is if you're sure."

David stood. He realized that Tony needed to make a dignified exit. "Two weeks will be just right. We'll see that everything is in order."

Tony stepped back, bowed slightly, and quickly moved to the door.

Once he was gone, David turned to his son. "That was very decent of you, Jim. I should have thought of it."

"It just makes sense."

"Yes, it does, and it shows great character. Thanks for suggesting it."

Jim was silent, lost in thought.

Black Canyon—March 1932

"HIGH SCALING AND TUNNEL BUILDING are certainly not the only activities Six Companies has been working on, even though they are the ones I'm most familiar with." David noted how quickly the correspondent from *Newsweek* magazine took notes. Glancing down at the fellow's notepad, he was startled to see a series of what appeared to be squiggles rather than words. "Is that shorthand?" Embarrassed, he started to apologize for looking at the fellow's notes.

"No problem. It is shorthand. I find it comes in very handy in my work, particularly when I want to get an exact quote."

David had been assigned to work with this reporter, who was writing a feature story on the dam. So far they'd toured the tunnels, visited the administration building in Boulder City, and were now standing on an overlook above the new concrete mixing plant.

Although the reporter was a pleasant enough fellow, David had the sense that he was looking for something sensational, and so he found himself being more guarded than usual. Particularly when they talked about conditions in the tunnels.

"You were talking about the other projects . . ."

"Yes," David responded, quickly organizing his thoughts. "Thousands of workers have been busy at a variety of sites in the desert building railroad tracks, roads, rock crushing operations, and bridges. What you're looking at now is the concrete plant."

"Concrete is just another name for cement, right?"

David shook his head. "Not exactly, although people often mix the two up. Concrete is a mixture of cement, water, sand, and crushed rock. The concrete required for the dam has very exacting specifications, requiring at least twenty-five thousand pounds of compressive strength for the main structure itself." The blank look on the fellow's face prompted him to add, "That simply means the concrete has to be mixed very dry, which also means that it will start to set up quickly. Consequently, it's vital that the mixing plant be as close to the dam site as possible."

"It doesn't seem like it's very close to the dam site to me."

"Three quarters of a mile. The problem is that the canyon is so narrow that we had to come back this far just to find a shelf we could carve out of the canyon wall large enough to support a four-story concrete plant, complete with five mixers. We call this the 'low-mix plant,' meaning it's situated low in the canyon, and it will supply all the concrete needed for the diversion tunnels and up to two-thirds of the concrete used in building the dam itself. Once we reach that height, this plant will be decommissioned and mixing work will be transferred to a 'high-mix' plant that will be built on the Nevada rim."

"So you guys aren't just building a dam, you're building a small country."

David laughed. "Railroad tracks and bridges, a small city, and eventually a steel fabrication plant to manufacture the thirty-foot-diameter steel pipes designed to line the tunnels that will carry water around the dam to the powerhouse. We really are pretty self-sufficient."

"Very interesting. What should I see next?"

"Well, if I were you I'd visit the rock crushing plant at Three-Mile Junction. It's an incredible operation. Then, if you'd like to learn about the most dangerous job on the project, you could interview a high scaler."

This got the reporter's attention. "One of the guys who dangles from the ropes?"

An aerial view of the low-mix concrete plant

"The very same. It turns out that my brother runs a crew. Maybe I could set something up for you."

PETE GLARED AT DAVID. "THANKS a lot for sending that reporter after me. Talk about a pain in the butt."

David smiled. "I figured you two would hit it off. The fact is that I needed to get back to work . . ."

"So you pawned him off on me. He ended up asking questions I didn't want to answer, like what happened to Jeremy Stephens and Salty. Now he'll make it look like that's what happens to all of us." Pete growled as he reached for another buttermilk biscuit. It was Sunday and they were enjoying one of David's home-cooked meals.

Jim, ignoring the banter, interjected himself into the conversation. "I believe we were talking about finishing off the tunnels? What comes next for both of you?"

"You probably know the answer to that better than I do," David replied. "Woody Williams is the boss, and I'm sure you've heard him talk. Besides, there's still a lot of work left on the tunnels before the water can be diverted.

We need to scoop out the bottoms and line them with three feet of concrete. I have to make sure there's enough air circulating to cure the concrete. After that, I honestly don't know."

"So you could lose your job?" Jim asked anxiously.

David raised an eyebrow. "And do you ask that hopefully so we can go back to Boise?"

"What? No. I mean, you need the work. Right?"

David nodded but didn't say anything.

Jim endured the silence as long as he could before adding, "Besides, it's not so bad here."

Pete smiled ever so slightly. "I assume you're also worried about that young lady—what's her name?

"Carol," David replied.

"Carol. That's it. I assume you're worried about her father losing his job as well?"

Jim blushed. "Sorry I showed any concern about you guys. I just figured you'd be a little anxious. Sheesh . . ."

"It's all right," said David, sensitive to Jim's embarrassment. "The fact is that once we finish the diversion tunnels and start routing water around the dam site, the real work begins. All of this has just been getting ready to start work on the dam itself. In addition, if Frank Crowe likes me working on tunnels, there is still plenty of drilling to do to accommodate the plumbing the dam needs after it gets built. You have to bring water through penstock tunnels to the powerhouse, plus build overflow tunnels in case the river runs too high. So, for better or for worse, I think we're here for at least a couple of years."

"That's all I wanted to know . . ." said Jim sullenly.

"So how's school going?" Pete asked, perhaps a little embarrassed himself for putting Jim on the spot. "Carol" was obviously a sensitive subject.

"It's all right. I should finish in May, and then I'll be a high-school graduate. Thank heavens."

Pete laughed. "And then you'll be even with me. But I'm sure it will be off to college after that so you can design those dams and tunnels of the future."

"It will be off to high scaling," Jim said firmly. "You promised."

David sighed, and Pete shrugged his shoulders. Jim clearly had his own plans for the future, regardless of what his father may have hoped for.

Black Canyon—April 1932

"I think we're all right here, Tony. They're not going to do any more blasting before the end of our shift."

"Are you sure, Mr. Fisher, sir? I can stay until the end."

One of the little ironies of the workplace was that older men, like Tony, who would usually receive the deference of a "sir" or "mister" instead used those honorific titles when addressing much younger men who happened to be foremen or managers.

"No, it's fine. You should be off to Las Vegas to meet your family."

Tony felt uncomfortable. While some four thousand men were now working on the dam site, nearly three times that number had been employed at one point or another, and the workers were always left to feel uncertain about their employment—even when they were highly competent and valued.

"All right, then. But I'll be back tomorrow. You don't need to worry about that."

"I'm not worried. Now go." Even with all that, Tony moved off slowly. Because he was not leaving at a normal shift change, he had to ride one of the cable slings up the canyon face rather than take a bus up to the rim. The slings were rather disconcerting and made him uncomfortable, even though he'd never admit that to anyone.

Back on the canyon floor, George Fisher stood watching as one of the great movable forms that held the concrete in place while it bonded to the canyon wall was shifted inside the tunnel they were working on.

"Even knowing how it's done, it still seems incredible to me." Fisher jumped at the sound of David Conroy's voice.

"You startled me, Conroy. Quit sneaking up on people."

"Sorry."

Fisher looked back at the tunnel. "You're right. It is incredible—a concrete lining three feet thick all the way around the tunnel. That alone will reduce its interior dimension from fifty-six to fifty feet in diameter. Who knows how much concrete that will take?"

"Four hundred thousand cubic yards."

Fisher laughed. "Of course an engineer would know that."

"It's got to be satisfying to know that you and your crew are making all this great progress possible, George. It's looking ever more likely that we'll get the tunnels finished by this winter, which means we'll be a full year ahead of schedule. The company could not be more pleased."

"I've got good men on my crew."

"That's an understatement. Particularly given the working conditions inside the tunnels during the original blasting. It's remarkable how well they held up to the temperatures inside."

Fisher was quiet for a moment before speaking hesitantly. "Not all of them did so well, you know. The carbon monoxide and all."

David nodded. More than one man had been sickened by the gas. Even the healthiest of men had complained of weakness in their limbs and an occasional episode of profuse sweating. He shouldn't reply to Fisher, given his position with the company, but he decided he didn't care. "It should have been a scandal, George, but no one cared enough to stop it—not the Feds, not Six Companies, not even me. The job always comes first, doesn't it?" David shook his head in disgust, and Fisher was smart enough not to press him.

"Can I ask you a question, David? It's personal."

That caught David by surprise. "Sure. What is it?"

"It's about Tony. It seems you're pretty good friends with him."

"I consider him a friend. Why? He's very intelligent."

"And a good worker. He may be the best Cat operator we have."

"So is there a problem?"

Fisher cleared his throat nervously. "Not a problem, really. It's just that a lot of people still wonder about him getting the job. There are not many Italians working on the site, you know."

David decided to avoid giving the lecture on how Tony was an American citizen. "I'm surprised to hear you talk about it. You seemed to have been supportive of Tony."

Fisher turned. "That's just it. I am. But I try to be subtle about it."

David blushed as he realized what the conversation was really about. He didn't expect this from George Fisher, of all people. "So you think it's a mistake for me to be so public with him? I really don't talk to him all that much, you know. Certainly no more than any of the other men in the canyon."

George's eyes widened. "It's not that, David. All of that's fine. The only reason I ask is that I'm worried about what happens to Tony when we finish the tunnels. I suspect I'll move onto the upper tunnels, but I don't know that there will be much Cat work involved because of they are far up and inaccessible to heavy equipment. I just don't know that I can keep him on my crew."

"So how am I adding to the problem?"

"It's about his family. I've heard some of the men talk about how it's not right that they should come into Boulder City. Even some of the men on our crew have said that, and they all like Tony."

David nodded as full understanding dawned. "I see. How will that affect his future employment?"

"People get even, David. Not directly, where you can challenge them on it, but they do get even. If I lose him I won't be able to do anything to help, and I'm not sure it's smart for you to step in, either."

By now David's face was burning in anger. He forced himself to take a few breaths, realizing that it wasn't George Fisher he should be mad at, since he was only trying to help. It wasn't even the men; they were doing nothing worse than Six Companies was doing. With more than four thousand men at work, they were down to only eleven who were black, and they were all American citizens, just like Tony. The blacks had it even worse than the Italians, since none of them was allowed to even live in Boulder City. Instead, they had to take a bus from the far side of Las Vegas every morning and every night. It was miserable and unfair, but it was company policy.

"I don't know what to do," said David quietly. "Tony needs a place for his family to stay, and he asked me. I personally have no objection since I think he has every bit as much right to have his family with him as any other man, but I don't want to make more trouble for him either."

George inhaled slowly and then took even longer to let the air out. "I understand. I know that it's too late to make any changes." He turned and looked at David earnestly. "The point is that maybe you'd better explain to them that they really shouldn't go out of the house very much. Not everybody knows about this, and if they're quiet, people may not talk as much. At least when his wife isn't here Tony gets to live in the men's dormitory, so people are used to seeing him around. But his family may well be a different thing. I'm just saying that maybe you should caution him." The sentence ended awkwardly, Fisher not knowing what else to say.

But he didn't need to say anything more. David finally understood the danger. "I understand. If those two morons find out about this visit, they'll make no end of trouble, will they?"

"Marv Denney and Chick Flemming?"

David nodded.

"As it turns out, I may have already done something about that."

David raised an eyebrow.

"Frank Bodell is a third cousin of mine. I hate to admit that to people. But he told me the other day that the company has secret plans to hire him away from the sheriff's office. It seems there are some troublemakers they want investigated. So, knowing this visit with Tony was coming up, I quite innocently suggested that maybe he ought to send those two thugs out to do some of the work. I think they'll be in California during most of the next two weeks."

David smiled. "Why, you are a rascal, George Fisher!" Then he added,

"But thanks. I believe I can take care of my neighbors if I don't have those two around."

"And the city manager?"

"Sims Ely doesn't really cross me very much. He's certainly the man in charge, but he doesn't pick fights with Frank Crowe's men unless he has to." David savored that for just a moment. "I guess this is yet another time it's an advantage to be on Frank's team, even though I don't know how he feels about such things."

George nodded. He'd said what he needed to say.

"Well," said David. "The tunnels really are something. Now that the outer edge is lined with concrete you can visualize in your mind how sleek they're going to look when they're finished, all three and a half miles of them. For my part I don't have to worry about how to keep the blasted things ventilated much longer." He laughed. "Who knows, George, I may have worked myself out of a job as well."

"There are other tunnels to be built."

"I know. I hope Tony gets to work on them." He turned to leave. "Or at least that he gets as decent a foreman as you." Before George Fisher could reply, David left. He didn't like it when emotion crept into his voice.

JIM SAT BACK IN HIS chair and put his hands on his belly. "This is the best food I've ever eaten in my life." He desperately wanted to eat one more bowl of pasta, just because it tasted so good, but there was simply no room left.

"I think I'm going to die," said Pete contentedly.

"It really is delicious, Mrs. Capelli," David added. "Although part of their praise may be that it's your cooking, not mine."

"Please, I insist that you call me Louisa."

"Louisa it is," said David. He watched as Tony's wife cleared his plate from the table. She had refused to eat with the men, preferring to serve them as they ate a magnificent meal of prosciutto ham wrapped around fresh asparagus that she had brought from the Imperial Valley, together with some rich spaghetti. David had never tasted a tomato sauce so juicy and flavorful, nor had he or any of the others had an authentic Italian meal. When asked about it, Louisa said that she'd learned to cook from her mother, also a first generation American like Tony's father.

"Your wife is a beautiful woman," said Pete quietly to Tony, "and gracious and kind."

"Thank you." It was obvious he was pleased at the compliment.

For his part, David thought that Pete had understated the case. Louisa Capelli was short and slender, with dark, penetrating eyes and flowing black hair that fell down around her thin, angular face. She was, he decided, one of the most beautiful women he'd ever laid eyes on, and their son was every bit as handsome.

"So you're a farmer, Paul?" David asked, turning to the boy.

"Yes, sir. With my father." He said this with absolutely no trace of a dialect.

"I always thought I wanted to be a farmer," said Pete. When both David and Jim laughed, he added, "But it turned out that I can't stand being alone much, so that didn't work out."

"Well, if I can keep up this steady work for another two years we should have the farm fully paid off," said Tony proudly. His smile quickly faded to concern, which tipped the others off that he hadn't really intended to reveal this part of his personal life. David had always assumed that he already owned the farm, but apparently there was a mortgage on it.

"There's still plenty of work to do, so I can't imagine why you'll have any trouble," said Pete.

"Tony sends too much money home," Louisa said. "We have more than we need, and I'm afraid he has nothing up here."

"Quiet," said Tony.

"But it's true," Louisa continued, obviously not intimidated. "Still, we are making great progress, and it looks like he hasn't starved."

"The company feeds me well and gives me a place to sleep. That's all a man needs when he is alone."

David nodded. "His foreman told me the other day that Tony may be the best Cat operator we have on the project. He places a high value on Tony's skill." Again, Tony was pleased. Even more satisfying was the look of affection Louisa cast him.

"Well, we'd better get going," said David, standing up. "I want you folks to have some time to yourselves . . ."

"Please don't leave," Louisa said. "It's your home, and we shouldn't impose." Paul seemed to agree, and David was sorry that they were embarrassed by the Conroys being there.

"No, really. It's all right. My brother's house hasn't been cleaned since he moved into it, so it's good that Jim and I are there. By working on it every day, we may be able to help him avoid getting evicted. So take your time." David was pleased when the Capellis laughed, which meant they'd caught his sarcasm.

With that, the three men moved toward the door, with Tony following them out onto the porch. David shook his hand. "Thanks for inviting us over, Tony. It really was the best meal I've eaten in my life." Pete and Jim nodded their agreement.

"It's good to have her here, although it makes me nervous." This was an unusual sign of uncertainty in Tony.

"I know. I'm sorry they have to stay in so much. But I think it's going to be fine. No one has said anything to me."

"Nor to me. But I do get looks. They'll leave this weekend, and then everything will get back to normal."

"Good. And bad. I'm sorry they have to leave. Your wife is a marvel, and your son is so polite. You have every reason to be proud of them."

THERE WAS AN URGENT POUNDING on the door. At 3:00 a.m. it was unnerving, and David found himself stubbing his toe on Pete's kitchen table as he stumbled toward the door. Doing his best not to curse, he pulled the door open. "What is it? Who's there?"

"It's me, David. You've got to come fast."

"George . . . George Fisher?"

"Yes, Come quickly, there's a problem!"

David was wide awake now. So were Jim and Pete. "What is it, George?" Pete asked as David made his way back to the bed to pull on his trousers.

"It's Tony's boy; some people beat him up, and Tony is ready to kill someone. A couple of my men saw it happen and moved in to protect the boy. Now they're holding Tony, but I don't know how long it will last."

David was on the porch while Jim and Pete were still pulling on their shoes. "But what was Paul doing out at this hour? He shouldn't have been out."

"Tony was going to take them out of Boulder City. He'd heard some threats, and so he wanted to move them out at night so no one would notice. Some men coming home from the card game saw them and took the occasion to grab the boy. The others held Tony and forced him to watch. He hurt one of them before the others held him down and beat him, too. I'm just glad we showed up, or the boy might have been killed."

"Have you called the doctor?"

"I thought maybe you'd do that. As an official you stand a much better chance of keeping this quiet."

David nodded. "Let's go." Fortunately, Pete lived only a block away from David's house, so the four of them were able to jog over. They knocked on the door and then stepped in. There was just one light on inside, and for the moment everything was quiet. When David's eyes adjusted to the light, he saw two men sitting on each side of Tony, who was sitting on the sofa clasping and unclasping his hands, the look of his earlier fury still evident on his face.

"Where's Paul?" David asked.

"In here, Mr. Conroy," Louisa replied.

When David stepped into the bedroom he was appalled to see Paul writhing on the bed. His face was bloody, even though his mother had done her best to wipe it clean, and it looked like he'd been kicked in the ribs the way he was holding his side.

"I'm so sorry about your bedding . . ." Louisa started to say, but David just shushed her.

He went over to Paul, who looked up in terror. "It's all right . . . you're all right now. No one will dare to come in while we're all here." He rubbed the boy's good cheek. "You're going to be okay." Paul seemed to calm down but then started coughing. The handkerchief turned crimson. The tortured sound of his coughing brought Tony to his feet in the other room, but David stepped out and motioned for him to sit back down.

As David moved to the kitchen, he heard Pete trying to find out who had done it, and Jim was urging him on. Clearly, they were spoiling for a fight.

"Okay," said David sharply. "Here's what we need to do, and there will be no discussion of it!" He said this with such authority that even Pete shut up. "I'm going to call Dr. Watkins and have him come over. Pete, you'll take my car and go get him. Jim, you're going to call your tutor and ask her to come over. She's going to stay with Louisa while the doctor does his work. I want another woman in the house." He then turned to Tony. "You're going to stay right where you are. When the doctor gives us his opinion, we'll decide whether to take your family out tonight or tomorrow. Pete will go with you into Las Vegas and rent you a room if it's too soon to move your son. George will put you on the sick list tomorrow, and Dr. Watkins will confirm it."

"How do you know he'll do that," Pete interrupted.

"He'll do it!" No one chose to question him any further.

"Now, here's the most important part, and I want everybody to listen. Everybody!"

All the men turned to him. "Tomorrow, no one will say anything about this to anybody. If someone brings it up, you will act as if you know nothing about it. If some of the men who did it start bragging, you simply ignore them and act like they're making the whole thing up. And, most important, there will be no recriminations."

"No recriminations!" This was spoken simultaneously by both Tony and Pete.

"Shut up, both of you!" David said this with just as much volume as was required to quiet them. "I said no recriminations."

"But they tried to kill my boy. I have to do something."

"No, Tony, you don't. You don't have to do anything. You want to do something, and you deserve to do something. I'm sure you feel it's your duty and honor to do something. But if you so much as make a single move against any one of these men, you'll be fired on the spot. Sims Ely has a simple policy: no fighting in Boulder City. When there is, both parties are immediately ordered to move out. If you get kicked out of Boulder City, Tony, I can promise that you'll lose your job. Even worse, you'll come under the jurisdiction of Bud Bodell and his lackeys Chick Flemming and Marv Denney, and you can count on them to find a way to take you on. So unless you want to go back to California with your wife and son right now, you have to let this go. If you want to stay, you have to do what I tell you. Do you understand?"

Tony could hardly keep his legs still, and he continually flexed his hands. It was obvious that he wanted to smash something. "I understand. I don't know how you can ask this of me, but I understand," he said.

Before David could reply, Louisa responded, "He asks this of you to save us. He is our friend, and you should treat him with respect, Tony."

Tony flashed a look at his wife, but then he returned his gaze to the floor. And then, in what had to be the most embarrassing moment of his life, he suppressed a sob. All the anger and despair had to find its way out somehow, and if he couldn't get his revenge on those who had wronged him, he had to release his emotions. It was embarrassing to him and to his friends, so they looked away to spare him.

"This is very hard for him," Louisa explained. "Men in our culture feel that they should avenge a wrong."

"It would be difficult for any of us," Pete replied.

They had no time to lose, so David quickly composed himself and said, "Okay, let's move." He went to the telephone as Pete and Jim made their way to the door.

"YOU SAW THEM OFF ON the train?"

"I did," said David. "Paul's doing fine. His rib is cracked, but the doctor said he had few internal injuries, and those he did have would heal. Even his face should heal without scarring."

"How's Tony doing?" said Pete

"He's all right. He went to work this morning, and his crew treated him like nothing had happened, just like we planned. Louisa wanted him to quit and go home with her."

"It may have been the best idea. This thing is getting ugly. Has there been any gossip about it?" David asked.

"A little the first day, but when people figured out there wasn't going to be any response, they quieted down. I've heard that the guys involved had been drinking. If that comes out they'll be kicked off the reservation pronto, so I don't think they're going to say anything about it."

"So you know who they are?"

"I have my suspicions."

"Is there anything we can do about them?"

Pete blinked a couple of times. "One of them has already been fired."

"Fired? By whom? And on what grounds?"

"Insubordination. It seems he didn't like it when I told him to transfer to another crew, so he took a swing at me. He's on his way back to Portland right now."

David shook his head. "A guy on your own crew? What a sorry mess this is."

"The worst of it is that my man O'Donnell was ready to punch the guy out, so I had to restrain him and tell him to leave it alone. Have you heard anything?"

"You mean at company headquarters? No. A couple of odd glances, which tells me that folks have heard about it, but no one has been stupid enough to confront me."

"Do you think Tony will be able to hold it together? If any of those guys say something to him . . ." Pete shook his head.

"I talked to him about it. I think he'll be all right. He's pretty quiet. But at least his own crew stood by him. He's got to give them credit for that."

"What about his boy? I know he's going to be okay physically . . ."

"He's a good kid. When I apologized for such a thing happening, he tried to comfort me. I think he's worried about his dad more than he is about himself. They know how to fit in down where they live, but he and his mother now understand just how tenuous it is for Tony up here. But Tony is determined to stick it out."

"I was really proud of you, Davy. You took control of a bad situation and brought order to the place in a real hurry. You had people going in every direction. I was impressed."

"Thanks. I don't really know where it all came from. I just knew that if we didn't shut it down it would blow up on all of us, including me and you."

"Come on, you didn't resolve these things for you and me. You did it for Tony, and you know it."

David was quiet for a moment. "Maybe. I certainly hope that's why I did it."

CHAPTER 13
The Cofferdams

Boulder City—November 12, 1932

Welcome to Nevada, Mr. President." E. O. Wattis, Chairman of the Six Companies consortium, extended his hand to the Honorable Herbert Hoover, soon-to-be former-president of the United States. "It's our privilege to have you visit us."

Hoover returned the handshake and then turned to Interior Secretary Wilbur, who introduced him to Walker Young and Raymond Walter of the Bureau of Reclamation.

Photo of the upper cofferdam, which diverted Colorado River water into the diversion tunnels during construction of the Hoover Dam.

"And this, Mr. President, is Mr. Frank Crowe . . ."

"I know who Mr. Crowe is," the president said confidently. "It's a pleasure to meet you after all these years. The government has certainly entrusted enough of its money to your care."

Frank Crowe replied simply, "Mr. President." He then introduced the members of his personal staff and managing engineers, including David Conroy. When finished he turned to the president and asked, "Well, then, shall we be off on the tour?"

"I've been looking forward to it with great anticipation," Hoover replied. "I'm an engineer myself, you know." Of course, everyone knew that. It was one of the reasons the president had just received one of the soundest drubbings in the history of the Republic, with Franklin Roosevelt winning by a landslide just one week earlier. Hoover's even-tempered, analytic demeanor was greatly respected; when elected to office he had been one of the most admired men in the world. But his perceived lack of empathy and aloofness toward the plight of the common man had become a great liability as the Depression worsened. This, even though he'd pushed the government far harder than ever before to increase the money supply and to provide liquidity to the economy. Plus, he'd funded public works projects like the Boulder Canyon Project in spite of criticism that he was spending too much money. Still, it wasn't enough, and by 1932 the economic slowdown had turned into a full-fledged depression, with banks failing across the country.

Now the president was traveling to his home in Palo Alto, California, south of San Francisco, for a short break before turning the government over to the Democrats in the spring. He'd surprised everyone with his announcement that he wanted to stop by the dam site on his way home through the West. One of the most embarrassing aspects of this visit was

An alternate view of the upper cofferdam which diverted Colorado River water into the diversion tunnels.

the fact that even though Six Companies had campaigned actively on behalf of Hoover, quite rightly judging that he was the better man to protect the Boulder Canyon Project, their own employees had voted against Hoover by more than a two-to-one margin. Hoover's defeat was one of the most humiliating in national history because the voters had to blame someone for their woes, and Roosevelt's bright demeanor and cheerful optimism held something that had been missing for a long time: hope.

"Well, gentlemen," the president said stiffly to the engineers who would not accompany him on the tour. "It's been a pleasure meeting you. I envy you, getting to work on this great project. Good luck."

After Hoover and his party left the administration building, the men inside relaxed. "I don't care if he is a lame duck, he's still a president, and I've never met one before. That was exciting," one of them said. The others nodded their agreement.

After chatting about it for a few minutes, another fellow turned to David. "So tomorrow is the big day."

David nodded. "It is. After all the work I did to get those tunnels ventilated, Frank is going to fill them with water." That brought a laugh. But it really masked the excitement of what was going to begin the very next day. When the appropriate signal was given, trucks would begin to file out onto the wooden trestle bridge upstream from the diversion tunnels, where they would start to dump hundreds of truckloads of rock and gravel into the riverbed. When this small earthen dam got high enough, the water would inevitably pour over the dikes that had been built to isolate the Arizona diversion tunnels, and water would start flowing through the tunnels on that side of the river. That was step one of a multistep process required to isolate the Hoover Dam construction site from the river. Step two was to build a much larger earthen structure, known as a cofferdam, that was heavy enough and high enough to hold back anything the river could send against it. After all, flows had been below ten thousand cubic feet per second so far in

President Herbert Hoover, an engineer

the season. But spring floods had been known to deliver as much as fifteen times that amount in heavy runoff years, so it was crucial that the cofferdam was hefty enough to make certain no water leaked into the dam site, no matter the volume of water in the river. Yet the trick was that they didn't want it to be too big, since it would be impossible to remove the material in this construction dam once the reservoir started backing up behind the Boulder Dam. The cofferdam would then remain submerged forever.

Like most tasks connected with this project, speed was essential. They couldn't start excavating the permanent dam's foundation and preparing the site for the massive mountain of concrete that was to grow up toward the canyon rim until the cofferdam was in place.

"I'd better get down there," said David. "Frank wants me to take a hand in staging the delivery of fill material, so I need to meet with my foremen. See you guys tomorrow." David left with a feeling of great anticipation for the day to come.

"Well, Tony, again you're at the heart of the operation."

Tony didn't smile. As far as David knew, he hadn't smiled in the six months since the incident with his son. He never talked about the beating and would only say, "He's fine," when asked how Paul was doing. Finally, his friends had stopped asking.

"Gotta go, Mr. Conroy. The shovels are ready." David tipped his hand to the rim of his hat and watched as Tony climbed up on his bulldozer. His job would be to continually shove fill material into large piles that the scoop shovels could claw into the dump trucks. The dumping operation for the initial diversion dikes was expected to take nearly thirty hours, and David had already told Jim not to expect him to come home, as he planned to catch a few naps during the operation in one of the supply buildings. At this stage there was no way he was going to be caught offsite if something went wrong.

"Ready, David?" He turned to see Frank Crowe standing next to him. The man was an absolute phantom in his ability to sneak up on a person.

David laughed, "Yes, sir." As if Frank Crowe needed his permission.

"All right, then . . ." Frank lifted his arm to give the signal.

David glanced at his watch and noted that it was eleven thirty a.m., November 12, 1932. The first truck in the line gunned its engine, a great cloud of bluish gray exhaust belching out of the stack, and the lumbering machine started out onto the trestle bridge. "That's got to take a lot of guts to go out on that bridge with such a heavy load." Of course, David said this quietly, so no one would hear. After all, not everyone shared his paranoia about bridges.

When the truck reached the appointed spot, the driver pushed a lever that forced open the side dump mechanism of the truck bed on the downstream side, allowing the contents to pour out and into the river. The seemingly placid water swallowed it up easily, and the river continued on its ancient course as if nothing had happened. Little did the river know that this was just the first of many thousands of such loads and that the ultimate objective of this intrusion was to force the river from the bed it had formed many thousands of years earlier and into a smooth-walled artificial channel that would swallow it up whole and spit it out three-quarters of a mile downstream.

When the first driver had emptied his load, he pulled ahead and to the side, then backed off the bridge and over to the material pile so the next truck could make its attack on the river, and then the third truck, and on and on. As the drivers became more familiar with the exercise, they shortened the time required to dump each load to just fifteen seconds, which was really rather remarkable given the trucks' size and weight.

It looked almost like a dance, and it continued all through the first day and night, hour after hour, four loads a minute, 240 loads an hour, in an endless stream that lasted through the night and into the next morning. The day shift was replaced by the swing shift, which was replaced, in turn, by the night shift. None of the switching interfered with the procession.

Finally, as the dark of night started to yield to the first intimation of dawn on the second morning, David saw ripples forming in the water. They were illuminated by the powerful arc lights that had kept the work area ablaze throughout the process. The ripples were a sure sign that the small mountain of rubble was getting close to the surface.

"You didn't get much sleep, David." He turned at the sound of Woody Williams' voice.

Not knowing what to say, David tried to be clever. "So, do you think your tunnels are up to the task?" It was a stupid question, but he was tired.

"I hope so. If not, let 'em fire me and I'll go off to Burma or someplace where they don't really care how well you build something, just as long as you finish it on time."

David felt bad about the perceived insult, so he responded, "You built it right, Woody, and a year ahead of schedule. Six Companies headquarters has to be pleased."

"*Ecstatic* is a better word. They've had so much cash flow that they're already declaring a dividend. Can you imagine that? A dividend this early in the project?"

It was impressive. Unheard of, really. To think that they had undertaken a project unlike any other in history, and yet in spite of theirs being the lowest bid, Frank Crowe had been so conservative in his calculations and so innovative in his processes that they were a full year ahead of schedule. It was amazing.

"Look there," Williams said excitedly, pointing to the river. "That load of fill just stuck its head above the surface, didn't it?"

David strained in the early light. "I think you're right." They watched as another truck dumped its load, and then another, and then another. By now it was clear that the water was flowing around that spot.

"Two more hours. I predict two hours, and water will breach the dike," Woody said excitedly. David said he thought it would be two and a half, as much to keep the conversation going as a real estimate of the moment. But Woody got animated by that. "That's not a bad idea, David. We can start a pool on when it's going to breach."

"Wait a minute, Woody . . ." But Williams was way too excited to stand still.

"Hey, everybody, I'm starting a pool on when the river will break through the Arizona dike. Who's in?"

David laughed as a group of excited men rushed forward to get in on Woody's pool. People really would bet on anything. "Thank heavens old Sims Ely isn't in charge of the canyon," said David to himself.

"Want a ticket, David?"

David raised an eyebrow then laughed. "Sure. Why not?" He looked at his watch, then out at the swirling water, and made his best guess. "Is 7:35 a.m. available?" Williams looked down at his sheet. "Seven thirty-five goes to David Conroy."

Which was why it was so exciting for David when, at precisely 7:30 a.m., a small finger of water finally crawled its way over the dike on the Arizona side. Slowly it formed a muddy trail on the top of the dike and then, reaching the downstream slope, started to meander down the inside face of the dike. As yet another truckload fell into the river, even more water followed the initial trail over the Arizona dike until, in a matter of moments, the water started crawling its way across the mud flat leading up to the entrance of the tunnel.

It was excruciating to watch as the water slowly reached the mouth of the concrete entrance. But the wait for it to mount the necessary depth to get over the lip didn't take long after that. Having found a new, more hospitable channel, the river quickly adapted to its new circumstance and washed out the dike in a matter of moments. Water from clear across the nearly nine-hundred-foot expanse of the canyon started flowing toward the Arizona side, where the beautifully finished concrete walls started to turn a muddy sienna red as the water started its way down the tunnel that would be its new home for the next two or three years.

You'd think that men would cheer on such an occasion, but instead they all just stood there, dumbfounded. When you considered all the work, sweat, and broken bones that had gone into this moment, it was overwhelming. More than a year of drilling and blasting, of building concrete plants and laying railroad tracks and paving roads had passed, and all that work was merely necessary preparation to the real job of building the dam. Not a single shovel full of concrete had been poured on the new dam, but all that was about to change. Water flowing through the tunnels was the most important single event necessary for the real project to begin.

So, as the realization soaked in, someone finally let out a cheer, and then everybody was shouting. In the relative blink of an eye, the river was turned, its ancient bed abandoned. It was an amazing sight to see the water start rushing into the tunnel, and David now wished he could be at the other end to witness the water as it emerged from the mouth of the lower portal. He also wondered how long it would take the main channel to dry out once water was no longer flowing into it.

An exciting moment—the initial diversion of the Colorado River into the tunnels, one year ahead of schedule.

"So who won the pool?" someone shouted. Woody looked at his watch, consulted the chart, and then let out a curse. "It's David Conroy by a minute. A single minute! Oh, that's rich, Conroy. You didn't even want to be in the pool, and you win."

David grinned. "Just good engineering, Woody."   .

"Yeah, well, I expect to see you at the card tables soon so I can win it back."

"Mind if I send Pete?"

"That shark? Keep your rotten two hundred bucks if that's your attitude."

David's eyes widened. "Two hundred? I can't believe it. You only had a few minutes to put the pool together." Two hundred dollars was, after all, about a month's income for an engineer.

Williams grinned. "You stick to engineering, Conroy. I'll stick to managing projects, no matter what they are."

Lower Portals—January 1933

"That is one big pile of dirt," said Pete.

"It's like a giant pyramid," Sean replied. "I guess I never realized just how huge a dam had to be, since you only see the downside face of it."

"Kind of like an iceberg—most of the weight and mass is under water." Pete always liked it when he could come up with a metaphor to describe something.

"But it's made out of rock and dirt. How is it that the water doesn't just turn the dirt into mud so that the whole thing starts leaking?"

This conversation was taking place on a break as Pete and Sean dangled on their cables downstream from the huge cofferdam being constructed just below the dikes that were diverting water into the tunnels. They were now working on scaling the canyon walls where the lower cofferdam would be built to prevent any backflow from moving upstream from the lower tunnel portals once work on the big dam started. Of course, the lower cofferdam would be much smaller than its upstream counterpart since it wouldn't bear the full force of the river.

"How is it, O'Donnell, that I'm supposed to know the answer to all your questions? I'm no expert on dams."

Sean smiled. "Ah, but you're a foreman, and foremen know everything. They're famous for it. So why doesn't an earth-fill dam leak?"

Pete shook his head. "Well, as it turns out, I do know the answer to this one—don't look smug—and I'll be happy to explain it to you, but at the cost of a beer on Saturday night."

"It always comes down to a beer with you, doesn't it?" Sean took a deep draft of water from his canteen. When the sun was in full blaze as it was right now, the canyon walls heated up quickly, even though it was January and the temperature on the rim was near freezing. In other words, it was hot, and he was thirsty. Wiping his mouth, he replied, "All right, then. A beer."

Pete smiled contentedly. "It's all in the materials. You use a combination of gravel, sand, and rock to get the weight of the dam great enough to resist the pressure of the water, and you use the density of the material to form an impenetrable core at the center of the triangle that water can't seep through. It's largely a function of the weight of the materials and the pressure of the water on the upstream side compressing the fine-grained material until it's packed so tight that nothing can get through, including water."

"Wow, foremen really do know everything."

"Nah, their little brothers do. At least in this case. Besides, with this particular cofferdam they're going to line the upstream face with concrete, so there's no chance of water getting through it anyway."

"Ah." Sean was quiet for a time, munching on his sandwich. "So why didn't you become an engineer like your brother David? You obviously like this stuff."

"I couldn't stand school. It's easy for me to understand things conceptually, but I don't want to do all the mathematics involved. Besides, the engineers bear the responsibility for the success of the whole thing. Just think of how terrible you'd feel if a bridge you designed or a dam you built were to fail and people got killed. It happens, you know."

Sean nodded. He knew of instances in New York City where buildings had collapsed or bridges had failed. Not so much in the twentieth century, but many in the nineteenth. "I guess I'm like you; I'm happy to do the work, but I want somebody else to figure it out." Sean again looked at the earthen dam taking shape and marveled. "So if that's one hundred feet high, how big is the real dam going to be?"

Pete laughed. "Seven times that tall. It will practically fill the whole canyon up to the rim. It's going to be made entirely of concrete, yet still be classified as a gravity dam. That means the concrete has to weigh enough to hold back a lake full of water that will back up for more than a hundred miles! Just try to picture all that in your mind."

Sean couldn't. It was one of the things that annoyed him most. He simply could not visualize things in his mind. When working on the skyscrapers in New York City, he had no clue what they would look like when they were finished, aside from the artist's drawings. It always amazed him that people could form a picture in their mind, reduce it to lines on blue paper, and then have the completed structure look almost exactly like the drawing.

"Well, this cofferdam has certainly kept a lot of men busy," said Sean. "Tony told me they've been managing to fill and dump nearly four thousand truckloads of fill per day. That's amazing."

"You've talked with Tony? How's he doing?"

"I see him at dinner occasionally. I try to sit with him at least a couple of nights each week. He's doing fine. He's been using his bulldozer to pull the big studded rollers that compress the fill material. I think he likes working on the cofferdam since it's out in the open. The tunnels were hard on him because of all the fumes."

"Has he said anything about his boy? How he's doing?"

"Not a word. I think things like that are really private for a person like Tony. He keeps all his problems inside."

"Well, the cofferdam should be finished in a week or so. Does he know what he's going to do after that?" The fact that the project was completed in phases was always a big worry to the workers, since it was not always easy to move from one job to another.

"His boss told him that he planned to move him to excavating the base of the big dam. They figure they may have to go a hundred feet deep, or something, to find bedrock."

Pete nodded. "That's good. I'm glad he has a job lined up. Well, break is over. We have to finish the scaling on this part of the canyon so they can start to build the downstream cofferdam."

Sean laughed. "I thought I was coming out here to build just one dam. Who knew I was going to build three of them—big, little, and gigantic?" With that, he put the wax paper from his sandwich into his pocket and started to swing himself into position to start chipping away again.

Muck crews excavating mud and soft material from the exposed riverbed prior to pouring the foundations of the Hoover Dam.

Exposed riverbed after the Colorado River was diverted through the tunnels.

CHAPTER 14
Mucking

Black Canyon—January 1933

George Fisher called his crew together. "Okay, the night crew is bragging that they're up to nearly one thousand truckloads of muck per shift. We want to beat that. It means nearly four trucks per minute. Any ideas on how we can speed things up?"

The stench at the bottom of the canyon was almost overpowering. The diversion of the river had exposed the riverbed to air for the first time in human history, and the accumulated decay and muck was like an open, oozing sore in the desert. Underground springs kept the air moist, and great pools of stagnant water kept the material soggy and muddy. The silt from thousands of years of erosion had formed a thick gooey mess, mixed with gravel that had to be excavated one shovel load at a time. No one knew how deep they would have to go before hitting bedrock. While it had been all right to simply excavate the ground beneath the cofferdams to the point where the compacted soil could support the weight of that intentionally temporary structure, that was not an option for the great concrete dam. The more than six million tons of weight that would bear down on the foundation had to be planted firmly in the bedrock.

George Fisher noted a raised hand. "Yes, Tony? You have an idea?"

"The trucks drive in to be loaded and then back their way out instead of turning around as one way of saving time. Perhaps we could do something like that on a modified basis with the bulldozers."

Fisher pondered this for a moment. "I'm not sure I understand exactly what you're proposing." He moved closer so Tony could draw it for him on his clipboard. As they were chatting a messenger came up to them, handing a piece of paper to Fisher. He looked at it, scowled, and then handed it to Tony.

"The paymaster? Why do I need to see the paymaster?"

George shrugged. "You know as much as I do. You better go."

"But when will I go? I'm in the middle of a shift?"

Fisher took the paper back. "It says immediately. So I guess you're off the clock."

Tony's face clouded, but he knew better than to argue. "I'll be back as soon as I can."

"You won't make it today, so we'll see you tomorrow." Tony turned to leave.

Noting his scowl, Fisher added, "I like your idea, by the way. We'll talk more in the morning."

By the time Tony found a ride up the side of the canyon and back to the men's dormitory to get his documentation, he almost missed making it to the office before it closed. When the clerk tried to brush him off, he got pushy. "This is bull. You took me off the clock, and I will not miss another day. Now what is it you want?"

The clerk huffed but finally directed him to an assistant paymaster. With more than four thousand men on the job at any given time, the company had many assistant paymasters. "This message says you want to see me?"

"What message? I don't even know who you are. Why would I want to see you?"

"This message. It says to come to the paymaster and to bring my documentation." He held out the message.

The fellow studied the sheet of paper Tony had handed him. "You're Capelli?"

Tony rolled his eyes. "Tony Capelli. I run a Cat on the mucking crew."

"Who's your supervisor?"

Tony was growing even more impatient, particularly since the guy hadn't started shuffling for papers or anything. "George Fisher."

The man nodded, then got up and moved to a filing cabinet. He fumbled for a few minutes, then pulled out a folder and studied it. Finally, after what seemed way too long, he turned and said, "Listen, Capelli. I don't know who sent this to you, but we didn't. It's on official stationery, so I see why you decided to come. But the fact is that we don't need to see your documentation. Everything in your file is fine. You've been here since the beginning, for crying out loud. If there was a problem we would have dealt with it way before now."

"But if you didn't send it . . ."

"Is somebody trying to play a joke on you? If so, you better tell them to knock it off because forging the paymaster's signature is going to get them fired, and pronto. Is this a friend of yours?"

"I don't have any friends."

"Well, then, somebody is playing a nasty routine on you, and we need to find out who it is. We will not have people sending out bogus communications. Do you mind if I keep this?"

"What about my pay?"

"Your pay is fine. I told you there's nothing wrong."

"I mean today. I've missed two and a half hours of work already, and I can't make it back down the canyon before the shift ends."

"Ah, your pay for today. Well, I'm afraid there's nothing I can do about that. A man's either working or he's not. Whoever did this to you just cost you some money. Sorry."

Tony clenched his teeth. "I understand." There was nothing more he could say.

"Listen, do you have any idea who would do this? I'm serious that we want to catch him. It won't give you your money back, but at least you'll have the satisfaction of knowing that he's gonna get his butt fired."

Tony shook his head. How could he possibly choose just one person out of all those who had given him trouble? "This won't cause problems for me, will it?"

The fellow shook his head slightly. "No. We won't record it as an absence since it was on official stationery. You're clear to go back to work tomorrow. Listen, if we ever need something from you, I'll make a note in here that we need to send a second confirmation. That way if you get just one notice, you'll know it's bogus and you can ignore it."

"Thank you."

"Wait a minute. I've got a better idea. If you do get a single notice, don't just throw it away. Instead, have your foreman send the bogus message to us by his usual messenger but marked confidential. That might help us track this down."

"Has this happened to anyone else?" Tony hoped the answer would be yes, but, of course, the answer was no. He thanked the assistant paymaster and left.

As he walked back toward the dormitory, the fury he felt inside seemed to swell like great waves on the ocean, and his face burned from the indignity he had suffered. What made it worse was that he had done what David Conroy had asked of him and not retaliated when someone had hurt his son. Now this. "No more, David Conroy. I will not take it anymore." True, he needed the job. "But a man must be a man," he said to himself, almost as if in a trance. "What am I, if I am forced to play the role of a coward?" The words felt salty on his tongue, repugnant like vinegar.

It seemed unnatural to the people who walked past him to hear a man talking to himself in such low guttural tones. So much so that no one said a word to him. "Crazy Italian," one man said to another, who nodded in agreement.

THE COLORADO IS AN ANCIENT river, carefully carving the great canyons of the far West over the course of many millennia. As it cut its way through the various layers of solidified silt and debris that formed in the ancient sea beds thrust up in some violent past geological event, canyons emerged, creating a multicolored spectacle that is beautiful almost beyond description, with brilliant hues of red, pink, ochre, and orange forming horizontal bands that line the canyon walls for hundreds of miles. Down at the bottom of this thousand-foot gorge lie the dark waters of the Colorado River, which also changes color with the season. When the river is calm and placid, the water is turgid brown. In spring, it is a violent muddy red as the force of the current erodes the sandstone channel. In the fall, it looks a lazy green.

Most of all, it is settled. In an almost paradoxical way, the river simultaneously erodes its way to the Gulf of California, leaving great deposits of silt in the riverbed along the way. And it was into this ancient strata of deposited silt that the men of the Boulder Canyon Project now found themselves descending.

It was because of the distinctively unpleasant odor of this ancient ooze that comments started to infuse the dormitory cafeteria—laments like, "I can't take it down there . . ." and, "There isn't enough bleach in North America to get the stains out of my shirts. They're ruined."

"It's the smell that bothers me," said Pete to George Fisher, who had been cursing the river. "Nothing personal, but you guys don't smell so good."

"Feel free to join us down there anytime you want to experience it for yourself, Pete. Maybe the smell won't stick to you."

Pete smiled. He and Sean O'Donnell had joined George Fisher's crew in the dining hall. "What about you, Tony? Have you figured out how to stay clean in the Colorado's outhouse?"

"Never step off your Cat once you leave the riverbank."

"Fine advice for those who get to spend their whole day sitting on their butts," Fisher responded. "But for those of us who actually have to wade in the stuff, it's a real treat. Ten thousand years of rotting trees and algae."

"And fish. Dead fish." Pete couldn't help but throw that one in. He took a long draught of water. "Beer would fix it."

Fisher looked up. "Beer would fix the muck?"

"No, this food. It's criminal to make us eat this stuff without something strong to wash it down."

Fisher shook his head as Tony smiled. It had been a couple of weeks since the payroll incident, and while he hadn't found out who the perpetrators were, nothing like it had happened since. It was only now that he was finally starting to relax again.

"So have you hit bottom yet?" This was the first time Sean had joined the conversation.

"We have," Tony replied with an uplift in his voice. "Forty feet on both sides."

"Seventy-five in the center," Fisher added gravely.

"So is that good? Will it make my little brother happy?"

Fisher shifted his gaze to Pete. "It should. From what I understand, the shape of the slope is practically perfect for a structure this size. The bedrock extends out from the canyon walls at a gentle slope almost to the center, where it suddenly angles sharply down to seventy-five feet. That forms a deep V-shaped wedge in the center of the canyon floor, which will help us anchor the dam more firmly."

"So that's what Davy was talking about the other day. I heard him mumbling something about a toe for the dam."

"Exactly. If you think of the foundation as the footing for the dam, the V gives it a little something extra to hold onto."

"Hold onto?" Pete laughed. "With a concrete base that's two football fields thick, that dam won't be floating away. The finished product is supposed to weigh something likely seven million tons."

"Yes, but water is resourceful. It can find its way around, under, and through even the smallest crack. The dam will be under a great deal of pressure at the base."

They ate in silence for a few moments as Pete tried to form the picture in his mind of what the foundation of the dam would look like. It was to be five hundred feet across from canyon wall to canyon wall, and 660 feet thick when measured from the upstream face to the downstream face, tapering to just forty-five feet thick at the top. It really was incredible, even for someone like Pete, who loved to play the role of cynic.

"Yeah," Pete continued, "Davy should be ecstatic. That seventy-five-foot depression is a made-to-order anchor for the dam."

"Excuse me, Pete, but why do you call your brother Davy?" Tony seemed somehow offended. "I get the feeling he doesn't like that name very much."

Pete turned toward Tony. "Exactly. That's why I use it. Older brothers are meant to irritate their younger brothers. It's natural. Certainly they do that in California, don't they?"

He was lucky he had phrased it that way. He had caught himself just in time. He'd almost said "in Italy" instead of "in California," nearly forgetting how crucial it was to maintain the distinction that Tony was American born.

"I suppose. I thought I was just being a good brother when I chastised the younger kids. But to hear them talk today, they think I was mean."

Pete turned and grinned. "See, even someone as mild-tempered as Tony picked on his little brothers. It's a tradition."

"It's a tradition that stinks," George Fisher interjected.

"You must be a younger brother."

My older brother was a great big pain. I haven't talked to him in years," George said.

"It's true," said Sean. "No matter how old you get, they're always older and they continue to treat you like you're still a dopey kid, even when you're old."

"Another younger brother?" Pete responded. "Well, I do feel sorry for all you little whiners . . ."

Tony waved his hand in the direction of George and Sean. "As you see, Pete, younger brothers can hold grudges. You should call him David, as he prefers."

Pete shook his head. "Can't do it. He's always been Davy to me, and he always will be. I like it that way. But," he said, looking up ominously, "if any of you thinks you can call him that I'll knock your heads off. Understand?" Pete felt that this was more than an appropriate nod to his filial responsibility and assumed that everyone would accept it, as such, but instead they gave him guff.

"Just like a big brother. Muscling everybody around, including his kid brother and all his friends." Fisher said this while gazing longingly into his glass of water as he considered Pete's earlier comment about the appropriate beverage for a meal like this.

Sean spoke up. "That, plus the 'rules don't apply to me' attitude. They're all like that."

"Why, Sean," Pete replied. "Even you turn against me? *Et tu, Brutus?*"

"When you're wrong. Absolutely."

"What about you, Tony?" Pete pleaded. "You're an older brother. Step up and help me out."

"I'm sure you mean well. Still, the other Mr. Conroy ought to have a say about his own name."

"He should not!"

Tony smiled. "I see your point when you put it that way." It sounded good to hear the others laugh with him.

"Of course, it may be that those who cause others to suffer first will get theirs in the end . . ." George Fisher said with a sneer in his voice.

"And just what do you mean by that?" Pete asked, suddenly suspicious.

"Well, it just stands to reason that once we hit bedrock, the trench will have to be scaled, just like the walls and the tunnels, so that the concrete can form a strong bond with the floor. It's certainly been pointed out to us in endlessly boring conversations that the only men qualified to do such highly skilled work are the overpaid scalers. So it just stands to reason . . ."

"You're kidding, right?"

Fisher smiled. Soon enough, he'd be the one wearing the clean shirt.

CHAPTER 15
Transitions

Boulder City—May 8, 1933

Gentlemen, if I could have your attention."

David and the other engineers looked up from their desks in the administration building at the sound of Woody Williams's voice.

"We've received a telegram from Secretary Ickes of the Department of the Interior. In it, he directs that from this point forward the dam we are building in Black Canyon is to be known as the Boulder Dam, not the Hoover Dam. Here is a relevant section: 'The name Boulder Dam is a fine, rugged, and individual name. The men who pioneered this project knew it by this name . . . These men, together with practically all who have had any first-hand knowledge of the circumstances surrounding the building of this dam, want it called Boulder Dam and have keenly resented the attempt to change its name.'" Williams looked up. "The secretary then goes on to suggest that former President Hoover really didn't have much to do with the dam, which I think is a load of nonsense, as well as saying that public works shouldn't be named after individuals, although I doubt he'd fight it much if we named something after him." The men in the room laughed. "But since he's the guy who ultimately signs our paychecks, I feel like I should paraphrase Moses: 'Thus it is written, so shall it be.' So from this point forward you're all working on the Boulder Dam. Any questions?"

"Isn't that what it was called in the first place?"

Woody nodded. "It was, until they changed it to Hoover. Now it's Boulder again. Who knows what it will be by the time we finish it. But since the federal government is paying for it, they can name it anything they want. Any other questions?"

No one had any, but someone piped up. "I'm just glad that the politicians have plenty of time to worry about the really important stuff while leaving the trivial details like building the thing to us."

All nodded in agreement.

Black Canyon—June 1933

"I'M NOT VERY GOOD AT this sort of thing . . ." Pete cleared his throat. "I mean, you're all a bunch of lazy no-accounts, but still . . ." Pete's crew shifted uneasily. They were feeling the same emotions he was, and it was uncomfortable. "Still . . ." he looked up. "In spite of that, you're the best crew on the canyon walls. 'Smooth as a baby's butt'; that's what Woody Williams said when he inspected your work. That's a lot to say, considering what we started with."

"Now it's finished. The scaling, the cutting of the wedge, the trench in the bedrock." Sean was surprised at how confident he felt saying this. "And we were there for all of it. Even the stinking mess in the trench."

Pete looked over at him and nodded. He always hated saying good-bye to a crew since no matter how hard he tried not to care, he couldn't help but feel melancholy. "Well, I guess that's it, then. Turn in your time cards and check with the paymaster on Friday. They'll muster you out." He looked around the group one last time. Some were moving on to other government-sponsored jobs in the West, such as building the new multispan Bay Bridge between Oakland and San Francisco or the flood-control projects in Los Angeles. Others were going to their homes in the Midwest in hopes of finding something that would let them stay closer to their wives and children. A handful, including Sean and Pete, had managed to find new work on the dam site.

Pete took a deep breath and slowly scanned the faces of each of his men. What he saw as he looked at them were men who had become like brothers to him. He could take that; what he couldn't take was the smile he received from each man as his gaze passed over them. "Well, all right, then. Why don't you get out of here before I have to turn you in to Bud Bodell and his goons. You're on government property, you know. What are you waiting around for, anyway?"

"Three cheers for Pete Conroy! Best foreman on the job!" Pete hated Sean for doing that, but the cheers were genuine, and Pete found that he had to wipe his nose on his sleeve.

Everybody laughed.

And then it was over. In a single instant they were no longer a cohesive group but rather a disconnected collection of individuals as each man receded into his own set of fears and hopes for what the future held for him. One by one they came up and shook Pete's hand and then made their way to the truck waiting to take them up to the canyon rim.

Pete and Sean lingered a moment. "I ought to paste you for that . . ."

Sean smiled. "I know. If it helps, you should know that I've never done that for a foreman before. That's because they've all been jerks."

"And I'm not?"

"Not all the time. Although you did have your moments."

They started to walk together in silence.

"So you're going to be a rigger?"

Sean nodded.

"As far as I can tell, that's even more dangerous than scaling."

"That's what they tell me."

"So do you have a death wish or something?"

"Nah, I figure I'm immortal or expendable. I just can't imagine being down there in the concrete where it's all closed up inside the casing blocks."

At this point they reached the truck where Sean had to go back with the crew while Pete stayed behind to close out the books. Pete stuck out his hand. "Best of luck to you, then. Maybe we can have dinner together once in a while?"

"I hope so." Sean smiled as he accepted Pete's handshake.

DAVID CLIMBED INTO THE DRIVER'S seat and put his right arm behind Pete's side of the seat as he turned to back the car out of its parking stall. Once centered in the right lane, he turned forward, changed gears, and let out the clutch so they could start the twenty-mile journey back to Boulder City.

"So, why is it again you had to cut your trip to Boise short? I thought you've been planning this for months."

"I have, but we just learned that we're being sued. A half-dozen men allege they were victims of carbon monoxide poisoning while working in the tunnels. When the papers were filed, Frank wanted me back here immediately. They're asking for $50,000 in compensation and $25,000 punitive damages."

"Seventy-five thousand? You've got to be kidding! Divided by six men, it's indecent! They won't get it, will they?"

"It's $75,000 each." David's reply was subdued, but it still had the effect of causing Pete's eyes to widen as he shook his head in disbelief. After all, the highest-paid job on the work site, apart from senior management, brought in $2,300 a year.

"That's more than most of us will make in a lifetime. It's ridiculous—and I'm the guy who's always on the worker's side."

"We did our best to ventilate the tunnels, but we didn't use electric trucks. The State of Nevada is against us, since they tried all along to stop the work and force us to modify the trucks to comply with their regulations. The feds let us go ahead, but the lawsuits are filed in state court. It's bad."

"How does this affect you?" Pete didn't even pretend to be upbeat.

"I bear much of the responsibility. It's absolutely certain I'll be called to the witness stand. The problem is that if a single case wins, the damage to Six Companies could be crushing since even more workers are bound to come forward."

Pete observed how tightly David was holding the steering wheel. "So I may not see much of you for a while?"

"Probably not. It's really frustrating since they're starting the cuts on the various intake tunnels, and I should be spending my time there rather than meeting with lawyers."

They drove in silence for a while. Pete was willing to talk, but only if David wanted to. Finally David spoke up, but not about lawsuits. "So it's back to concrete work for you?"

"Curbs and gutters. That's where I got my start."

David laughed. "I hardly think of the Boulder Dam as curbs and gutters."

"It's more like it than you think. The deepest the wet concrete will ever be poured is eighteen inches—just about the depth of a good curb. Anything more than that and the chemical heat would mess up the curing."

David raised an eyebrow. "Eighteen inches? I didn't know that. It'll take a while to pour more than seven hundred feet of the stuff at that rate."

"You'd think so. But as I listen to Frank and Woody talk, they've figured out how to accelerate the curing. It's going to be something to behold."

"Are you really glad to get back into concrete, or are you just settling for it?"

"I do need the job, but I'm also kind of glad to get it. I'm getting too old to dangle from a rope all day long. It hurts my butt to sit on that little board for hours at a time, swinging like Tarzan across the face of the cliff when its 120 degrees outside. So I guess I am looking forward to a change."

David nodded but didn't say anything.

"It'll be all right, David. I don't know how, but somehow you'll come out all right."

His voice tight, David replied, "I hope so. I left Jim up there in Boise, and he and Mary are at it again. I feel bad that men got sick, even though I do believe we took reasonable precautions to protect them. I did what I could . . ."

"I'd be glad to buy you a drink before we get back to the monastery."

David smiled. "I probably should have a drink. Woody thinks it would help me relax if I did."

"But you won't, will you?"

"I guess not after this long. I have to remind myself just how bad it was before I quit drinking. Why start up again now?" He tried to sound lighthearted. "Besides, I need all the money I can get; Mary's mother and father have lost everything, and it looks like they're going to move into our place for a while. You can count on her brothers to be there every Sunday. So on top of everything else, I have new mouths to feed. Can't go wasting my money on booze—"

"Or women. Don't forget that you can't waste money on women."

David smiled. "You're right. In some ways my life still isn't as complicated as yours, is it?"

Pete laid his head against the side window and closed his eyes, glad that he'd gotten his brother to smile. Then he opened his eyes and added, "Actually, knowing Mary's brothers, you should be glad for these lawsuits. At least it keeps you out of Boise."

David laughed. "That's just what Mary said. She may be moving down here after all. Just leave the house to them without a forwarding address."

Cableway in action, carrying a bucket of concrete for placement in one
of the construction forms.

CHAPTER 16
Cableways and Riggers

Boulder Dam—August 1933

H ey, Sean, wait up a minute."
Sean smiled at the sound of Pete's voice, stopped, and turned to
wait for him.

Huffing a bit, Pete jogged up. "So how's it going?"

"Fine. Those are amazing contraptions Mr.
Crowe designed," Sean said, referring to the unique cableway system to
which he'd been assigned. "Have you ever seen anything like them?"

By this time the two men had started walking toward the changing
room at the base of the dam where the footings had started to take shape
as massive amounts of concrete were lowered in great buckets, each holding
sixteen tons of concrete.

"I have. He pioneered the idea of cableways on a dam just outside Boise
nearly twenty years ago. Both Davy and I worked on that one as well. It's
where we got to know Frank Crowe."

"Well, it's the most sophisticated system I've ever seen for delivering
concrete, people, and any other thing you can think of to precisely the right
spot in thirty seconds or so. The other day we lowered a diesel generator right
down to the canyon floor. There was nothing like this, even on the Empire
State Building, and those folks knew how to organize things."

Pete shook his head. "The thing I can't get over is how those skinny little
cables can hold all that weight. Davy could tell us, but he's tied up with a
bunch of lawyers."

"The gas lawsuits?"

"Yes," said Pete

"Well, I feel sorry for him and for all those guys who had to work in the
tunnels. Even though it's hot as Hades out here, I'm glad to be out in the
open air."

"So maybe you can tell me how the system works in its day-to-day operation. I've applied to be a spotter, and I'm feeling a little underprepared."

Sean was surprised and pleased. His mentor was now seeking his instruction. "A spotter? Well, let's see. It's pretty straightforward. There are ten cableways in all. Most are strung between two movable ninety-foot towers on each side of the canyon. The towers are mounted on steel wheels that ride on railroad tracks. The operator controls the movements of both towers in the upstream and downstream direction by activating electric motors in the wheels. What else do you want to know?"

"The cables. I think I get it, but I'm going to be tested on it, and I don't like tests."

Sean nodded. "There are five cables on each rig that control the movement of the buckets or platforms as they move side to side and up and down. The sixth is a dump cable to open the concrete bucket when it's dropped into position.

"Let's see if I can name the cables." Pete scrunched his forehead in concentration. "The track cable is the one that the carriage rolls on. It's the strongest."

"Right, it's the fixed cable that's strung between the two towers, and the one that bears the weight of the load." He then went on to name the other cables, forgetting only one.

"That's five. You've almost got it."

"I hate this. I always forget the last one."

"Concrete weighs a lot . . ."

"Right, Sherlock, it does weigh a lot."

"It's a hint. Think about it. As the carriage rolls out on the track cable . . ."

"Sag! Of course. The button line is the cable that adjusts to the carriage's position on the track cable to offset any sag in the line."

Sean smiled. "You've got it. But why a spotter? That's a pretty tough job. Sometimes you can hardly even see the operator, and yet you're giving him the directions needed to move the thing out and over the canyon and then down to wherever your crew is working, stopping just inches from where it needs to be, and all as fast as possible. It's a tense job. One misstep and sixteen tons of concrete comes crashing into the dam itself, maybe killing somebody or worse, damaging the thing. Six Companies might forgive a man for dying, but not for slowing down their construction timetable."

Pete reached down and pulled on the high-topped rubber boots he used on the job. "An eighth of a mile. That's how far it is from the work area to the operator sitting in his little cab on top of the towers. It really is crazy."

"The only way you have to signal is with bells and hand signals."

Pete smiled. "High risk, hairsplitting precision, primitive communication, and wet concrete. What's not to love about that?" Then he added, "But the truth is, I'm getting old. Handling the concrete is hard on old bones and muscles. So this seems like the best way to stay with my crew and keep on working."

"I'm glad it's you, not me."

"As if you don't have your own challenges. I've watched you guys ride the bucket. You're out there dangling a thousand feet above the canyon, without even the canyon wall to steady you, and you want to lecture me on high risk?"

"It is exciting. Probably the best job I've ever had. Each tower has over 650 feet of steel cables, all of which have to be lubricated and inspected to make sure they're not going to fail."

"That would be the tough part for me." Pete shook his head. "Some of the crew platforms have, what, upwards of twenty men on them? If your cable separates, it's a free fall to death."

"That's a low probability. The greater danger is that we get them traveling out on the cable toward the far side of the dam, and the operator misses the signal to slow the carriage down. We had one carriage slam into the canyon wall on the other side. A couple of men nearly fell off, which would have been sure death."

"I heard about that. Rumor is that a couple of the men quit on the spot, they were so shaken up."

"It's not a rumor. It happened." Sean shook his head. "I guess one man's adventure is another man's worst nightmare."

"So have you had any close calls?"

"A couple. Not really all that close, but enough to scare me. One day I was working on one of the head towers, standing up there in the wind. Suddenly we started moving as the operator started positioning a bucket at exactly the same time as a blast of wind hit me from the opposite

Initial forms to hold concrete at the base of Hoover Dam. The thickness of the base is greater than the length of two football fields.

direction. I very nearly lost my footing. I did lose the wrench I was working with, which irritated me no end."

Pete smiled. "And probably scared the heck out of anyone who was near the point where it landed in the canyon. Any others?"

"Believe it or not, I get a little vertigo each time we start moving out over the canyon while simultaneously moving upstream. Somehow the travel in both directions disorients me."

"You? Get vertigo? After the buildings you've worked on?"

"The buildings are planted squarely on terra firma. It's a lot different out on a cable that swings its way out to where it's going."

"Well, who'd have thought? Still, you must love it to stay with it in spite of that . . ."

"I do love it. You're totally free up there."

Pete nodded. "And that's something the boys behind the desk will never understand."

Boulder Dam

"TONY, CAN I TALK TO YOU for a minute?"

Tony's stomach tightened. "Yes, sir." It didn't help his anxiety that George Fisher had a solemn look on his face.

"What is it, Mr. Fisher?" George motioned for him to move to the side of the room where they could talk without others overhearing him. Even though he had no reason to believe he was in trouble, he felt the blood rush to his face, particularly when he saw the grin on Chick's and Marvin's faces.

"Sit down, Tony." Tony's eyes followed George's hand, and, even though he didn't want to sit down, he moved into position and settled lightly on the front edge of the chair.

Crew begins concrete placement for a portion of the cutoff wall at the base of the dam.

Pouring concrete in multiple forms that fit together to form the dam

"Listen, Tony, there's no good way to say this, so I'm just going to say it. The new rosters came out for the dozer work that will be done on the new Penstock tunnels, and your name isn't on it."

"What? But—'"

George held up his hand. "I put you on my list, but the crews are much smaller, and so they've shifted some of the other, more experienced, operators onto my smaller shift since theirs were eliminated."

Tony didn't remind George that there was no one more experienced than him, except at being white. "So I'm done?" The mix of anger and terror that registered on his face was disturbing.

George shook his head. "You almost were. But Pete Conroy happened to be there when I was challenging the decision. He's going to become a spotter, which opens up a position on his pouring crew. He said that he wanted you to take his place."

Tony inhaled deeply, doing his best to keep his hands from trembling. "But a concrete crew earns a third less . . ."

"I know," George replied, "but it's the best we can do. I hope you'll take it."

Tony looked down and tried to control his hands, which were shaking so badly that he slid them between his thighs and the chair. "It always comes down to you or the Conroys. If it wasn't for you, I'd have been gone a long time ago."

"That's because we know what a good worker you are. Six Companies always gets good value out of you."

Tony understood that what he was saying was true; George did champion his cause because he was a good worker. He sighed. He could make a scene, of course, and appeal the decision. But it would go nowhere. So he looked up and then stood. "Well, then, I guess that's that."

George stood as well. "So you'll take the job?"

"I have no choice. I still have a family to feed, and obligations."

"Okay. I'll let the paymaster know."

Tony started to walk away, but his heart told him that George deserved better. So he turned to face him. "Thank you, Mr. Fisher. It's been an honor to work on your crew."

George's lips were white and narrowed. Tony suspected that it was his way of suppressing his urge to tell Tony just how hard he'd gone to bat trying to keep him on his crew. That made Tony appreciate his boss even more while his contempt for Six Companies grew even deeper.

"I feel the same way, Tony. Good luck." George then turned and walked off quickly, intentionally brushing against Marvin as he left, which prompted a suppressed curse. But even the dim-witted Marvin was smart enough to see that it wasn't a good time to tangle with George Fisher.

CHAPTER 17
The Great Pour

Boulder Dam—September 1933

Seven million divided by sixteen. That's how many bucket loads of this crap we've got to wade through." Pete looked up and saw Tony's lips moving silently. "Forget it, Tony. I don't want to know how many that is."

"That's 412,000 loads, for those who do want to know."

Pete shook his head. Although he'd initially been a little anxious about having a friend come onto the crew, it had actually been good to have Tony on the team. Tony's quick wit and powerful work ethic helped him gain acceptance from most of the guys. So much so that Pete decided that Tony might have gotten along better on the job in his previous positions had he not been off on the bulldozer by himself all the time. Once the men got to know him, they seemed to like him.

"So, 412,000, huh? Why don't you count 'em down in your head as each one splashes into the platform?"

Tony looked over at one of the buckets zipping down toward the Nevada side of the dam and said, "411,999." Everyone laughed, including Pete.

"Well, there you have it. We're already one behind that other crew. So let's get at it."

Getting at it was the easy part. The hard part had been designing the process that would allow them to build the dam in such a fashion that it could be put to immediate use. The biggest problem was the chemical reaction that caused concrete to heat up as it cured, which, in turn, caused expansion. When a roadway or sidewalk is poured, expansion isn't much of a problem, since the surface area of the concrete relative to the depth allows it to quickly dissipate the excess heat. But in a structure the size of the Boulder Dam, at a depth of 760 feet, it would take decades for the heat to cool, and the fracturing that resulted from the eventual contraction would turn the structure into gravel.

"About 120 years, David says."

"What was that, sir?"

Pete looked up. "My brother says it would take 120 years for the concrete to cool if we didn't lay down the piping."

Tony looked down at the large square in which they were standing. It really was amazing how they had overcome the heat problem. Before each layer of concrete was poured, they would lay down a lattice of metal pipes through which they circulated Colorado River water to draw off the heat. When the concrete cooled enough to add another layer in the block, they injected grout into the water pipes that had been covered up so that the structure itself would be solid. The metal lattice then became a permanent part of the dam.

"Was it your brother's idea to use the pipes?"

"No, he's not really a concrete man. The idea came from Frank Crowe and some of his other boys. It really is ingenious, don't you think?"

Tony looked across the expanse of the dam's base, which now lay before them—a giant grid of plywood squares being filled with heavy concrete. "I think the whole thing is amazing. The idea of building the dam like a giant set of building blocks stacked one on top of the other is remarkable."

"And the way the blocks fit together with the striated grooves—now that's real engineering." The upstream and downstream sides of each pouring block had vertical grooves, while the canyon-facing sides had horizontal grooves. Thus, each block would be locked together with the blocks on each of its boundaries, with grout extruded into the grooves at the end of the process to make certain that the interlocking columns formed a solid mass of concrete that would present an impermeable

Workmen opening a bucket to release concrete into the forms. The wet concrete was never deeper than eighteen inches. After drying, more was poured until the form was completed.

barrier to the water in the lake.

Pete shook his head as he looked out across the checkerboard of columns rising to different heights and widths around him. Complicating the pattern even further was the curve of the dam, which meant the upstream side of each column formed a wider arc than the downstream side. The whole thing required an army of skilled tradesmen, including carpenters, plumbers, steel men, and concrete tampers.

Pete moved into position next to the spotter who was training him. "Let's get at it, then."

Tony moved to the outer edge of the box, along with some of the other men, as they awaited the spidery cable that would bring the first bucket of the day. It was nerve-wracking to see the bucket come flying toward them, particularly since the cable was often invisible. As the bucket appeared above the rim of the canyon, it looked like a thimble swinging out and into the air. Then, as it moved to the center of the canyon directly above them, it appeared to be the size of a child's sandbox pail, growing larger as it started its precipitous descent down into the bowels of the canyon, growing in size until it came to an abrupt halt just a few feet above the designated box. By that point it was deeper than two men standing one on the other's shoulders. The bucket held the volume of a small water tower—about eight cubic yards. Of course, in time it became routine, and no one paid particular attention, at least until the bucket was nearly at their level and ready to dump its load.

On this occasion Tony and the others watched as Pete raised his arms and gave the signal. Following the arc of his motions, they watched one of the towers up on the ledge start moving to pick up a bucket from the mixing tower. When it was connected, the bucket swung out and over the canyon, moving along the track cable as it made its way toward them. At the same time, the towers themselves were moving downstream on their heavy metal wheels. Another signal from Pete and the bucket came to an abrupt halt, with just the slightest pendulum motion. Before the eye could even follow what was happening, the bucket appeared to grow larger, the main indicator that it was descending.

"Stand clear!" Pete shouted. As the bucket continued its descent, he held his position then gave an authoritative swing of his arms to signal the operator it was time to bring it to a stop. The bucket turned up in front of the men, two of whom moved into the center of the box to a position at the bottom of the bucket where they used heavy sledgehammers to knock out the safety clips. They then jumped back and out of the way as Pete signaled the operator to take the slack out of the dump cable. The screeching sound of metal on metal was followed by a great whooshing noise as a mound of wet concrete sloshed out of the bottom of the bucket, forming a small, rounded pyramid in the center of the box.

"Perfect!" Tony shouted to Pete, and then he and the other puddlers rushed out into the box to start spreading the concrete evenly throughout the square. They didn't even notice as the bucket arced its way up and out of the canyon to be refilled and then deposited in some other crew's box. Meanwhile, the puddlers had to move quickly to get the concrete formed up properly and tamped down so that any air pockets were punctured and the concrete formed into a dense, even mass. Given the time it took to move the concrete from the mixing plant to the box, the time left to the puddlers before it started to harden was very limited, so they had to work fast and hard.

But by now they had a bit more experience and had this particular load tamped out in better time. Then they prepared to move to another box. As they did, Tony stepped in front of Pete. "Good job on the spotting," he said.

"Thanks," said Pete humbly. He wasn't often humble, but in this case he'd been nervous enough that he really was subdued at his success.

"Are they ready to let you do it on your own?"

"A couple more shifts and only periodic checks, at that. But I'm pretty well there."

"Well, congratulations. It's a very responsible position."

Pete was amazed at how unfailingly polite Tony was, even with all he'd been through.

"So how is your boy doing? Is he in school or working on the farm?"

"Oh, there's no work on the farm. Not until the rainy season. There is some year-round water coming into the valley, of course, but until the Imperial Dam is built to divert water to the new canal, our property is pretty much unusable."

"Does he have much farm experience? Do you?"

"I do. In the early days, I was amazed what we could grow when we had water. Pretty much anything you wanted to put in the ground."

"But Paul?"

"Limited to our small crop and going out to pick the harvest in the fall, along with all the other boys in the school. He'll have to learn real farming from the ground up, once we get water."

"And is that something he wants to do?"

"That is not really a question we would ever ask. It's a family enterprise, and so, naturally, everyone in the family will work on it. That's what my father intended, and that's what we must do."

"Ah. Sorry, I didn't know."

Tony was quiet for a time. "I always assumed that's why you and your brother worked together on construction jobs. I just thought that it was what your father did, and so you followed in his footsteps."

"Our father?" Pete laughed. "He owned a small business. He was shocked when he first learned that I wanted to work in construction. But as much trouble as I gave my parents, he finally agreed I needed something physical. I don't know why David decided to become an engineer; I always thought he was the accounting type. But it turns out he's more rugged than that."

"You got to decide for yourself what you wanted to do?"

"Of course, but that's the way it's always been for our family. To tell you the truth, I never even thought about going into a 'family business.' My father and I just didn't get along. So I couldn't wait to get out on my own."

"It's not like that for us," said Tony. His good cheer had evaporated. "We do what we must—what duty requires of us."

"I guess that's got its own set of advantages. At least you don't have to spend your life wondering what to do. I think David's struggling right now with what Jim wants to do with his life. David wants him to get an engineering degree, but Jim is more like me. He just wants to get out there and hammer something."

Tony's mood lightened a little. "I see both of you in him. He's a good young man. He's back from Boise, isn't he?"

"Yes, he's over working on Tom Sim's crew on the Nevada side. He's a puddler, just like you."

"Not on your crew?"

"Nepotism. They try to discourage it."

"Nepotism? What's that?"

"Family working for family inside a corporation. It's looked down on since it's assumed that the foreman will show preference to his own family."

Tony shook his head. "I really don't understand some things. In my culture it would be expected that you would work for a family member and that you would be the last one to receive preference since it would be dishonorable. Plus, you'd be expected to be the hardest worker on the crew to uphold the family name. To do otherwise would be a disgrace."

"You folks take things seriously, don't you?"

Tony eyed him, suspicious that he was being mocked, so Pete quickly added, "I don't say that in a bad way. I mean, it really seems important to uphold your family's good name."

"There is nothing more important, Pete. Nothing."

Deciding that this was all getting pretty heavy, Pete looked up and said, "Well, I think it's time to order another bucket of slop. Are you ready to go stomping through the mud?"

"I'm ready."

Pete shouted, "All right then, let's get set!"

"How many do we have to pour, Tony?"

"Well, I think I saw ten other buckets lowered while we were working on ours, so that makes 411,985, counting ours. Of course, I could have missed some. I was looking down most of the time."

"Well, that's still a lot of concrete. Let's take another whack at it." And with that he raised his arms to extend the signal.

CHAPTER 18
Despicable Allies

Boulder City—October 1933

"I suppose it's possible for you to be a bit quieter, Davy. But you'd have to be dead to do it."

David looked up from the table. "Sorry. I've just got a lot on my mind."

Pete cast a quick glance at Jim, who simply shook his head. It was the lawsuit, of course, that was bothering him.

"So how are things in Boise? Are your grandparents doing okay, Jim?"

"It's really weird. My grandfather was always such a take-charge guy when he ran the moving-and-storage business, but now he's completely passive. It seems like my grandmother has to tell him everything, like when to come to dinner, when to get dressed. It's really pretty pathetic."

"I don't think I'd say it like that, Jim, particularly when your mother comes down to visit. Your grandfather is like many people who lose their job, except that in his case he lost a business and all his life's savings besides." David didn't look up when he said this, and Jim cast a quick glance at his uncle.

Trying to lighten things, Pete added, "And how are your uncles?"

Jim burst into a grin. "Don't even make me think about that. You know those two."

This caused David to look up, and even if he wanted to suppress a grin, he couldn't. "I can't disagree with that. Mary says they're making her life crazy. Neither one of them has a job, but they still stop by the house to complain about how hard their lives are."

"Well, I'm glad some things don't change," said Pete wryly. "As far as I can tell, they've never worked an honest day in their life yet, so why start now? But that's enough about Boise. How are things going for you and your lawyers? I assume that's why you're so quiet."

"They're going far better than I could have expected."

"What?" Pete and Jim exchanged glances. "Then why are you so gloomy?"

David looked up. "They're not going well because of anything I've done or said. It's because Six Companies hired Bud Bodell and his cronies as special investigators, and they've been busy digging up dirt on the plaintiffs."

A period photo of a police car

Pete rocked his head back. "So that's what those idiots have been up to. I saw Marvin and Chick the other day, and they acted like cats that had swallowed canaries. Are they part of it?"

David nodded. "They and a couple of other Bodell thugs. They've been following the lead plaintiff, Ed Kraus, around for a month, and they've dug up some incriminating things."

"Tell me more; I love gossip."

David looked from side to side, as if checking to make sure that no one else was listening. Which was preposterous, given that they were having Sunday dinner together at David's house. But both Pete and Jim followed his movements with their eyes, part of the natural sympathetic response humans share with one another.

Finally, hunched forward but looking directly up at them, David replied, "All right, but you've got to keep it under wraps. No leaks. Do you agree?"

Pete crossed his heart, which made Jim laugh, but David simply glowered. "I'm serious. It will all come out soon enough, but if it gets out in advance, his attorney may be able to turn it against us."

"Sorry," said Pete. "I promise. I can keep confidences, you know." Jim swore his oath of silence as well.

"All right. Kraus is from Utah, and he's a real character. It turns out he has a criminal record there. Besides, he's been limping around town showing everyone how disabled he is. Yet Bodell and the others have found him dancing the night away in Las Vegas clubs a couple of times, even though he's supposed to be so sick he can hardly get his breath."

"So a little bit of gold digging on Mr. Kraus's part?"

David cracked a small smile. "It's a lot worse than that. And this is the part that I don't like very much. It seems that Kraus's attorney, Harry

Austin, plans to put Ed's wife on the stand to testify that because of carbon monoxide poisoning he has lost all interest in having normal sexual relations with her."

"What? You've gotta be kidding. She'll talk about that on the stand?" Pete was grinning from ear to ear. "Kraus must be pretty desperate for money to have that little secret aired in front of the whole world. He'll be a laughingstock."

"He's been overheard to say that he can act mighty sick for seventy-five thousand."

"Well, I can tell you this," said Pete with a smile. "If I were on the jury I'd give him the seventy-five grand and more. If it's true that he can't take advantage of his marriage vows any more, then Six Companies ought to pay through the nose."

Jim burst into a grin until he saw his father's glower.

David shook his head. "Not everyone centers their life in that particular activity, Peter."

"Ah, but they should. It's ranked the number-one vice for a reason, you know."

"Well, in this case it turns out that Mr. Kraus may not be quite the tragic figure he makes himself out to be. Besides dancing, word was passed to the company that he really has quite a sexual appetite and that he's been seen with prostitutes on more than one occasion."

"Oh, so Six Companies is going to get one of them to testify?"

"This is where it turns pretty disgusting." David shook his head. "It's actually a blot on the company as far as I'm concerned."

Pete turned to Jim. "It must be bad to get your father to say something negative about his employer. It just doesn't happen in the normal course of events."

Jim worked very hard to suppress a smile. He was amazed that his father was talking so candidly in front of him. He was pleased because it meant he thought of him as a man. Still, if he started carrying on with his uncle, his dad would probably clam up.

Pete turned back to David. "Well, what's this other news? Come on, you can't bait us like this without giving the full story."

"Well, just to make sure they can make their case about Kraus's lack of moral turpitude, Bodell actually hired a fellow to cozy up to Kraus and to befriend him. Kraus is not particularly bright, so he accepted. Since then, this guy has lured Kraus into multiple sexual liaisons with prostitutes, taken him dancing and drinking, and even maneuvered him into participating in an extortion scheme in Salt Lake City. Chances are very good that he'll be hit with criminal charges once his civil suit is over."

Pete sat back against his chair. "Amazing. And you're right—that is pretty lousy. I'm all for taking a gold digger down, but it sounds like the company is fighting the gas claim by diverting attention."

"Exactly. If you can paint this guy as a creep trying to steal money with a false claim, then the burden of proof on all the other claimants becomes that much harder to establish. It will be easy to paint all of them as pikers as well."

"But if they really didn't get hurt by the gas, what's the problem?"

David shook his head. "It's just that I'd like to win fair. Conditions were bad in there, but it's hard to tell if it was from the fumes and vapors or simply the heat. Most of the conditions the men are complaining of could be attributed to heat exhaustion. The fact is that thousands of men went in and out of the tunnels without getting poisoned. I just think it would be better to win on those grounds rather than by making villains out of the men who complain."

"Is it possible that the company could lose, even if they are on solid ground?"

David stood up and stretched, a sure sign of stress. "Of course it is. Think of how it would play out to the jurors and the newspapers: 'Great big company making millions of dollars pitted against puny little workers who are sick and incapacitated.' It makes for a compelling story. Of course, it all depends on the jury and whose side they are naturally sympathetic to."

"So what the Six Companies lawyers are doing may be kind of sleazy, but it's also necessary."

"I suppose so. But it's still rotten. Plus, the fact is that whether by gas or by heat, we really did make a lot of men sick, and then we rewarded them for their incapacity by firing them if they didn't immediately report back to work in what the doctor considered a reasonable time. I really don't see how any one is standing on the side of right and truth in this."

"And I'm always labeled the crusader in the family, when in reality you're the real idealist." David didn't respond, so Pete added, "Come on, little brother. You're going to kill yourself with stress. Let's go for a walk."

"Or some pick-up basketball?" Jim asked brightly.

"Oh, please, Jim. I said a walk. Your father and I are getting old and frail. You don't want to kill him, do you?"

"Actually," said David, "a little basketball would feel good."

Pete raised an eyebrow. "Uh, oh. We're in for it now, Jim. Your dad has some steam to work off, and I'm afraid we're going to be the safety valve." Pete stood up from his chair. "Okay, then, let's get it over with. If I live through this, you owe me dessert."

"Done," David replied quickly.

Boulder Dam—March 1934

Tony Capelli wiped his forehead with his shirtsleeve. Even though it was barely spring on the calendar, it was already hot in the concrete blocks, particularly since the concrete itself gave off a great deal of heat. The usual chemical heating was intensified by the fact that the block they were working in was bounded on three sides by taller ones that were just now ready to have their plywood forms broken down and moved to another section. To an uninformed spectator, it looked like the dam was being built helter-skelter, with crews working at apparently random sites around the base. But it was more like a well-orchestrated symphony that periodically arranged and rearranged the work site to avoid overlap in the various cableways and to allow recently poured concrete the time it needed to cool down while the workers poured a new column in an area that had been previously poured.

"Is it this hot in Southern California?" Tony turned at the sound of one of his co-workers' voices, Max Henry.

"Sometimes hotter. Of course, it's not red rock down there, like it is here. More like a parched desert."

"With cactus?"

Tony smiled. "Some cactus. Scrub brush mainly."

"Whatever scrub brush is. Personally I can't imagine why anybody would want to live there. I miss trees. For that matter, I miss ferns and moss and clear running streams."

"In the West we call them creeks. I've never been to Pennsylvania, but I hear it's beautiful."

"It's amazing compared to this place. If you want to plant a garden, you have to cut down a half dozen trees. And move rocks. But it's always lush and green—and cold in the winter. Sometimes I just plain miss being cold."

"Well, if that's the case I can see why you wouldn't like it in California. But the fact is that the desert has its own beauty. In January it comes alive with color as the flowers start to bloom and non-flowering plants green up before the summer heat arrives. It really is something to see, and the sunsets are fantastic."

"And the farming's good?"

"It will be. All you've got to do is put water on the ground and just about anything will grow. Depending on the crops, you can grow things all year long."

"Do you have a big place?"

"Four hundred acres."

"Wow! That's more than a man can handle by himself, isn't it?"

"Probably. But when we get Colorado River water to the farm, I'll buy a tractor, which makes managing a place that large a lot more practical, and I've got my family."

"So you're going to be rich?"

Tony laughed. "I hope to be solvent before I'm rich." He was thoughtful. "But if things work out like I think they will, we should be very prosperous."

He would have added more, but they were interrupted by Pete Conroy, who strung together some extremely creative expletives to point out the fact that another load of concrete was on its way.

At that point Six Companies was up to more than 1,100 buckets of concrete each day, with each bucket weighing some 32,000 pounds. To deliver that many buckets, a bucket had to be deposited somewhere on the dam at the rate of one every 75 seconds, 24 hours a day, 7 days a week. Under that kind of relentless onslaught, the mammoth dam was steadily growing toward the canyon rim.

Boulder Dam—April 1934

"HEY, O'DONNELL! UP TO TRYING something new?"

"Depends on what it is. Some of the stuff you do is just plain crazy."

Sean's supervisor, Mike Wood, smiled. He was a cheerful fellow who managed to take everything the job could throw at him in stride. He had even handled the tragedy of a bucket loaded with concrete breaking loose and crashing into the dam when a cable had snapped,; killing a man in the process. He'd personally gone to the man's family to tell them the bad news and to try to explain how an accident like that could happen.

The thing that made the cabling system so dangerous was that on the rare occasions where a cable broke, there were few signs to indicate it had been stressed, such as fraying or stretch lines. This was why it was so crucial workers like Sean follow a strict maintenance program on the many miles of cables, pulleys, and carriages for which they were responsible.

"Crazy, you say?" Sean's supervisor responded. "Another guy who doesn't trust me. I don't know what a man has to do to gain respect around here."

"Okay, I'll trust you. What am I signing up for?"

"It's quite interesting. They've started blasting out the tunnels for the penstocks, and we're going to have to lift the pipe that will line the tunnel. In some instances the pipe is going to be thirty feet in diameter."

Sean whistled. "Now I've heard everything. Concrete, human beings, and construction cranes. Now we're going to hoist thirty-foot steel cylinders? Is there anything we don't plan to lift out into that expanse with Mr. Crowe's cables?"

"Haven't had any orders for a kitchen sink yet, but I wouldn't be surprised if they didn't throw one in for good measure."

Sean laughed. "And what does this penstock thing have to do with me?" Before Wood could reply, Sean added, "And what is a penstock anyway?"

"It's the system of valves, pipes, and tubes that will drain water from the reservoir and channel it through the power plant. Four intake towers will be built into the canyon walls on the upstream side of the dam, with stainless-steel drums that can be opened and closed based on demand. The penstock pipes will sit inside the tunnels. Getting the pipes positioned is the challenge."

"Okay, so what about me?"

"Well, it's kind of specialized work, and we need someone who has special training. I thought maybe you'd like to take a week off to meet with the team that will bring these monsters to the canyon and drill with them on how to use the cableway to hoist them into position. What do you think?"

View of the two Nevada Intake Towers under construction.

"I think I'd like that." Sean smiled in anticipation.

"Then the job is yours." Report to the headquarters building in Boulder City on Monday at 0800 sharp.

"WHAT IN THE WORLD?" PETE gave a signal, although it proved redundant. In a moment the carriage came gliding to an easy stop, just a foot above the concrete. Inside the railings of the platform were two familiar figures.

"O'Donnell? Hank?"

"Nice to see you too, Pete. You might want to close your mouth. You're gaping."

Pete slammed his mouth shut. "And maybe that's because you're supposed to be a bucket of concrete instead of a bucket of . . ."

"Temper, temper . . ." Sean clicked his tongue, certain that it would annoy Pete even further.

Pete chose to ignore him. "I expect crap from you, Sean. But from you, Hank?"

"Official business, Conroy. Mind if I step off?"

Pete motioned with a sweeping gesture. "It's still a little soggy, but

Note the superb finishing work to the concrete lining the penstock tunnel. These tunnels now house metal pipes to carry the usual flow of the Colorado River.

please, feel free to join us." After Hank Toombs stepped down into the concrete, Sean asked if he could signal the operator and leave, but Hank indicated he should wait.

"I'm not a taxi driver," Sean sniffed, but Hank simply ignored him.

"So what's your official business?"

"I need to talk to Tony."

Pete's face clouded. "You leave him alone, Hank. He's doing a great job here."

"Knock it off, Pete. I'm not here to hurt him. Now, can I talk to your man?"

Pete grimaced but motioned for Tony to come over. When Tony saw who it was, he too clouded up. "What is it, Mr. Conroy?" he asked, purposely ignoring Hank.

"Mr. Toombs, here, has something to say to you."

"In private," Hank added.

"No, not in private. Tony is on my crew, and anything you have to say to him, you can say to me."

"Is that all right with you, Capelli?"

Tony nodded. His face betrayed him with a look of anxiety mixed with a generous helping of anger.

"All right, then. I know you're doing well here, Capelli, and I'm not going to mess that up for you. So you both can relax." Neither Pete nor Tony did. "Here's the meat of it. We've started to excavate the penstock tunnels, and it's turning out to be a pretty dicey operation. Although the tunnels are just half the size of the diversion tunnels, they're being cut at a steep angle that's miserable to work in. It calls for a skilled Cat operator."

"I'm a concrete man now," said Tony defiantly.

Hank nodded. "And if that's what you want to keep doing, you can. But I'm here to tell you that I've been authorized to offer you a transfer. At a 50 percent increase in pay."

Even Pete staggered at that. "I thought all the jobs were scale?"

"Not this one. We have some very tight schedules to meet and some very precise cuts to make. I need the best man I can find, and I insisted to the company that Tony is the guy. I don't have time to wait around, so if you don't want it, tell me right now. If you do, you'll need to transfer tomorrow morning. What do you say?"

Pete turned to Tony. He knew that he had to take it, but he also knew it put him at risk again.

"You've got a solid job here, Tony. The men like you and you're doing great work. You can stay, or you can go. I won't stand in your way."

It was odd to see Tony's emotions play out over his face. He'd clearly expected the worst when he was called over, and now he was being offered a promotion. The change in status was so abrupt that it must have thrown him for a loop.

"I like it here. I like the men and I like the fact that the job is predictable . . ."

Hank nodded. "Then you should stay."

"No . . . that's not what I'm saying." Tony was clearly flustered, but he did a good job of composing himself. "What I'm trying to say is that I'm grateful to Pete and the others for standing up for me and making me part of their team, but I miss the skilled work, and I need the money." He turned to Pete for support. And he got it in the form of a simple nod. Not a smile. That could be misinterpreted, but not a nod.

Hank smiled. "Good. That's what I wanted to hear. So tomorrow morning go to the paymaster and turn in your card for your work here. He'll give you a new card, and you'll spend the rest of the day in training. Then I expect to see you on the job early Friday."

Tony nodded. "Friday then."

Hank hopped up on the platform and grabbed the railing to steady himself as it started to rise. "By the way," he called out, "you'll like the new crew as well. They're excited to get you."

Before Tony could ask why, the carriage was accelerating up and away.

"Well, I'll be," said Pete. "The company finally got its head out of the sand and did the right thing for a change." Pete was shaking his head and alternating between a grin and a grimace.

Tony turned to Pete, bit his lower lip, and then smiled, if ever so slightly. At first it looked like he might cry, but instead he did something much better. He smiled openly. "I think you're right about that, Pete. They finally did get it right, didn't they?"

Pete laughed. "Hey, everybody, Tony's leaving us, and it's a good thing!" Of course, everyone crowded around him to congratulate him. Tony did his best to keep his composure, but it was obvious that he was moved by this display of friendship.

CHAPTER 19
Home

Boulder City—June 1934

Davie glanced up from the Sunday paper. "You'll drive carefully?"

Jim sighed. "Yes, Dad. I'll drive carefully."

David folded the paper into his lap. "Carol's a nice girl, Jim. So treat her with respect."

"Like there's anyplace in Boulder City where we could get into trouble. We're going to a concert at the high school auditorium, for heaven's sake."

David picked the paper up and mumbled, "Just doing what fathers are supposed to do: irritate the tar out of their kids."

"Yeah, well, I'm sure it's gratifying to know you're a success." To make sure David didn't have a chance to add anything else to this scintillating discussion, Jim called out, "See you tomorrow, Uncle Pete." Since Jim had transferred out to the dam site to work, he and Pete had fallen into the habit of having breakfast together every morning before going to work. David's schedule was too unpredictable to allow for such regularity. So in many ways Pete was closer to Jim than David was.

"Don't do anything I wouldn't do . . ." Pete called out cheerfully.

"That leaves the door wide open, doesn't it?" David's sarcasm was punctuated by the slamming of the front door.

"You're rather surly today. Still smarting from the court decision?"

David put down his paper. He really had been quiet, showing little passion for their weekly poker game, which Pete had won handily. "We didn't lose."

"You didn't win. After everything Six Companies threw at that Kraus guy, including perjury and attempted insurance fraud, it took something of a miracle for a jury not to find for Six Companies."

"A hung jury. Who'd have thought such a thing possible? It means we're vulnerable if the next fellow turns out to be even halfway respectable."

"The part I liked best was the testimony about the blue haze at the mouth of the tunnels. I remember seeing the weird rings around the lights at night."

"But that means we were exhausting the stuff . . ."

"I know, I know. I'm not piling on. Still, it's going to be a while before the next suit comes to trial, isn't it? So why are you so worried right now?"

"It's not the lawsuits."

"The job, then?"

David shook his head. "No, the new work building the penstock tunnels is interesting, and we're using the right kind of equipment this time around."

"How's Tony doing?"

"Fine, from what I can tell. He's there every day, and the chatter around the work site is that he's really good at what he does."

"So if it's not the job and not the lawsuit and nothing more than the usual with Jim, it's got to have something to do with Boise."

David didn't answer, but his face clearly showed that that was the problem.

"So what's up?"

David shifted in his chair. "Mary asked me not to talk about it."

"But it looks to me like you really should. I'm not the type to talk out of school, you know."

David shook his head as if measuring his loyalty to Mary's wish to his need to talk. Finally he said quietly, "It's her brothers. Mary's got the feeling that they're somehow taking advantage of their father."

"Well, that's no surprise. Those oafs have lived off him their whole lives."

"No, this is different." David didn't mean to emphasize it as much as he did, but that simply showed how angry he was.

Pete rocked back just a little. "Sorry. I'll listen. I can see that this is serious."

David took a deep breath. "It's just that her father took out bankruptcy. He had to, mostly because he kept employees on the payroll long after revenue fell short. He just couldn't bring himself to hurt all those families. But nobody's moving these days—and even the few who do are usually moving out of a house because of foreclosure, rather than to a nice new one."

Pete got a sick feeling in his stomach. "In a bankruptcy you're supposed to go through all your assets before the court provides relief."

David got a surprised look on his face. "How did you—"

"A lot of people have done it, Davy. They transfer assets to their kids or someone else to hide them from the bankruptcy court. If they get away with it, the creditors suffer . . ."

"And if the court finds out about it, they go to jail."

"So, is that what's got Mary upset? She thinks her father did that?"

"Remember how I told you the boys don't have jobs?"

"Yeah."

"Well, it also seems they've been gambling a lot. One of them let it slip the other day. When Mary asked them how on earth they got money to gamble, they both got red faces and changed the subject."

Pete nodded. "So they took dad's money, and now they're not giving it back."

"Mary thinks he feels so guilty and angry about it that it's just eating him up inside. Guilty that he cheated the court, and angry that he's living on our welfare while his sons are out living it up."

"Yet he can't say anything about it, or his fraud will be discovered."

David nodded. "Of course, we don't have any proof. But I do have a miserable wife, a despondent father-in-law, and potential felons visiting my family."

Pete grew serious. "Listen, David. You've got to call Mary and tell her to stop looking into this. If she ever comes into proof that this happens, and she doesn't turn them in, then she could be considered an accessory. So it's better if she just minds her own business." When he saw the effect this had on the color in David's face, he hurried to add, "But, of course, she's not involved, so the real problem is for her father. Still, you've got to be very careful about this."

David took a long breath and sighed. Pete couldn't help but notice the lines in his younger brother's face. Between the gas suits and this new mess, he had aged a decade in the past year. He was just about to suggest they go for a walk when there was a sound on the doorstep, and suddenly Jim appeared in the doorway.

David got quickly to his feet. "Jim? What happened to the concert?"

Jim helped Carol over the doorstep. "It got cancelled. That old battle-ax said it was too provocative."

"Jim, don't talk about the city manager that way. You may not like him, but he can make life miserable for us. Besides, you need to show respect for people even if you don't like them." On another day, when David wasn't so distraught, he would be among the first to criticize Sims Ely. But this wasn't the day.

Jim fired back, "Yeah? Well, he made our life miserable today."

David started a retort but caught himself. Pete watched as David purposely lifted his shoulders to stretch them while he gained control. Then, softly, he said, "Maybe I can make some dessert."

"What we were hoping is that you'd play some songs. Carol's got a great singing voice, you know, and I told her that you play."

Pete smiled. "I've heard Carol sing. Now that would be a classy way to spend a Sunday evening—listening to you and Carol sing while your dad plays."

"I don't sing so well, Uncle Pete."

"Neither do I, unless I'm drunk. Then I sound like a nightingale."

They all laughed—even David, who said a little more brightly, "I'd be glad to play for you, Carol. Do you have any favorites?"

"I love George Gershwin songs."

"Wonderful. I just got a new Gershwin songbook in the mail."

As David settled onto the bench and started playing, Pete leaned against the wall. Good for you, little brother, he thought. The bad mood had passed, at least for a while.

Westmoreland, California—June 1934

"WE'RE DOING FINE, TONY. YOU don't need to worry." Louisa Capelli listened intently since it was hard to hear on the payphone at the local drug store. "Paul is all right. He's working hard." A burst of static on the line hurt her ears, and she had to pull the earpiece away for a few seconds.

"The girls, too. No, I understand. I know why we can't come see you, and it's all right that you stay there. I'm glad you like your new job. What?" Telephone service was a modern miracle and a source of frustration at once. "Yes, yes, we're making the payments, just like you want."

Paul watched as his mother strained her ear for a moment, and then she shouted into the phone, "Are you there? Are you there?" She shouted with such intensity that other customers turned to look at her, even though she was sitting in the telephone booth with the door only slightly ajar.

"He's gone." She looked out of the phone booth at Paul and accepted his help as she pulled herself to a standing position. "But he sounded happy."

"Good. I think it's great that he's back on a bulldozer."

"Yes, but he's not with those Conroy men, and they're the ones who seem to watch out for him."

"He doesn't need watching out for," Paul said with an intensity that surprised Louisa.

"I didn't mean . . ."

"It's all right, Mother. It's just that if you ever talk like that and it gets back to him, it would embarrass him. A real man doesn't need other men to fight his battles. It's hard enough on Dad without having to think about that, particularly since he really does need their help. We just don't need to remind him of it."

"Paul, I understand much more than you think I do. I married into the Capelli family and had to learn the hard way. Italian men are loving—but they are proud. I watched your uncle nearly kill himself from heat exhaustion rather than ask Tony for help after they'd had a disagreement. Now I've watched your father sacrifice nearly everything to keep that piece of ground out there, even though I don't think he even wants to be a farmer. I know your father, and I would never do anything to embarrass him."

"But the Conroys—"

"Are good people. That's all. No matter how strong your father is, or how strong you are, sometimes prejudice is even stronger. All I want is for him to survive so he can come back to us with his head held high. That's all."

"It's hard . . ." Paul was still young enough that he couldn't help but resent the pain that came into his throat as he tried to talk. "It's hard with him up there all alone, now that I know what people can do to him. Yet, if we go up there it just makes it worse."

"Which is why we have to stay cheerful down here, and write him letters, and tell him everything is all right. That's how we can help him."

Louisa heard Paul sigh. "I'll be glad when he gets to come home." Paul started to rest his head on his mother's shoulder but caught himself. He too was turning into a man.

Then Louisa sighed. "I'll be glad too."

Top: Intake towers under construction. The base of these towers penetrate the canyon rock and divert water around the dam through penstock tunnels. The dam is a solid concrete monolith.

CHAPTER 20
Intake Towers

D ad, I have something exciting to tell you."

David looked up from his desk. He had a harried look on his face, which usually meant he was lost deep in thought about some technical problem at the dam site. But Jim was too excited to worry about interrupting him.

David shook his head to clear it. "Exciting? What's up?"

"They've asked me if I'd like to work on the intake towers."

David nodded and smiled. "I think that's great, Jim. While there's nothing wrong with being a puddler, it certainly isn't teaching you a lot about engineering. The intake towers are a far more complicated pour, with some pretty intricate plumbing. You can learn a lot there."

"I'm more interested in how much I can earn than in what I can learn."

"Ah. The interesting thing is that in the long run you'll make far more money from what you learn than from the day-to-day wages." He held up his hand to stop his son's retort. "But it's all right. I understand. In this case you get to do both, so that's a positive thing."

"So you can teach me what I need to know about the towers?"

David felt a little guilty at the pleasure he took in this question. It still felt good to be needed. "I think so. I certainly understand the engineering. Let me grab one of my construction diagrams." He went to his worktable and fumbled to find some diagrams that could help him explain the layout of the dam and how the water would flow.

"It's really quite remarkable given that the full flow of the Colorado River will be diverted around the dam and through the canyon walls. The dam itself is a monolith—just one great big chunk of concrete. But those four elegant towers you're going to help build will be mounted on the canyon walls, with intakes that use gravity to feed water into the penstock pipes, where it will flow down to either the powerhouse or to the needle valves in the outlet works. It's going to be one of the most amazing plumbing jobs in the world." David looked up and smiled. Jim simply looked bemused. "You want to know about building them, don't you?"

Jim nodded in a good-natured way. He was used to the fact that his father would eventually get to the point but not until he thoroughly set the stage for the discussion first. So it was natural to assume that's what was happening now.

The assumption was correct.

Boulder City

"YOU'VE GOT TO BE KIDDING me. Of course I'll come." There was a pause as David listened on the phone. "Yes, I'll leave today if I can get a ticket. I don't know how, I'll just do it. Oh, Mary, I'm so sorry . . ." As the conversation drew to an end, he set the phone down and put his head in his hands for a moment.

"Trouble, David? Did I hear that you need to go home?"

David looked up at Woody Williams and nodded. "I hate to ask, Woody, but . . ."

"You don't need to tell me why. Just make sure Henry is briefed on your assignments. He can cover for you. Any idea how long you'll be gone?"

David felt a wave of gratitude sweep over him. Few men could ask for time off, no matter what the problem was at home. And Woody was giving him time without even asking why. "Just a couple of days, I think. Mary's got a problem in her family . . ."

"I said you don't need to tell me. Just stay in touch so we know when to expect you."

David nodded. "Thanks. I promise I'll keep it absolutely as short as possible, and I'll call every day, just in case things come up where I need to talk through a problem or something."

Woody nodded. "That would be good."

David struggled with his thoughts for a moment. Then he said, "Oh, who cares, Woody? Let me tell you what's happening. I don't want you to think it's a problem between me and Mary. The truth is I'm so angry right now that I'm liable to kick a cat or something."

"Well, I am curious, but it's your business."

"It's those two idiots I have for brothers-in-law. They talked my father-in-law into hiding assets in a bankruptcy proceeding, and now he's been arrested. Those little thieves are putting the blame squarely on him, even though it was their idea. I have to go home to help Mary get an attorney for her father and to maybe get a restraining order on her brothers. It's a mess unlike anything I could ever imagine."

"Wow. That's one you don't really expect to hear. I've heard of men going home because their wives are cheating on them or their kid is in trouble, but never anything like this. It sounds like you've got your hands full."

"Mary does, and it angers me that those jerks would put her in a bind like this."

"Well, you go. No one else needs to know why." Woody paused. "Maybe I'll tell Frank, if that's all right."

David nodded. "Of course." Then he shook his head. "And just when I have so much to get done."

"Go." Williams said. "Just go. We'll try not to finish the dam before you get back. I'm sure there will still be something left to do."

David smiled. "Thanks." Then he started organizing his papers so he could hand them off to Henry Ward, a junior engineer who had been working under his direction.

Boise, Idaho

"THE DEFENDANT WILL ARISE." THE judge's voice betrayed no emotion. Painfully, Mary's father stood up next to the lawyer David had hired for this initial hearing. "How do you plead, Mr. Covington?"

"The defendant pleads guilty, Your Honor. But there are extenuating circumstances, as noted in the filing."

David was pleased that his father-in-law had accepted his attorney's advice to plead guilty. He was, after all. But now came the anxiety. Since the bankruptcy, and particularly since being arrested, he had gone from a vigorous, optimistic soul to a shrunken, hollowed-eyed wreck.

"Yes, well, the court is sensitive to the issues involved—and to the fact that others may share the defendant's culpability." He looked up from the papers. "And I judge that there is very little risk of flight involved. Therefore, I set bail at one thousand dollars until a full hearing to determine all relevant facts prior to sentencing."

David winced as Mary squeezed his hand so tightly it hurt.

"Thank you, Your Honor." The attorney turned to Mary's father to explain what that meant. David and Mary watched as even more color drained from his face—since it would be virtually impossible for him to come up with $1,000.

"What can we do, David? We don't have that kind of money." Mary's voice was desperate.

"My life insurance. We'll take a loan on my life insurance."

"No—you said we should never do that."

David turned and faced her squarely. "I never had this problem to consider. Now I'm saying we should." He smiled. "Besides, the judge is right, you know. There is no flight risk. So we'll get the money back." David truly hated going after the one solid financial asset they had, but he knew he had to.

"Thank you, David. Thank you." Mary wiped her cheek, and David leaned over to kiss her.

Boulder Dam

"CONROY! GET OUT OF THE WAY!"

Jim turned his head quickly from side to side at the sound of the foreman's voice, and then jumped back as the cable brought a bucket load of concrete screaming down from above. The buckets were much smaller than the ones used on the dam itself, because the towers had much smaller forms to fill, but they still weighed more than a ton. The irony is that Jim had been standing precisely where he should have been. It was the bucket that was coming down in the wrong place. Even though its descent was off by just a few feet, it was an error that had the potential to be fatal.

"MOMMA! DADDY! COME QUICKLY. THERE'S a long distance phone call! Uncle Pete said there's been an accident. Jim's hurt!" Elizabeth's voice was desperate, undoubtedly made more so because she'd had to wait at home while they returned from the courthouse.

"Jim! What's happened to him?" Mary's voice bordered on panic. "What's happened, Elizabeth?"

"I don't know, momma. I don't know." Elizabeth was crying now and David felt a wave of sheer desperation roll across him.

"Did Pete leave a number?"

Elizabeth nodded and thrust a piece of paper at David.

"Will he be all right, Daddy?" asked Katie, her eyes as big as saucers.

"I don't know, honey. I don't know." And then they all were crying.

"OH NO! WHAT HAVE I DONE?"

"What happened?" the operator called out in alarm, almost leaping from his platform as he strained to see what was happening down on the

Nevada intake tunnel number two. He knew something was wrong by the way the line had gone slack before he had received the signal to stop it.

"I did it," Sean called out in a panic. "I let the bucket crash into the tower. It's all my fault." Sean rushed to the button that would sound the emergency alarm. Even though the alarm would sound throughout the construction site, the flashing beacon would signal that it was related to their particular cableway so that the emergency medical crews would know which direction to head.

By now the cable operator had joined him, and they were peering over the side of the canyon wall. Because the four intake towers were being built almost halfway up the side of the canyon, at a point where the rock tapered out from the canyon rim, it took two spotters for each load, one on the tower itself, the other on the canyon rim, to interpret the signals and relay them to the operator.

"What do you make out?" Sean asked anxiously. He was far too nervous to try to sort it out.

"Well, the bucket has dumped its load all down the side of the footings of the tower."

"Can you see if anyone is hurt?" Sean was shaking so badly it's a wonder the operator could even understand him—he knew that someone must have been involved by the way the other men were frantically clawing through the spilled concrete. "We need to find out if we can raise the bucket, O'Donnell. Make the signals so we can see what they want us to do."

"It was a letter. My mother's sick. My sister said she may be dying. I was thinking about a letter. I may have killed a man. Oh, dear Lord. Please—"

"O'Donnell. Shake it off! I need you now." The cable operator was harshly abrupt, but it worked.

Sean shook his head and then turned to the operator. "Right. Sorry." In an almost mechanical fashion, Sean turned and made his way over to his spotting point, where he made the signals to the crew below. Meanwhile, the operator had moved back to his controls. "They want us to raise the bucket and get it out of the way," Sean called to him. He watched as the operator gently started the electric motor that put tension on the hoist cable. Slowly the bucket started to lift away from the side of the tower's base.

The biggest danger at this point was the risk that the bucket would swing once it was clear, raising the potential of hurting even more men. But the operator was highly skilled, and the bucket righted itself and then lifted up and free, with hardly any swinging at all. When Sean received confirmation from the spotter below that it was clear, he relayed it to the operator, who quickly and expertly accelerated the speed of the cable as the bucket ascended skyward and away from the site of the accident. Once the bucket was settled on the rim, the operator moved out of his cabin and over to Sean.

"You better report to the superintendent."

"It was my fault. I did it. I wasn't paying attention."

"It's all right, O'Donnell. What's happened has happened. You need to focus on the next step. Go report to the superintendent. They'll know what to do."

As Sean moved away he heard sirens coming toward them. He also knew that the next step would be to get a carriage down there to lift anyone who had been injured up to the ambulance. It wasn't going to be him giving the signals. Not after he'd screwed up like this. In something of a daze, he walked away from the job site, his heart racing. *I shouldn't have read the letter. I should have waited. Why did I bring it here to read?*

CHAPTER 21
Shattered Dreams

Boulder City—July 1934

David Conroy's heart pounded as the car made its way through the twilight. There was nothing in the world quite like a desert sunset—the sharp angle of the sun's rays striking the sandstone of the rocky landscape in such a way that the entire mesa glowed as if it were iridescent. With a hundred million fractures in the rock surfaces, the shadows formed intricate patterns that deceived the eye. These mingled with great clefts in the rock that receded into impenetrable shadows, conveying a sense of danger and excitement. Usually David was fascinated by the scene, but tonight it felt ominous and foreboding.

"How much farther is it?" David turned at the sound of Mary's voice. He was sad that she had to leave her father in Boise at the moment of his greatest crisis, but she had insisted, and the truth was, he was grateful. He wanted her at his side.

"Only about five minutes. We'll be pulling up to the fence shortly." The car groaned as they turned a corner, perhaps faster than David had intended.

Mary looked around, seeming to notice the desert for the first time. "This is a barren place, isn't it? And so desolate. The hills are all rock and empty." She shuddered. "It makes me feel lonesome."

"It grows on you," said David quietly. "There's a marvelous solitude here. And I find a special kind of beauty and grace in the way the desert cactuses and other grasses somehow manage to survive the scorching summer weather to blossom in January. And how the animals can make such a place their home." He seemed to catch himself. "But of course this isn't the time."

Mary put her hand on his knee. "I've been wrong not to come down here. We should have shared this, like so many other projects . . ."

"It's all right. Things have worked out with Jim—" At the mention of his son's name, David voice caught.

"Pete told me that he's doing better than he looks. The doctors are encouraged."

"I know." David smiled. "I'm glad. He'll be surprised to see us—"

Mary shook her head. "He'll be shocked to see me is what you mean." She looked up at David. "Like I said, I should have been here." David wondered how people ever knew exactly where they should be. How did you choose among all the demands on your attention?

"SORRY TO HEAR ABOUT YOUR SON, Mr. Conroy." David rolled down the driver's side window, pulled out his identification card, and explained to the guard that the woman next to him in the car was his wife. The guard, sensitive to why they were there, waved them through immediately.

As they approached the infirmary, David slowed the car and found a place to park. Then he helped Mary out of the passenger side.

"I don't know if I can do this," she said. David couldn't tell if she was referring to seeing Jim or about talking with Pete, who was now approaching them from the steps of the little building.

"Hello, brother. Hello, Mary."

Mary managed a weak smile. "Hello, Peter. Thank you for taking care of my boy."

Pete nodded. "Let me take you to his room." As they walked down the short hallway, Pete started to explain that Jim looked worse than he was, but David raised a hand to stop him. "Thanks . . . I think we're ready."

"Well, here we are. I'll just stay out here while you two say hello." David was grateful that Pete had been there for Jim. "By the way, Carol's in there with him."

David nodded, appreciative of the notice.

"Who's Carol?" Mary asked.

"A girl Jim's been dating. She sings with our little group once in a while. Let me introduce you."

As they stepped into the room, Carol looked up from the chair she was sitting in by Jim's bed and immediately stood to move to the door.

"Hello, Carol. Let me introduce you to Jim's mother. Mary, this is Carol Mitchell. Her father is an engineer with Pacific Bridge out of Portland. She's been a good friend to Jim while we've been here."

"Pleased to meet you, Mrs. Conroy." Carol's voice was tinged with uncertainty.

"And I'm pleased to meet you." Mary's voice wasn't quite as warm as usual, but that was to be expected given the circumstance. David hoped Carol wouldn't misinterpret it.

"Who is it, Carol?" This came from a sleepy sounding Jim.

David was grateful for the distraction and moved over to the bed. Jim's eyes were closed, which David was also glad for. It gave him a moment to compose himself. Lying in front of him was the battered body of his eighteen-year-old son. Jim's shoulder and left arm were in a full cast, as was his left leg. His arm was held up by a pulley and a cable, which had to be uncomfortable.

"Hey, Jim," said David. "It's me." He gently brushed Jim's face. It startled Jim, who jerked as he came to, causing him to let out a yelp of pain.

"Sorry, boy. Sorry."

"Dad? Is that you?" Jim did his best to turn, but the way the cast was positioned made it impossible, so David quickly moved around the foot of the bed and toward Jim. "It is you." Jim smiled, which melted David's heart.

"Oh, Jim. I am so sorry . . ."

"It's all right. I feel better than I look." That made David laugh.

"What's so funny?" Jim asked. David shook his head. "It has to do with your Uncle Pete . . ."

Jim smiled, even though he didn't know exactly what Pete had to do with it. He just knew that it would be funny.

"I have a surprise for you."

Jim looked up expectantly. "Good, because I feel like I deserve something nice."

Rather than explain it, David simply stepped back and motioned to Mary.

"Hello, Jim." At the sound of his mother's voice, Jim's eyes widened.

"Mom?"

"It's me. I had to come see you."

"Boy, I must be hurt bad." Jim didn't intend to hurt her feelings, but Mary was clearly stung, and she stepped back a bit.

"I didn't mean it to sound like that. I'm glad you're here."

Mary allowed her breath to escape. It was only then that David realized just how hard it must have been on the two of them before Jim came to Nevada. Now, even though they loved each other, they were uncomfortable.

"I'll tell you what," said David as cheerfully as he could. "I've been on an airplane and in a car winding through the canyons at night . . ."

"And you're motion sick . . ." Jim completed the sentence.

"So you think you know me, do you?"

"Oh, David. Everybody knows how you get sick." Mary said this matter-of-factly, and he recognized that it was her attempt to establish some common ground with Jim.

"Well, since you both understand, then you won't mind if I take a few moments to go outside and breathe some fresh air. I need to get my head stabilized." He saw the look of distress on Jim's face, but he knew he'd be all right. The truth was that Mary deserved some time alone with Jim, and David needed to talk to Pete to find out the whole story.

"I'll come with you, Mr. Conroy," Carol said quickly. That brought Jim's eyes fully open, but he didn't protest.

Once outside in the hall, David turned to Carol. "I can see that his body's been beat up, but how's he holding up emotionally?"

Carol smiled. "He jokes about it. I think it must be his way of dealing with fear, but he's always cracking jokes."

David smiled and nodded. "I'm glad you're here for him."

She blushed. "Yes, well. As it turns out, it's good that *you're* here, because I really need to be going home."

"Of course. Can I arrange a ride?"

"No, I've got my father's car. Thank you."

David walked her to the entrance of the hospital, where she made her way to a Chevrolet parked by the curb. Once she started the car and turned on the headlights, he turned and walked over to Pete, who was smoking a cigarette and staring out into the coal black sky. "Lots of stars up there," said Pete absentmindedly.

David nodded, although Pete couldn't see it in the dark. "And who can guess how many of those stars have planets like ours circling them?" David added. "Maybe somebody's building a dam on one of them."

"Well, he's a sorry piece of work if he is." Vintage Pete, but it had broken the ice, and Pete turned to David. "I'm sorry about Jim. The only good news is that it could have been a lot worse."

"I'm glad you were there. How did it happen?"

"Human error, plain and simple. They were in an odd spot on the tower where the operator couldn't see them directly. Sean O'Donnell was spotting from above. He let his mind wander for a moment, and the bucket dropped into the side of the tower. Jim had no way to know it was coming."

"Sean O'Donnell? He's the one responsible?"

"He's absolutely broken up about it," said Pete defensively. "He resigned this morning."

"But that doesn't do anyone any good. The damage is done."

"Yeah, I know. But it's not just about this. He's got troubles at home. That's what he was thinking about when he missed the signal. His mother's dying of cancer. So he'll be leaving for New York City. Six Companies docked him a week's pay for the mistake."

"What exactly happened to Jim? Did the bucket hit him directly?"

"No. That would have killed him, no question. It hit just above the place where he was standing and tipped. The upper edge of the bucket smashed him on the left side, which knocked him something like five feet. That turned out to be what saved his life. Had it not sent him flying, the bucket would have tipped right on top of him and crushed him."

David tried to force that image out of his mind. "So the injuries were from the impact?"

Pete nodded. "A crushed shoulder, broken ribs, and multiple fractures in his legs. The most dangerous thing was that one of the ribs punctured his right lung. He was really struggling for air by the time I got there."

"You were close?"

"Close enough that I was able to ride in the ambulance with him." Pete paused. "It's funny how you think at times like that. Before I found out that it was Sean who made the mistake, I was cursing the cable operator and the upper spotter, all the time promising Jim that I'd personally beat the two of them to death. Of course that did no good. He was struggling for air while I ranted. Then, when I found out the true story and who it was, all the fire went out of me and I was in shock. I wanted to hate Sean, but I knew him well enough to know that he'd never do something like that intentionally."

"I'd like to talk to him before he leaves. Can you set something up?"

"What are you going to say? He's been through a lot already."

David turned on Pete. "Come on, you know me better than that. We've all had momentary lapses that could have turned out badly, but for a little luck. For example, you look down while driving your car and nearly hit a pedestrian; you get distracted while chopping vegetables and almost lose a finger. It's something that could happen to any of us."

Pete took a deep draft of the desert air into his lungs. "I'll make sure Sean takes time to talk with you. It will probably be good for him."

"Good. Now what do they tell you is going to happen to my boy? Do they think he'll fully recover, or will there be permanent damage?"

"The doctor tells me they just don't know. They had to do surgery to reset some of the bones. And the facilities here aren't exactly the best. I think his leg will be fine, but I don't know about his shoulder and arm . . ."

"I'd better get back in there. I left him alone with Mary. She needed time alone with him, but they didn't part on the best of terms, so I'm not sure about Jim."

"How did things work out in Boise?"

David shook his head. "Her father pled guilty. We posted bail so at least he can go home. Fortunately, the judge issued a restraining order to keep his brothers away so they can't collude on what happened. At least that keeps them away from our house." David felt his face start to burn. "But that's a story for another time. I'm just glad Mary came with me." Pete nodded, even though he was curious to hear the whole story. "Thanks again for taking care of Jim. I'm sorry I wasn't here."

"Not a problem, little brother. It was special for me to be put in the role of caring for someone. It was almost—for lack of a better word—spiritual."

David put his arm around his brother then squinted as he reentered the brightly illuminated hallway of the hospital. As he approached the partially open door, he paused as he heard Jim say in a tightened voice, "I'm sorry, Momma. I'm so sorry I was rotten to you . . ." And then he heard Mary comfort him. Perhaps Jim would heal from this accident in more ways than one.

The Nevada Spillway overflow basin is shown at the right of the photo. Note the exposed opening to the sharply angled spillway tunnel that drops water nearly seven hundred feet to the river below the dam in periods of extremely high runoff.

CHAPTER 22

Looking Forward

Observation Deck at the Boulder Dam—August 1934

This is so neat!" The excitement in Katie's young voice was sincere, although her use of the word *neat* was certainly overused by this point.

"You want me to show you what we did as high scalers?" Pete asked. "There's still a spot where we have the eyehooks on the canyon rim, and I could take you over the side." David wanted to smile at what could only be characterized as excitement in Pete's voice, since it was not a usual part of his repertoire. But what he was suggesting was preposterous.

Katie's eyes widened. "Would you really let me do that?"

"Ask your dad."

David shook his head. It was inevitable that it would come to him. "Life is so unfair. You, the bachelor uncle, get to come up with the harebrained ideas, and I, the responsible father, get to bear the odium of saying no."

Pete's eyes sparkled. "You can always say yes . . ."

"Oh, Dad, I would be careful. You know I'd be careful, and Uncle Pete knows what he's doing; you said so yourself."

"You know that your mother would faint dead away if she saw you in a harness going over the side of the canyon wall."

Much to their collective surprise, it was Elizabeth who picked up the next line. "I think you should let her go, father. When will she ever get a chance like this again?"

Katie squealed in delight, Pete shrugged his shoulders, and David raised an eyebrow, although he quickly dismissed the thought that maybe Elizabeth was interested less in Katie's welfare than in getting a reprieve from attending to her little sister. The look in her eye convinced him, however, that she meant it.

"But what about your mother?"

"I think mother has plenty to worry about with Jim. Why would we add something like this to her worries by telling her about it?"

David laughed. "Well, Elizabeth. You are certainly full of surprises. It's awfully dangerous." Turning to Katie, who by now had the common sense to hold her tongue, he asked, "Are you sure this is something you'd like to do? He could just show you how it's done."

"I'm sure." Apparently Katie realized what was obvious to everyone else; if even cautious old Elizabeth thought it was all right, then David had no reason to stand in the way. "All right, you can go, but do not bounce around or get ahead of what Pete is telling you. Do you understand?"

She expressed her understanding by letting out another squeal, and then she tackled him with a hug. "I'll be careful." David still felt dubious. But when he cast a glance toward Pete, he saw that it was Pete who now looked worried. He hadn't really thought the offer would be accepted.

"Well, brother. She's all yours. And if anything happens to her you have to answer to both me and Mary."

Pete gulped. "We'll be all right." Then he mumbled, "I hope." It was obvious he hadn't thought that David would really allow it, and now he was the one responsible for his enthusiastic little niece.

Katie noticed none of this but rather raced over to Pete and took his hand. As they moved off she was chattering the whole way about how excited she was.

David leaned his arms on the railing and looked out over the dam site. The concrete pouring was almost 80 percent finished, and the dam was more massive than he had pictured it in his mind. At this point it was as tall as a fifty-story skyscraper but with a squat base that could have supported a dozen skyscrapers. He doubted it would ever look more impressive than at this moment.

"In fact, it will actually start to look less imposing as they complete the taper to just forty-five feet at the top," he said quietly.

"Why is that?" He was startled by Elizabeth's question.

"What? Oh, I was just saying that right now you can gain a sense of the full heft of the dam. But when it tapers up to the top, and the finishing work is applied to the face so that the columns disappear into a continuously smooth surface, it won't seem nearly as large, particularly when there's water in the reservoir submerging the large footprint." He regretted using the word footprint but didn't know how else to describe it.

"I think it's the most beautiful thing I've ever seen."

"You do?" asked David, surprised. "But I always thought of you as a connoisseur of the fine arts, like music and poetry and painting."

"I know that's how you think of me. You think that because I'm quiet, and because you still think of me as a little girl. But I'm not anymore."

"I didn't . . . I don't . . ."

She turned to face him directly. "It's all right. I've never done anything to make you think otherwise. I know that we never talk. You've been gone so long that it would be hard for you to know what interests me. But along the way I've learned to love mathematics and solving complex equations. And I like to picture things in my mind, like this dam, and try to imagine how something this huge can be reduced to blueprints. I think it's fascinating that people can picture something in their minds like this, draw it on paper, and then watch it become real in the world."

David nodded and formed his response carefully, not wanting to spoil this moment. "I like the puzzle of trying to figure out how all the millions of little details get anticipated and dealt with . . ."

"Like how to form an impermeable barrier between the side of the dam and the canyon walls?"

"Why, Elizabeth, my dear, you're an engineer at heart. I had no idea."

She looked at him earnestly. "It's true. I think I might want to be an engineer. I've thought of it, and now, looking out on this . . ."

David's shook his head to clear his thoughts. It had been a stressful week since his mother had brought Katie and Elizabeth to Boulder City to visit Jim. Between David's work schedule and visiting Jim and trying to keep things interesting for the girls, he had been at his wit's end. This was really the first quiet time he'd enjoyed in days.

"So, Elizabeth, I don't know what to say about this interest that you've developed. I hoped that Jim would follow me into the profession . . ."

"Jim doesn't want to be an engineer. He wants to be a doctor." She said this in a matter-of-fact voice, seemingly oblivious to the effect it would have on David. It seemed there was no one quite as candid as a teenager.

"A doctor? Jim doesn't want to be a doctor—he doesn't even like school."

Elizabeth shrugged. "Well, that's what he told me this morning. He's kind of afraid to bring it up with you. He said that he's been watching what the doctors do for people while he's been laid up, and he says that he figures he might not have made it if it weren't for the doctors helping him with his broken rib cage. So now he wants to do that."

David shook his head. "A doctor? Who'd have thought of Jim as a doctor?"

"And for your part, you can't think of me as an engineer, can you?"

"What?" He turned to look at her again.

"It's true. You think that I'm just a girl and that things like mechanical engineering or civil engineering are too much for me."

"I guess I always thought that you'd want to get married and have a family."

"Maybe, but probably not. I'm not pretty enough. Besides, I'm not that interested in boys. It's too hard to figure out how to make things work with them." She looked down again at the dam site. "I'm not like Katie, a natural-born flirt. So I need to find some way to support myself."

"First of all, you are pretty, and secondly, you're still way too young to pass judgment on boys."

"Thanks, but you still haven't responded to my idea. What about me becoming an engineer?"

David pondered for a few moments. "It would be very hard. It's clearly a man's profession, with lots of onsite work around a horde of dirty, foul-mouthed men."

"I can put up with that."

"Besides, the universities may give you trouble."

"It's been fifteen years since women first got to vote in a presidential election. Don't you think it's time they got to work in a profession?" She looked at him earnestly.

David smiled. "I think that if anyone can do it, you can. I wouldn't have thought that before today, but there's a lot more to my oldest daughter than I realized." He was pleased at her smile, even as he felt a tinge of regret that he had been absent from her life so long. He grew quiet again. "It will be hard. I'd love to help you, and I will if you ask me. Have you thought about being an architect rather than an engineer?"

She nodded. "Maybe. I might like architecture. But we don't have to make those decisions right now. Why don't you tell me about your dam?"

David smiled. "I'd love to." This had unexpectedly become one of the best days of his life. "What do you want to know first?"

"How big is the dam?"

"Six hundred and sixty feet thick at the base, 726 feet high, with a width of 1,244 feet at the crest." He answered this in staccato, much like a soldier responding to a sergeant.

She laughed at the way he answered. "But help me understand this taper thing."

"All right. Maybe I can show you." David fumbled in his leather briefcase for a moment then smiled. "It just so happens that I have a diagram with me. I have a small set of them I carry with me whenever I'm working onsite, away from the office." He laid out one that showed various cross sections of the

View of the dam with the Arizona overflow valves at full force. In extremely high water years water can exit around the dam three ways: thru the powerhouse; the overflow valves; the massive overflow tunnels.

dam. "The key to this type of dam is for the dam itself to weigh more than enough to hold the water back. Because the water pressure is greatest at the base, the base has to be really thick. See how it looks?" The two of them pored over the diagram. "Plus, to add some redundancy, we give it an arch design. The arch doesn't show up well on this cross section. But believe me, this dam can operate at peak capacity with no problem."

Elizabeth studied the diagram for a few moments, pointing to various parts and asking questions. Finally, she concluded with, "Okay, so that's really big, but how does it handle all the water? Does the water go through tunnels inside the dam?"

"Ah. An unusual question. You do have the mind of an engineer." Pointing to the intake towers, he said, "See those towers your brother was helping to build? They can handle more than twice the highest recorded flow of the river, something like four hundred thousand cubic feet per minute. The water enters the tower and flows into steel pipes—very big steel pipes."

At this point a couple came over to them, and the woman said, "Pardon me, but it sounds like you know a lot about the dam. Would you mind if we listened in?"

"This is my father. He's one of the engineers building the dam." David heard a pride in Elizabeth's voice that he'd never experienced before.

"We don't mind at all," he said simply. He then proceeded to talk about the penstock tunnels and how water from the reservoir would flow through two-million-pound steel gates in each of the four intake towers into steel tubes that narrowed as the water approached the turbines that spun the electric generators.

"Why narrower?" the man asked.

"To increase the velocity. If the tubes are handling the same volume of water in a restricted space, the water has to move faster, which increases force. By the time the water reaches the blades of the turbine in the electrical generator it will be traveling more than eighty-five miles per hour."

"Wow!" The fellow nodded as if he understood. Realizing that he did not, David added, "You need the additional pressure to turn the turbines."

"But where does the water go?" Elizabeth sounded a bit impatient as she said this, since this was the original question that she'd posed to David.

"It goes through . . ." He started to point. "It goes through . . . why don't we ask him?" Elizabeth saw a dark-complexioned man approaching them.

"Who is he?" It was the woman who'd asked the question, and the look on her face showed that she was startled by Tony's appearance.

"This is Tony Capelli." By that time Tony had reached them. David introduced them and said, "My daughter was just asking me about the plumbing, Tony. Maybe you can tell her."

Tony smiled and was about to begin when the woman rather abruptly said, "Please forgive us, but we really should be running . . ."

"But I thought you wanted to know about the dam," replied Elizabeth. She clearly understood what was going on.

"Maybe another time." The woman straightened and made it clear to her husband that they were to leave.

He mumbled something like, "Sorry . . ." but it was lost in the sound of her shoes clattering on the concrete.

Tony sighed, and David felt a knot tighten in his stomach. But he wasn't going to let that dampen the spirit of the day. "Well, now that they're gone, let me take a moment to introduce the two of you. Tony, this is my daughter Elizabeth, who has surprised me by expressing an interest in engineering. And Elizabeth, this is Tony Capelli, who has worked on the dam since the start of construction. He's one of the best bulldozer operators on the operation." He added, "And a very good friend." Tony and Elizabeth shook hands. "Now, Tony, you were going to tell my daughter about the work you do."

"Yes. Well, right now I'm working on the overflow spillways. Earlier I helped excavate the penstock tunnels. It's not likely that the spillways will ever be used, but if we have a particularly high water year, they could easily carry off all the excess water with no problem. The dam has been designed to handle peak water flows that may occur just once in any given century."

"How can you be sure?" Elizabeth wasn't skeptical, but she also wasn't going to accept things at face value.

"She's a lot like your brother, Mr. Conroy." Tony said this deadpan, but it was probably intended as a joke. When Tony saw that it didn't work, he quickly added, "The reason, I'm sure, is that each of the emergency spillways can route more water around the dam than flows over Niagara Falls, and with a three-times greater drop. You could float a battleship in each of the spillway basins I'm working on right now. That's a lot of capacity."

"Wow," said David. "I hadn't ever thought of it in terms of battleships and Niagara Falls. But you're right. Boulder can handle all that and more. I hadn't done the math on it . . ."

"Well, I think it's amazing," said Elizabeth. You two are very lucky to have worked on all this."

Concrete being poured at the rim, even as Lake Mead rises behind the still unfinished dam.

"We are, aren't we," said David. He then thanked Tony for his input. "We'd better be going to see if my brother has dropped Elizabeth's sister over the edge of the canyon. He was teaching her about scaling. That would be something to explain to Jim and his mother, now wouldn't it?"

Tony smiled. "I'm sure Pete is being careful." David didn't fully understand why he was always "Mr. Conroy," while Pete was "Pete."

"And please give Mrs. Conroy and your son my regards. I hope he's doing well."

David nodded. "He should be out of the hospital tomorrow or Thursday. Then I'm afraid he'll be leaving me to go back to Boise.

"Well, wish him well on his journey."

Elizabeth and her father walked away from the canyon wall, leaving Tony standing alone.

Tony gazed over the side of the canyon at the spectacle of the great dam growing below him. By this point it was clear that the battle had been won. The Colorado would never again flow free. "You'll never wash us out again, will you? I told you we would beat you." He took a deep draught of the desert air. "I told you, Rio Colorado." Then more quietly, "I told you."

Men's Cafeteria

CHAPTER 23
A Devil's Bargain

Boulder City—October 1934

Mind if I join you?"

Pete looked up from the table in the dining hall. "What are you doing here?" The shock was genuine, but he still managed to motion for David to sit down.

"It's lonesome at home. I decided I could use some company."

"You must be lonesome to choose this food over yours."

David set his tray on the table and then lifted his left foot over the bench to climb into the seat next to Pete. "A letter from an admirer?"

"It's from Sean O'Donnell in New York."

"Ah." The last time David had seen Sean was at the hospital where Sean had offered a tortured apology to Jim before leaving for Manhattan. Jim had been civil to him, and he'd been proud of his son for taking the whole thing in stride. David had done his best to reassure Sean that there were no hard feelings and that they understood it was an accident. "How's he doing?"

Pete folded the letter in half and held it out for David. "Why don't you read it? It's short." David took the letter.

> *Dear Pete,*
>
> *I'm not usually a letter writer, but I wanted you to know that I made it home safely. My mother's still alive but not doing very well. I'm glad I got here when I did because she seems so happy to see me, even though she doesn't always remember who I am. She's taking morphine for pain, and it leaves her disoriented.*
>
> *I've been out of work since I got here, but it looks like I'm going to get hired on a new bridge project. They're building a series of auto*

bridges to connect the Bronx, Manhattan, and Queens. It's called the Triborough Bridge, and it is going to be a terrific project. Lots of jobs for steelworkers. I guess I kind of like getting back into steelwork. Besides, the weather's a lot better here in New York than in Nevada.

Still, I miss the dam. I hate to leave a project before it's finished. Please tell the other guys hello. I hope your nephew is okay. Let me know.

Sean O'Donnell

"I'm glad he got a job. It had to be scary going home without anything."

Pete shrugged. "That's the life of a construction worker. You never know where the next job is coming from." He paused to take a drink of his Coca-Cola. "This stuff could kill you. It's too sweet. Beer's a lot healthier."

"So you say."

"I wish I could work on a bridge. I'm tired of getting my skin burned by the chemical action of the concrete. I hate the stuff, and yet it's all there is on this cursed dam." Before David could reply, Pete returned to the original subject again. "How is Jim, by the way? I may actually muster the energy to write a letter back to O'Donnell."

"It's incredible. He's actually taken the trouble to apply to a college, and it looks like he'll be accepted at the University of Washington. They have a medical school there, so chances are high that he'll be moving to Seattle. I find it all hard to believe."

"Well. Another educated Conroy. I'm clearly the no-account in the family."

"He's not educated yet. I hope he does follow through if this is something he really wants. The good thing is that he can do his undergraduate work and then change his mind about a graduate degree if he loses interest in medicine. By the way, ask Sean about the opera."

"The opera? What has that got to do with Sean O'Donnell?"

"It turns out he's a fan. He and I talked about it once."

"Okay. So what does it have to do with you? It's not like we've had a lot of opera in Boise—or in this godforsaken place."

"I can listen to records, can't I?" David was just a little put off.

"Sorry. I'll ask."

"What I really want is for Sean to know that I have no hard feelings. I know he was pretty shook up by the whole thing."

Pete nodded. "Okay. I'll ask."

They lapsed into a comfortable silence as they worked away at the pork chops and mashed potatoes. In spite of Pete's complaints, the food was pretty good at the mess hall. David continued to look at some papers he'd brought along, and Pete started reading the sports section of the company newspaper. They were both startled, however, when the silence was shattered by the sound of a loud crash a few tables away. Leaning out into the aisle, Pete could see that someone had tripped, sending his tray of food splattering across the floor and onto the pant legs of some guy at a nearby table who jumped up, cursing. The poor fellow who had had the misfortune of tripping now lay flat on his belly as the other man stood up and brushed himself off. In spite of himself, Pete couldn't help but laugh. There was just something funny about a fall, any fall, since it was such an unnatural way to hit the ground.

As the man got up to his knees, Pete watched as the other guy moved out and toward him in a threatening way. "Uh-oh."

"What is it?"

"It's Tony. My guess is that somebody tripped him, and now the guy he spilled on is going after him."

Pete started to rise, but David pulled him back down. " I'm sure he can take care of himself."

Pete sat back down, reluctantly. He knew it irritated Tony when the Conroys stepped in. "All right, but if they gang up on him . . ."

"We'll do something then."

Pete saw Tony step forward to face the other fellow, and watched as he managed to somehow calm him down without taking or receiving a punch. "Score one for diplomacy." But then, in the instant he'd finished with that fellow, Tony turned and charged back toward another table. Almost faster than the eye could follow, he pulled somebody up and off the bench and started pounding him. Pete jumped up. "It's Marvin and Chick. The odds are bad now."

David sighed. "I asked for it, I guess. All that crap about being lonesome." So the two of them jogged down the aisle to where Tony, Chick, and Marvin were all in a heap on the floor.

Just as Pete was about to dive in, there was a loud whistle that about split their eardrums. "What's going on here?" a masculine voice bellowed. Pete didn't have to look up to know it was Bud Bodell. Catching his eye, Pete motioned in such a way as to request permission to pull them apart. Bodell nodded, and David and Pete reached into the pile and first pulled Chick off Tony, and then Tony off Marvin.

Chick came up swinging, forcing Pete to wrap his arms around him. "Whoa, boy!" That did nothing but exact a string of expletives from Chick. The cursing stopped instantly at the sound of Bodell's voice, as he repeated his earlier question. Tony was not ready to stop the fight until David stepped in front of him.

"What's going on here?" Bodell asked firmly.

Before Pete could say anything, Chick responded. "This filthy wop spilled his tray of food all over everybody and then came swinging at us. We had to defend ourselves."

"You tripped me."

Pete and David had positioned themselves between Tony and the "ugly twins," as Pete called them, and got ruffled for their kindness as Tony attempted to get past them.

"You shut up!" Bodell commanded. "You'll talk when I tell you, and not before." Tony's face reddened at this humiliation.

"Now wait a minute, Bud—" Pete started to say, but Bodell shut him down as well.

"I'm not talking to you either, Conroy. Let Flemming finish what he was saying."

"But what he was saying is a lie." Pete was not ready to be rebuked by Bud Bodell.

Bodell fingered his Billy club, but he didn't hit Pete. "You an eyewitness?" he said.

"Not exactly," said Pete, "but I'm sure all these people are." He looked around at the other men at the tables near where Tony had gone down, but they all ducked their heads or averted their eyes. "That is unless their cowardice makes them completely blind," he added.

"Fine. Since you didn't see it, we don't really need to hear from you." Turning to Marvin, Bodell demanded, "Well, what happened? Did you trip the man?"

"No, sir. It's just like Chick said. He was walking by and just fell. Food went flying, and the next thing I know he was on top of me. I laughed, it's true, but who wouldn't?"

"They're lying. I was tripped."

Bodell slapped his hand on the club. "I told you to shut up, mister! Do I need to make myself clearer?" Two of Bodell's men joined him, and they were armed.

Tony glowered and shut up, but only after muttering, "This is so much crap."

Bud whirled on him. "You know, I don't like your attitude. You've never been anything but trouble since the day you signed on to this job. I had a feeling at the time. It seems like I spend more time cleaning up after you than a dozen of the white men here."

"That's not true," Tony spluttered, but whatever he was going to say was cut short as Bodell reached out and slapped him. "I told you to shut up."

David moved forward. "Knock it off, Bodell."

"You knock it off, Mr. Conroy. This is a security matter, and you have no jurisdiction here." David's face flushed, but he had no choice but to back down because Bodell was right. "So what are you going to do?" David posed the question since both Pete and Tony had been gagged.

Bodell nodded his head a few times as if lost in thought. Finally, after picking up Chick's cup so he could spit out some chewing tobacco, he said, "I'll tell you what I'm going to do. I'm going to kick this little Dago right out of Boulder City. He's just not worth the trouble." As Pete started forward, Bodell raised his club and added, "Besides, you know that fighting is against the rules. I have every legal right to do it."

"But you don't have to do it. You know perfectly well that Tony is telling the truth here. These two have tormented him since the minute he came on the job."

"These 'two' are members of my security team. I'll thank you to watch what you're saying about them."

David took a deep breath. One quick glance at Pete told him the situation was explosive and just the sort of thing that could get his brother sent to jail if he didn't tamp down the fire right away.

"Look, Bud. It doesn't have to be this way. We'll clean up the mess, pay to have this man's clothes cleaned, and Tony will apologize to these two 'men' of yours."

"No, I won't, Mr. Conroy. I will not apologize. They've goaded me since the day I came on the job, and they did trip me. I won't apologize."

David shook his head. "Tony, this is not the time or place . . ."

"And it won't make any difference anyway," Bodell interrupted. "He's out. It's that simple."

"But if you kick him out of Boulder, you know he'll lose his job," said Pete through clenched teeth.

"That's not my problem."

David bristled. "Listen, Bodell. You can't single him out."

"I can. He's a troublemaker."

David rocked back on his feet. For a second, Pete thought David was actually going to go after Bodell. But instead, his brother got a determined look on his face. "So one more question."

"What, Conroy? I don't have time for this."

"Just one. Is it true that you're firing him for fighting?"

"Yes. I'm pretty sure I said that." Bodell looked around and smiled at the men at the nearby tables. "Or did you lose your hearing sucking up all the carbon monoxide that you were supposed to keep out of the tunnels."

"Shut your filthy mouth, Bodell."

"It's true. They had to turn to me and my people to win their lawsuit."

David shook his head and ground his teeth, but he was determined not to let himself be distracted by Bodell's bragging.

"Well, regardless of that, if you're firing Tony by the rules, then you have to fire Chick and Marvin as well. The rule is no fighting, regardless of who starts it or why. Your men are just as guilty as he is."

"We were defending ourselves . . ."

"Shut up, Marvin." Chick snarled, quickly adding, "We had no part in it."

"Oh, yes you did. He came after Marvin, but you attacked him. I was a witness to that. Marvin could have pushed him off, but instead the two of you started beating him."

"What are you driving at, Conroy?" Bud Bodell looked puzzled. "You know I'm not going to fire my own men."

"Then you better not fire Tony. Rules are rules, and they have to be applied evenly."

"They have to be applied the way I decide to apply them."

"Ah, but people would be shocked to think that the government's 'model city' is unfair in its administration of justice, wouldn't they? Particularly since it would appear like a racial issue."

"And just who would know or care?"

David stepped away from Tony and moved closer to Bodell, where he said quietly next to his ear, "Maybe *Newsweek Magazine*? They're brand new and looking for a story. Even worse, I can't imagine how the government and the morally upstanding citizens of the United States would feel if they knew that one of Six Companies' security chiefs has been running an illegal card game in Boulder City for nearly two years now. That would be a scandal now, wouldn't it?"

"*Newsweek Magazine?* Just what are you talking about?"

"It's just that the magazines are all in a lather about this project. It's the biggest news in the country now that we're almost finished with the dam, and people are eager to read anything they can about it. It turns out that I'm meeting with a reporter on Thursday. It would be a shame if your name came up in the story . . ."

"Blackmail?" Bodell shook his head and spat some tobacco juice at the floor next to David. "You wouldn't dare. It would cast a bad light on the company."

"Want to try me?"

Bodell set his jaw. "So what are you saying?"

"I'm saying that you let this go. Don't take action against any of them."

"I have to now. Everybody knows that I said I would."

"Then you'll have to fire all of them. All or none—your choice. It's a devil's bargain." David watched with some small pleasure as the emotions played out on Bodell's face. He was not a pleasant-looking man, and being backed into a corner was clearly not something he was used to or that he liked. Still, David expected he would let them all off.

Instead, Bodell's face went absolutely flat, showing no emotion, and David knew that he'd lost. "Fine. Then they're all fired." He said this loud enough so that everyone could hear.

"What? You can't do that. You can't fire me and Marvin!"

"Shut up, Flemming." Bodell turned on Chick with a vengeance as his two other thugs moved in closer. "The truth is that you've been a pain in my side since the day I hired the two of you. You're no better than the Italian. We'll all be better off without any of you. Now you three clear out of Boulder City, or I'll have you arrested for vagrancy."

"But we get to keep our jobs, right?" Chick obviously didn't believe that Bodell's decision was final.

It was amazing how fast a pack could turn on its own. Chick and Marvin had been nothing but loyal to Bodell, but that served them nothing now. "No, you don't keep your jobs, idiot. I said you were fired." He smiled. "It turns out that there was an eyewitness to Marvin tripping poor old Capelli here, wasn't there?" He turned sharply to one of the men sitting at a table across from where Marvin had been. The man got a shocked look on his face and then quickly nodded in agreement. "See, as much as I hate to agree with a Conroy, the truth is that you provoked Tony. His problem is that he should have reported it rather than turning on you. But he chose to fight, and now you're all gone. So get out."

Bodell turned and motioned to his two men, who moved in and grabbed the three combatants. Pete and David had no legitimate way to protest, so they stepped aside.

Pete gritted his teeth. "You're a sorry excuse for a human being, Bodell."

"Coming from Peter Conroy, I consider that a real compliment. Now, gentlemen, will you excuse me?" He brushed against David's shoulder as he pushed past him. Turning, he added, "By the way, I think you did me a real favor, Mr. Engineer Conroy. All three of these morons had worn out their welcome. Thanks for pointing out my duty to me. I'm sure Mr. Williams will be proud of us both." When David just stood there, trembling in anger, Bodell added, "And you can tell *Newsweek Magazine* anything you want. Six

Companies will only be half as mad at me as they will at you for ratting." Bodell then moved on and out of the door.

After he left, David was crestfallen. "What have I done? Tony has lost his job."

"Knock it off," said Pete harshly. "Like you always say, this isn't about you. You tried to help, but there was nothing you could do. Tony's fate was sealed the minute Bodell walked in. Now, I better get out there and find Tony. Who knows what he'll do."

"I'm coming with you."

When they got outside, they first saw Marvin and Chick trailing Bodell and his two men, gesticulating wildly as they obviously pleaded for mercy. Looking in both directions, the Conroys finally saw Tony striding down a side street toward the men's barracks.

"Why don't you let me take this one, little brother? I think it will be better if we don't double team him." David nodded, and Pete took off on a jog.

Boulder City

DAVID WIPED HIS FOREHEAD WITH his sleeve. It was an unusually hot October day, and the sun at the administration building was relentless. It left him feeling breathless. Still, he had to say something. Something profound and healing. Instead, all he could think to say was, "Sorry I can't come with you." He was disgusted with himself the moment he said it. All that was left was to extend his hand to Tony and add, "I'll miss you. I'm sorry it turned out this way."

Tony accepted his hand. "Thank you for all you've done. Do you mind if I call you paesano? It means kin or countryman in Italian."

David blinked a couple of times, and his voice was tight when he replied. "I'm honored." Tony did his best to smile. "I'll be okay. I've made good money here, and somehow it will work out."

David drew a deep breath and returned the smile, even though he didn't feel like smiling. He didn't say anything more. He didn't trust his voice not to break. Instead, he reached out and hugged the man, whispering, "Good luck back in Imperial Valley."

Pete slapped the top of the car. "Well, we gotta go. Trains in Las Vegas don't wait, and if we don't get moving we'll be driving right into the sun. I hate that." With that Pete climbed into the driver's seat, and David stepped back so that Tony could get in on the passenger side. Pete started the engine and quickly popped the clutch, squealing the tires and leaving a streak of rubber on the road. David watched them until the turn at the end of the street, and then he started walking toward the administration building. But at the last moment he decided he ought to pop into the café and get a soda first.

OUT ON THE ROAD PETE made a left turn and quickly accelerated north onto the Boulder City Highway. They traveled in silence for about five minutes. Normally that would make Pete uncomfortable, but it didn't. His good temper didn't last long, though. "Oh, for cripes sake. What is this all about?" As he slowed down they saw a row of barricades and a detour sign across the road. "This will take us ten miles out of our way and across that old wooden bridge. I hate that bridge!"

"You sound like your brother and the swinging bridge."

Pete smiled. "If you're right, it means he's wearing off on me. Which means I'm doomed to a life of boredom." He cursed the sign again and made a right turn onto the gravel road that would act as a bypass to the main highway.

In the early days of the project, the old road had been used by construction crews, but the old bridge had been deemed unsafe for such heavy vehicles. As he gunned the car he looked into the rearview mirror and was cheered by the billowing trail of dust it kicked up behind them. Somehow he liked the world better knowing

Above: A trestle bridge at the Hoover Dam construction site

Left: Six Companies administration building in Boulder City

where he'd been and how fast he was going.

As he settled in he turned to Tony. "Can I ask you a personal question? You don't have to answer if you don't want to."

"I don't mind. What do you want to know?"

"Well, you've talked a lot about your farm, and you've lived like a miser while you're here to pay it off. Did you make it?"

Tony shook his head. "Not quite. I paid most of it down, but there's still money owing."

"But you've paid it down enough that you don't need to worry, right?"

Tony's answer was strained. "Not really. I've paid it down enough to where the bank would love to foreclose on it. The value of the land is going through the roof, and a lot of speculators have come into the valley expecting the dam to provide a steady supply of water. The rumor is that the bankers like to foreclose so their friends can buy at a discount."

Pete wished he hadn't asked. "I don't have much . . ."

"No, and even if you did, it's my problem. You've done enough."

Pete knew enough about Tony to realize that this conversation had hit a dead end. And even though he'd help if he could, he also knew that he wouldn't want anyone to bail him out if he were the one in Tony's position. He thought about trying to turn the conversation, but Tony was so quiet now that he decided it was better to drive along in silence—at least for a little while. The trip was hard enough without having to pretend to be cheerful.

As they came over a rise in the road, Pete was blinded by the sun in his eyes. He grabbed for the visor, but it was still hard to see. This came at a particularly inopportune time, since he was about to cross the narrow wooden bridge spanning a gulley that drained down toward Black Canyon. The gulley wasn't that wide, but it was deep, perhaps thirty or forty feet, and it wouldn't do to have a wheel slip off the bridge. Instinctively, he slowed down as he made the approach to the bridge. It was at the time of day that the afternoon shadows were the deepest, and with the sun directly in their eyes it was impossible to see anything except the portions of the road that were illuminated.

"I'm glad you're slowing down," said Tony, his mouth sounding dry.

"You don't need to soft-pedal it. I know this bridge is a wreck, and it's going to be hard with the sun. You watch out your side, and I'll keep it straight on mine." Slowly he started out onto the bridge, a simple structure with no side railings, only the supporting trestles under the platform. The parallel boards that formed the roadway clattered in a distinct *click-clack, click-clack* as a wheel hit the leading edge of one of the planks and then again as it passed over and off the other end.

As they reached the midpoint, Tony spoke up. "Is that another car at the end of the bridge?" Pete did his best to shield his eyes, but the sun was still squarely in front of him. Squinting even more, he saw a black shape up ahead.

"What's wrong with that idiot? Everybody knows this is a one-lane bridge, and we were clearly on it first." He slowed to a crawl, waiting for the other driver to back off the end of the bridge, but as he got a little closer, he saw that the car was stationery. "Oh, for crying out loud . . ."

"What are you going to do?"

"Do? I'm going to get out and go have a talk with that jerk." Pete shoved in the clutch, put the gears in neutral, and engaged the parking brake. "I'll be right back."

He climbed out of the car. Since he had perhaps eighteen inches of timber to stand on, he had to step back in order to get the door closed. Then he started forward, still shielding his eyes. Even with the sun he was able to see the driver's side door of the other car open and a figure step out. As the door closed, Pete stopped, startled by the fact that the hair on the back of his neck stood up.

"Who's there?" he called out. There was no reply. "Come on, I know you're there. Who is it, and why don't you back off so we can pass? We've got to get to Las Vegas." Still there was no reply.

He decided that he needed a little something in his hand just for safety, so he turned and started back to the car to grab the Billy club he kept under the seat. As he did, he heard Tony's door open.

"Pete, we've got trouble. Look behind us." He turned, the sun was now behind him, and he could now see clearly that another car had pulled its front wheels onto the bridge behind them. They were boxed in at both ends. "He was probably hiding in a shadow until we came up on the bridge," said Tony.

"We've got to be cool here. Do you have anything you can use in a fight besides your fists?"

"No, not that I can put my hands on quickly."

Pete took a deep breath. He wanted to get to that club, so he started moving faster toward the driver's side door. It was then that he heard the voice he'd expected. "That's far enough, Conroy. I want you to stop right where you are." Pete was smart enough to stop. Then, very slowly and deliberately, he turned.

"I don't suppose it's out of line to think that maybe that detour sign wasn't put up by the state transportation department?"

"Smart, Conroy. You always were." Pete winced at the sneer in Chick

Flemming's voice.

"So what are you going to do now?"

"We're going to do what we should have done two days ago. We're gonna turn your face into a pile of mush so I don't have to hear you talk again, and then we're going to kill us an Italian. That's what we're going to do."

Pete's breath quickened. He had to find out what the odds were. "A gun I suppose. That's the fast and easy way. You never did like a real fight."

"Oh, we've got a gun. We'll use it if we need it, but that really wouldn't be any fun, would it? No, we want to hear both of you squeal a bit."

"Leave Pete out of this. It's me you want."

Pete turned at the sound of Tony's voice but didn't say anything. It was a noble but absolutely meaningless gesture on his part. These two could never leave a witness alive. They knew that if they didn't kill Pete, he'd hunt them down and get them. So this was a life-and-death struggle, with no way out, and Chick and Marvin held the better cards.

"So how do you want to do it?" Pete asked. "Take us on one at a time? Free-for-all? Do we get to choose our weapons? Is it that kind of a duel?"

"Dueling is pretty stupid, isn't it? You don't really want to start a fight you don't know you can win, so here's what's going to happen. My buddy Marv over there wants to take Capelli out, and I agree. Marv's the one you guys laughed at through the years." Pete knew that Chick said this just to inflame Marvin. "So we're gonna start with me and you. Marvin's holding a gun on us. Assuming I'm winning the fight, he'll let it go until I've pounded you into a bloody pulp. If, by chance, you get the best of me, he'll just shoot you and I still win." Chick laughed. "Then I'll do the same thing for him while he takes out Capelli. That's the best way to play the game, don't you think?"

Pete's heart raced. He wanted time. He didn't know why, since there was no cavalry to rescue them. Still, each minute he wasn't fighting was a minute he was living. The problem was that no matter how much he squinted, he couldn't see into the sun, and his eyes had started to water. Still, he had to appear calm.

"About the weapons, then?"

"Fists. Good old-fashioned fists. Except that I get to use a knife as well." And with that Chick lurched forward unexpectedly, lunging at Pete. His switchblade flashed in the sunlight as it sank deep into Pete's left arm. Pete let out a howl as Chick withdrew the blade. Pete couldn't help but fall back as he grabbed his arm with his right hand.

He expected Chick to come at him again, but instead Chick laughed and said, "You see, this is how they fight bulls in Spain. They keep jabbing them with swords to disable their main muscles. The bull's too stupid to stop trying to attack them because he thinks he has a chance to live if he can just drive them off. I know you're not that stupid, but we think we did a good job of making it impossible for you to withdraw. So, just like the bull, all you can do is bellow. I'm right about how bullfights work, aren't I, Tony?" He laughed again.

Chick apparently thought he could pull this maneuver off a second time, but this time when he lunged, Pete was able to sidestep at the last moment so that Chick stumbled forward and down to a knee. Pete used the opportunity to kick him in the side with all the force he could muster. Chick growled and rolled onto his side with a grunt. "That wasn't nice, Conroy. Still, I'm the one who said I wanted a fight."

Pete braced for the next attack. Then he heard some kind of rustling from Tony's direction, followed by the concussion of a pistol and, for the first time, Marvin's irritating voice saying, "If you move, I'll shoot you dead."

"What should I do, Pete?"

"Stay where you are. You're no good to me dead. Just stay there!" There was a searing pain in Pete's arm, like it had been cut with a hot steak knife, but he did his best to concentrate on Chick and what was coming next.

Because Chick had fallen forward past Pete, the sun was now behind Pete and in Chick's eyes. Still, Chick could see his silhouette, and Chick was bigger, younger, and uninjured. Which was why he was able to lunge directly from his crouching position. Pete reached out to deflect the knife away from his torso but at the cost of having his right hand cut. Still, he was able to use the force of his response to bring his body into contact with Chick's, and he seized the opportunity to head butt Chick's face. Chick roared in pain, and Pete felt the warm wetness of his blood as it spurted out onto his face. Chick staggered backward, grabbing his nose with his hand.

"Now we're both bleeding, you moron," Pete shouted, and Chick reacted, as Pete hoped he would, by raising his head in anger at the provocation while simultaneously dropping his right hand as he staggered to regain his balance. Now it was Pete who lunged and, knowing that he didn't stand a chance of taking the blade from Chick since his own hand was too injured, he used the palm of his right hand to slam Chick's hand, successfully knocking the knife out of it. The knife dropped between the cracks in the planks, falling harmlessly into the gulley below.

"Now we're a little more even," said Pete, and he tackled Chick again. It wasn't the smartest thing to do, since Chick was much bigger, but with an injured arm and a bloody hand he simply couldn't come up with anything else.

"You are a royal pain, Conroy. I'll be glad when you're dead." Chick was now the one with the advantage, since Pete's momentum proved inadequate to overcome Chick's greater mass, and Pete actually recoiled from the collision, leaving him off balance. Chick was quick to take advantage of it. He roared forward, reached out, and grabbed hold of Pete's neck with his right hand, his left hand grabbing the hair on the side of Pete's scalp. It wasn't exactly what he planned, but Chick was flexible. When he realized that he had Pete's hair, he simply yanked it as hard as he could, which was excruciatingly painful to Pete as well as effective in spinning him around and up against Chick's body. The bigger man immediately wrapped both arms around Pete's arms and chest in a crushing body hug.

"Now we'll see how you do without air." Chick then deliberately allowed one of his arms to move up Pete's torso until the massive arm was wrapped firmly around Pete's throat. He began to squeeze as hard as he could while Pete struggled in vain to break free.

Pete tried to work his right arm free so that he could bring his elbow back against Chick's ribs, but no matter how much he struggled he couldn't do it. As he gasped for air, Pete started to feel his strength fade, and his legs started collapsing under him. Tears were running down his cheek as an involuntary reaction of his body. He'd passed out before, so he recognized the blackness that started to envelop him and he felt himself slumping in Chick's arms. That was when Chick brought the arm he wasn't using to choke Pete up and away from Pete's mostly lifeless body. Then, with a satisfied roar, he brought his elbow crashing down on Pete's head. Pete registered a blinding flash of light as his optic nerve was crunched by the blow, and it felt as if his left eye had literally exploded out of its socket. He started to crumple to the deck of the bridge, but there was nothing he could do to stop it. As he lay in a heap at Chick's feet, the blood pounding in his ears, he braced for the final kick, blow, or blast that would end it all.

Instead he heard the sound of Tony letting out a roar. He also heard the sound of something at the other end of the bridge. He tried to roll to his back to see what was happening, but his left eye was totally useless and there was blood in his right eye. What he did register was the blurred image of two bodies colliding above him and then disappearing from view. Then he heard the slap of a gun going off, followed quickly by a second blast. He assumed it was Marvin shooting Tony, and he knew it would be just a moment before he too was hit. His mind moved in what seemed slow motion—something people talked about that he'd never really understood. He was surprised that he didn't feel the bullet. At the very least, he thought, a person should feel the bullet.

"PETE! PETE! CAN YOU HEAR ME?"

As Pete became aware of the late afternoon sun on his face, the light caused his eyes to sting, and it felt as if his head was going to explode.

"Pete!" There was a desperate sound to the voice. He tried to place it.

"Peter Conroy! Wake up."

A picture of his father came into his mind. He'd always been a mellow person. Never one to get this excited. It couldn't be him.

"We've got to get him to the car. We've got to get back to Boulder City fast."

"Davy? Is that you?"

"Pete. Pete, come on boy, wake up. We need you right now."

Pete shook his head, but the shaking hurt bad, so he didn't try it again.

"Davy, what are you doing here? Marvin is supposed to be shooting me right now. I think you're messing up his plans again."

"You're being sarcastic. That can only be good."

He felt David gently wipe his eyes with a piece of cloth, probably his own shirttail.

"Can you open your eyes?" Pete struggled but was unable to do anything with his left eye. Reluctantly, his right eye opened a bit.

"I can't see much. Am I blind?"

"No. It's getting dark." The relief in David's voice was palpable. Pete struggled to sit up.

"It's all right. Don't try to sit up. Now that I know you're alive, it's all right. We've got time before we have to get you up. Just lay there and get your breath."

"My arm . . ."

"Has stopped bleeding. I've bandaged it."

"That's good . . ." Pete felt like he wanted to go to sleep. In fact, he started to let himself go. Then he sat bolt upright. At least that's what his mind intended for him to do. His body didn't agree, the argument causing him excruciating pain in both his head and his ribs. So, unable to get up, he opted for a groan.

"I said you can be quiet. I know it's not natural . . ."

"Tony! What about Tony? Where is he?"

There was silence and, with what light there was, he saw David wipe his arm across his face. "What is it, David? What's happened?"

"Oh, Pete . . ." And then, in a voice Pete had never heard before, he heard his brother say, "He's gone. He's gone."

Pete jerked in spite of the pain. "Gone! What do you mean gone? Dead? Did Marvin shoot him?"

He saw David shake his head. "He . . . he . . ." David struggled.

Pete mustered all the strength he had. "David! Just tell me."

David reared back and his voice toughened up. "When Tony heard us drive up in our car, he used the distraction to tackle Chick just as he was about to kill you, and the two of them went over the edge of the bridge."

Pete tried to assimilate the thought for a moment. Finally, he asked, "Is Tony dead?"

David, contrary to anything in Pete's previous experience with him, started sobbing. As the realization of what had occurred started to sink in, Pete's eyes started watering as well, which proved to be an extremely painful experience.

David tried to choke something out, but he couldn't talk. When he could get a word or two out, the only thing he could say was, "Oh, dear Lord."

Pete felt a lump in his throat as the reality of Tony's death washed across his consciousness, and the pain was just too much to bear. "But what happened?"

"I'll tell you what happened . . ." he heard an unfamiliar voice say. "What happened is that Chick Flemming crashed off the bridge and landed on his head some thirty feet below—hit it on a rather pointed rock, which split his skull right apart. Tony fell with him, and we think he landed in a way that broke his back."

"And he died." Pete struggled for breath. Then he rolled his head to look at David and whoever the other person was. "But he shouldn't have done it. He has a family. I'm all alone. I should have been the one!" He suppressed a sob.

David finally got control of his voice. "I think he knew what he was doing, Pete. I think we should respect that."

"What about Marvin?" Pete asked.

"Your brother probably broke his jaw. Lucky he's not a police officer or he'd be in trouble for beating up a prisoner. As it is, we've got him in hand-cuffs in the back of the police car."

Now Pete let the tears come, not caring how they burned. "So it was all in vain. All the times we stood up to them, and they still won."

CHAPTER 24
Reflections

Southern California Desert—November 1934

D avid Conroy looked out the window of the railroad train's club car and sighed. Compared to this place, Boise was a tropical oasis—and Boise was situated in a first-rate desert.

"My theory is that God started vegetating the West Coast up in Alaska and went a little overboard on trees in Washington and Oregon. By the time He got down here to Southern California, He'd run out of seed, which is why the place is so barren." Pete smiled at his own creativity. "Or godforsaken, if you want to carry the metaphor through."

David didn't laugh. "It's not a matter of seeds. It's water. You can shove anything you want into the ground down here, and if you give it water it will grow. That's why Tony's farm will do so well once we get the lower Colorado projects completed."

Pete rolled his eyes. "Thank you for being so literal. It was a joke, David."

David laid his head back against the train seat's headrest and closed his eyes. "Sorry. I just can't get past Tony's family. They were so dignified. They didn't cry or moan, which made me want to. I felt like the blubbering fool."

Pete nodded. It had been the most remarkable experience of his life.

"I mean, here we are delivering the worst news of their lives," David continued, "and all they could do was try to comfort us and tell us how grateful they were to us for standing by him."

Pete got a faraway look in his eyes. "I wish I could have talked to him before he died."

John Shurtliff had been the first to get to the bottom of the canyon because David had rushed past Marvin to help Pete. So it was Shurtliff, a deputy sheriff, who'd held Tony as the last moments of his life had passed away. He'd told them how Tony had managed to say that he had a life insurance policy his wife didn't know about and that it was enough to pay off the farm. Then he said, "Tell the Conroys thanks . . ." and those were his last words.

David looked at his brother. "Something else is bothering you."

Pete started to say something but hesitated.

"What is it?"

"It's just that Chick had won. Another blow and I was gone. Then Tony went and did that."

"And you should never diminish his sacrifice by feeling guilty, should you."

Pete took a turn looking out the window. "Easier said than done."

David nodded slightly.

"I was just so stupid . . ." Pete started to say this at exactly the same moment David tried to say, "If only we'd have left five minutes earlier. I just couldn't find anybody to go with me. I should have come alone."

When they unsorted what the other one was trying to say, Pete concluded with, "Right, and then they'd have blamed you for everything instead of having a deputy as an eyewitness who could save my life and vouch that it was Chick and Marvin who were the perpetrators. Great idea, you coming all by yourself."

In spite of his sage advice for David, Pete couldn't help but talk about how he should have known the detour was phony.

"And how, exactly, should you have known that?"

"Because that road hasn't been used in almost three years. Maybe that was a clue."

"Maybe I should have moved a little faster when I heard the people at the café saying that Chick and Marvin had left town bragging how they were going to even things up."

"Yes, but if you hadn't taken time to find out the details, you wouldn't have known where to go."

Of course, it was pointless to continue. They'd been over all this dozens of times. The fact that David and John had showed up at all was a minor miracle, one that had certainly saved Pete's life. The fact that John had shot Marvin's arm just in time to keep him from shooting Tony was a second miracle. Unfortunately, the miracles ran out for Tony and Chick.

At this point they'd made it up over the San Bernardino Mountains and were passing through a cactus desert on their way back to Las Vegas. "It's kind of amazing that those big old cactuses can store so much water, isn't it?"

Pete could always tell when things were getting too tense for David, because he changed the subject to talk about some obscure fact of nature or engineering. "Yes, it is amazing."

"I mean, have you ever felt their skins? It's like rattlesnake leather. Once water gets inside a cactus, there's no way it can get out. Not through evaporation, at least. The cactus just stores it until it needs it."

They rode in silence for a while, listening to the *click-clack* of the train's wheels crossing rail sections. Then Pete spoke. "I admire Paul. His mother's been away from Tony for three years now, so while life will be difficult for her, at least she is used to going it alone. But Paul has had his life changed almost overnight. He is now the man of the family. He has to take care of Tony's family, and his own, if he decides to get married. That's a lot of weight to put on such a young kid. Yet he never showed any emotion at all at the funeral."

David nodded. "I think that's what's expected of him. His father had very specific notions of how the family was supposed to get on, and that included Paul working on the farm. I don't think Paul was given much say in it. He's a loyal boy, so he'll do what's expected. Probably even more so now that he has to show honor to a father who's gone. He'll spend his whole life trying to redeem his father's and grandfather's dream."

"It must be hard to come out of that culture. When you or I get fed up, we quit. People may think we're jerks, but they never question our patriotism or our ability. But Tony felt it every day. That's why he worked harder than anyone else."

The train slowed as they came into a small siding. It was so hot outside, even in November, that the railroad company had to have watering towers at regular intervals across the desert. The train would have to pause for ten or fifteen minutes to take on water for the steam boiler.

Now it was Pete who changed the subject. "It will be dinner in a while. For some reason I just love train food. I don't know why it tastes better than regular food, but it does."

"It's because it's prepared by Negro cooks. They can do more in a four-by-eight-foot kitchen in a moving railroad car than most chefs could do at the Waldorf-Astoria." David added sarcastically, "And yet we can't possibly have them work with us on a construction job since they're so inferior."

Normally this would prompt some kind of response from Pete, but he just sat quietly, looking out at the small animals that darted in and around the train while it was stationary. Sometimes one of the cooks would throw out table scraps while they were parked at a siding, and the local animals enjoyed the feast.

"There are two other things that amaze me about all this," said David. "The first is that we had to bury Tony in Las Vegas on the day he died. I had no idea that Catholics discourage embalming."

"I didn't either. But I guess it's pretty common in Latin American countries."

David drifted off in thought. Which irritated Pete just a little bit, since it was David who seemed to want to talk so much. "And the second thing…?"

David looked out the window. "It's that I can't help but wonder if we caused all this."

Pete raised an eyebrow. "And how would we have caused it?"

"Because we stood up for him. We ran interference for him. Maybe if we'd have stayed out of it, he would have gone home like his friend Nick, and that would have been the end of that." David continued gazing out the window, unwilling to look at Pete.

Pete was having none of it. "Go ahead and feel guilty if you want, but Marvin and Chick are the bad guys here. We stood up for the man. It's that simple in my book."

David nodded but didn't pursue the matter. Finally, he turned to look at his brother. "It's interesting that he had that insurance. After all his struggles, he ended up reaching his goal. He left his family with the farm. It's not like he was rich or anything. He had to pay the premiums out of his earnings."

"I wouldn't be so sure that he wasn't rich. Our incomes may have been higher, but with all that land I'm pretty sure Tony was worth a lot more than either of us—maybe even both of us put together. Do you have any idea how much that place will be worth when water reaches it again? Paul will be a millionaire some day. None of the Conroy relatives can say that."

"It just seems so meaningless, his death." After saying this, David noticed Pete drumming his fingers on the armrest, a sure sign that he was getting stressed but one that Pete seldom noticed while he was doing it. "What is it?"

"What?" Pete seemed perplexed.

"You're doing that thing with your fingers. What are you thinking?"

Pete's Adam's apple bobbed. "I'm just thinking that I miss him." He rolled his fingers even more furiously. "Isn't that the stupidest thing? It's not like we were best friends or anything. I don't really have best friends."

"But we were all good friends." David tried to think of something else to say. He felt the same way and was just as powerless to explain it. Perhaps it had something to do with the thought that except for an accident of birth, the persecution Tony had experienced could have happened to them. Maybe that was why Chick and Marvin couldn't stand Tony. Their entire view of the world was dependent on an accident of birth that made them white, along with the irrational judgment that skin color was what created value in a human being. Tony's competence and quality gave lie to all that, and it shattered their illusions. So they'd killed him, and now Pete and David felt bad because it was such a crappy world. David decided that was right. But it also undersold Tony. He felt rotten because they'd killed a friend.

CHAPTER 25
Air Quality

Las Vegas—May 1935

Y ou're back from Boise, David? Good." David looked up at the unexpected arrival of Frank Crowe. "Morrison-Knudsen remember any of us?"

David laughed. "Are you kidding? They've refurbished the lobby in solid marble and named it in your honor. They have wheelbarrows filled with cash to carry the profits to the bank."

Crowe smiled. "Hardly fair, is it? They haven't had to drag their sorry butts through the cactus these past four years."

David braced for whatever was coming next, knowing that this would be the extent of Frank's chatter. "What can I do for you, boss?"

Crowe looked around. "Is there some place private where we can talk?"

"We can go for a walk. That's what I usually do when I need to get away from people."

"Good. Let's go." David didn't even have time to set his pencil down before Frank had put his hand under David's arm to lift him up and out of the chair.

Once they were outside, Crowe started with, "I heard you and your group play the other night. You're very good at the piano. When are you going to turn professional?"

David smiled. "Just after I become independently wealthy so I don't have to worry about earning an income."

Crowe nodded, obviously not really all that interested in David's hobby. "I guess you've heard that these infernal lawsuits are still pending. It's a nightmare for us—the only real blot on our record." David nodded, suddenly sick to his stomach. "Here's the thing, David. I know perfectly well where you stand on whether we were right or wrong. I have my own opinion about that. But I would like your opinion on something that has nothing to do with the carbon monoxide in the tunnels."

David raised an eyebrow. "I'll tell you what I can."

"It's about Woody. I know you've heard that he shot his mouth off in a bar before we won the second verdict, telling everybody that we'd paid off enough jurors to assure an acquittal."

David nodded. It was a small scandal that had grown in scope. Now everybody, including the national magazines and major newspapers, seemed to know about it, particularly since Six Companies had, indeed, won that case.

"Well, the thing is that their attorneys are open to a settlement. We've resisted so far, since we figure that even more lawsuits will follow if we settle. But with this meddling Roosevelt Administration in office, the thing just won't go away. They're all over us, even though it was the feds who put the pressure on us to get ahead of schedule and who stood by us when Nevada was trying to shut the mines down unless we converted to electrics and diesel. So what do you think we should do? Do we fight it, or do we settle?"

David sighed. "Now that we're finishing nearly two years ahead of schedule, I know what we should have done: we should have done the conversion. Whether we poisoned the men or not, we made a lot of them sick. But it's easy to look back. It wasn't so easy looking ahead."

"We'd have lost a whole year. If we hadn't pressed on, we'd have finished too late to divert before the flood season, and then we'd have had to sit around on our keisters for nearly a whole year."

David was silent. He couldn't count how many times he'd tried to get the company to hold off for that year, in spite of the cost. Now, if they settled, it would undoubtedly cost ten or twenty times as much as if they'd just converted to electric shovels and diesel trucks when they could. He'd been for conversion at the time, but no one had listened.

"I take it by your silence that you'd settle."

"I think it's going to be pretty hard to get a jury to be sympathetic to us this time around, particularly since everybody knows how much profit we've made by ending two years early. All the production bonuses went our way, and so it looks like a classic case of the big company winning at the expense of the little guy."

"Oh, for Pete's sake, David! We're two years ahead of schedule because of good planning and execution." Frank did nothing to hide his irritation, but David decided he didn't care.

"Well, so don't settle. You asked my opinion . . ."

Frank stopped. "Don't get mad, David. It wasn't your fault. You told us that we should convert, and we went against your advice. Then you and the others did what you could to keep the air moving. No one holds you accountable."

David bit his lip. "I understand. But I don't take comfort from that—not at your expense."

Crowe was silent.

"So what do you think we'll do?" David asked.

"We'll settle. The exasperating part of it is that most of these guys are just whiners. Now they think they should be compensated for it. I suspect that the ones who really deserve a settlement have too much pride to say anything. They're the real men. They're the real heroes of Boulder Dam."

David nodded his agreement. In some ways, he was one of them. After all, he continued to go in and out of the tunnels through the whole process, even with knowing how dangerous it was.

Frank turned and faced him directly. "Well, I thought you should know that this is what we're thinking. If we make the settlement, we're going to insist on nondisclosure so none of the plaintiffs can go out and shoot their mouths off about how much they got. For our part, we're not going to admit guilt. So you need to watch what you say. Even though you may have been right, you can never say it like that. Do you understand?"

"I understand. I'll abide by the settlement in full."

"You're a good man, David. Given any thought to what you'll do when this is over?"

"I've thought about staying on to work on the final construction and initial operation of the power plant. I've never done that before. I'd like to learn more about electricity and the distribution grid."

"Great idea. I'll put in a good word with Walker Young, if you want. He's kicking me out of here just as soon as the dam is finished."

"Thanks. I'd appreciate that."

"What about your brother? Does he have plans?"

"He's been talking about going to Oakland to work on the new bridge they're building to San Francisco. Or up to Bonneville in Washington State to work on the new dams across the Columbia."

"Either one sounds great." Frank acted as if he wanted to say more, and David had a sense of what was wrong. Here was a man who had spent his whole life getting ready to build the greatest dam in the world. Now it was almost finished. What did a person do after that?

Frank shifted uncomfortably, so David took the initiative. "Thanks for letting me know what's happening on the lawsuits. I think it's for the best."

Frank nodded, then extended his hand. "We'll probably see each other again, but we may not have a chance to talk. So good luck, and thanks for coming down to work with us. It probably would have been a lot worse in those tunnels without you."

David smiled. He couldn't help but feel good at hearing an affirmation like that from a man as great as Frank Crowe—the man who'd built the Boulder Dam.

When Frank had left, Woody Williams came up to him. "So, how did things go in Boise? Were you able to straighten things out?"

David shook his head. "It was certainly nothing I ever expected to have to deal with. The judge was savvy, and he figured out that it was really the boys that got their father into trouble. The prosecutor managed to find some witnesses who talked about how they'd bragged about taking their father to the cleaners, so he brought charges against them. It looks like they'll serve at least a year in the penitentiary. My father-in-law has to serve six weeks in the county jail, mostly to calm the local newspapers down. They've had a field day with this. Mary's devastated."

"Were they able to get any money back?"

"They'd spent all of it. The only way we could get her father off with such a lenient sentence was for Mary and me to take out a mortgage on our house to pay back his creditors. Those creeps ended up costing me nearly five thousand dollars. But I don't know what else we could have done." He shrugged his shoulders.

"It's a sorry world. No question about that." Woody studied David for a moment, which was a little uncomfortable. But David had been through enough uncomfortable moments in the past month that it really couldn't get to him anymore. So he just waited. Finally Woody said quietly, "Listen, I'm not supposed to say anything, but I think you could use some good news right now. Six Companies is holding off on what I'm about to tell you until after the dam is dedicated and after the furor in the press dies down over these

Finishing work on the Hoover Dam before its dedication.

gas poisoning suits, but the plan is to pay a bonus to those of us who have worked on the project through the whole thing. I happen to know that Frank made sure your name was on the bonus list. I don't know how much it is, but it may make a pretty good dent in that mortgage of yours."

David's eyes widened, "A bonus . . . ?"

"Shh. You can't let anyone else know about this. It's not public, and it's not for everybody. I've heard that Frank is going to get a spectacular bonus—something like two hundred and fifty thousand."

David's eyes went wide, and he was speechless for a moment. Then he said quietly, "Well, he deserves it. He made all the directors millionaires. I hope they do something good for him. And I hope they take care of you, too."

Woody nodded. "It's been a great job, hasn't it?"

David smiled. "Thanks for telling me. You don't know what a relief it is. No matter how much it is, the bonus will help. Thanks for putting up with all the distractions in my life."

"Like Frank said, you're a good man. I'm glad I got to work with you."

David accepted Woody's outstretched hand.

On the Rim of the Boulder Dam—*September 1, 1935*

> *THE SIX COMPANIES CONSORTIUM CORDIALLY invites you to a brief reception with the president of the United States, the Honorable Franklin D. Roosevelt, and other dignitaries immediately following the dedication of the Boulder Dam on September 30, 1935.*

Pete handed the engraved invitation back to David. "I had no idea you were that well connected, little brother. I'm sitting in the presence of royalty. You'll get to meet the president himself."

The two of them were standing on top of the completed Boulder Dam.

"I'm not that well connected. Six Companies decided they needed to have at least a smattering of the working engineers at the ceremony, so they held a drawing for two assistant engineers, and my name was picked. Still, I think it will be rather neat to meet President Roosevelt. If half of what people say about him is true, he's a remarkable man."

"He's certainly done wonders for the working stiff. We had absolutely no rights or protection under the Republicans. But since the New Deal showed up, Six Companies has had to treat us with a minimal degree of decency. It's been kind of fun to watch Frank Crowe squirm under some of their regulations."

"They told me I could have two guests with me. I sent a telegram to Jim, and he's agreed to make the trip down. I'm hoping you'll be the other one."

"Me? You're kidding. Frank Crowe would have a heart attack for fear that I'd stick my foot in my mouth."

"I promised him you'd be on your best behavior."

"You're serious? You would actually invite me to associate with the president of the United States, along with every dignitary from the Bureau of Reclamation and Six Companies? And you're not a little worried?"

"You're a grown-up. Besides, they should have some of the working men there. It was your labor that built the thing."

"I'm honored, David. I really am."

"Good, then I'll put your name on the list."

"No. Don't do it. The fact is that I'll probably be gone by then. All that's left for a guy like me to work on is the administration building at the foot of the dam, and, frankly, that's pretty boring. So I'll have to pass."

"Ah. Sorry to hear that."

"What about Mary?"

"Nah, she's got her hands full in Boise. Her father just got out of jail, and he's a mess. Her mother won't leave the house—I think you get the picture."

Pete nodded. "Sorry a ticket's got to go to waste."

"Maybe not. I'll see if Elizabeth is interested in coming down with Jim. She surprised me the last time she was here."

"I know. Who'd have thought she would be interested in engineering?" Pete laughed. "Poor Mary. She's put up with you and construction jobs all these years, and now her own daughter is thinking about getting her hands dirty."

The two of them stood gazing over the crest of the dam. "It really is something, isn't it?" said David.

Pete nodded but didn't reply. He stood for a time looking down at the water that had already backed up behind the dam. With the three diversion tunnels sealed, the water master was allowing just enough water through the fourth to keep the river flowing downstream from the dam. David told him it would take about six years to fill the reservoir. Once the water reached the level of the intake towers, the fourth tunnel would be sealed forever. From that point on, all the water would flow through the intake towers and penstock tunnels. Most of the water would be used to turn the water turbines that would power the electric generators. "From up here it looks like a little wading pool, doesn't it?"

David liked it when Pete turned philosophical. "Yes, but come back in six or seven years and it will be a massive lake backing up 115 miles into fingers that shoot off into the hundreds of chasms that feed into the main channel."

"So you got that job working on the power plant?"

David nodded. "Thanks to Frank and Walker Young of the bureau. Have you decided where you're going yet? Off to Oakland or to Oregon?"

"You know, I've been thinking about that—I know, me thinking about my future is an unexpected shock, so don't keel over and fall over the edge of the dam. But I've about decided to go back to visit Sean O'Donnell in New York City. I've never been to New York, and I feel like I ought to see it before I die. And Boulder City is so oppressively boring that I have some money left in the bank."

"I think that's a great idea. New York's a great city. I love the energy and drive of the place, with its millions of people crammed onto an island only twenty-two square miles. You really feel alive there."

"Well, Sean said I could stay as long as I want, and he thinks I could get a job on that bridge of his."

"I've been reading about it. It's more than just a bridge, at least anything that we think of as a bridge. Connecting three boroughs and spanning two rivers. It sounds interesting. Maybe I should quit the power plant and come join you."

Pete shook his head. "No. It's better for you to stay here. At least for a while."

David raised an eyebrow. "And why do you say that?"

"Keeps you closer to your family. Mary's not going to want to move, and New York is a long ways away."

"Well, it won't be the same without you. At least I can come visit wherever you wind up."

Pete grinned. "You're always welcome to flop at my place, or whoever's place I'm flopping at. I'm sure they won't mind. What's mine is yours, and what's theirs is yours too."

David smiled. "I'll miss you Pete . . ." He stepped forward and hugged his brother.

"I'll miss you too, little brother. I'll miss you too."

The matchless Hoover Dam is finished. The outlets to the overflow tunnels show in the foreground. It remains the Western Hemisphere's highest dam and Lake Mead the largest manmade reservoir in the United States.

EPILOGUE

Imperial Valley, Six Years Later—October 1941

Y ou're awfully quiet, Dad."

"It's been nearly seven years since I was last here."

"And you're nervous about seeing the Capelli family?"

"A little." He turned and looked out the window of the University of Southern California automobile Elizabeth was driving.

"It's amazing, isn't it?" she said tentatively. "So much green after all the godforsaken sand dunes that the All-American Canal passes through to bring water to this valley."

Mary spoke up. "It's a miracle. I've never seen such abundance. Beautiful crops as far as the eye can see, and they're green in October. Usually this is harvest time in the rest of the country."

"This is probably their sixth crop of the year," Elizabeth added.

"Sixth!" said Mary in astonishment.

David laughed. "Well, it's what the early promoters promised. All that this desert requires for it to blossom is a steady supply of water."

"And now you've given it to them," said Mary.

"Me? Me and the people who built the Parker and Imperial Dams, as well as the nearly three thousand miles of canals since we finished the dam. The Boulder Dam is certainly the keystone, but it's a much bigger project than just our piece."

Elizabeth loved the fact that her father never fully accepted a compliment without deflecting most of the credit.

"And Elizabeth," he added. "Elizabeth's work on the desilting works at Imperial Dam made the new All-American Canal possible. Now the river water flows without all the sediment that used to clog the early canals. This one will be serviceable for decades."

An early photo of the upstream side of the dam at night. The reservoir is near capacity as shown in the reflected lights of the Intake Towers in the dark waters of Lake Mead.

"I was an intern, Dad. I'm hardly responsible for the de-silting works."

David smiled. "You tell the story your way, I'll tell it my way."

Elizabeth looked forward and smiled. This tour had been her idea. After completing her internship at the Imperial Dam de-silting works at the lower end of the Colorado River the previous year, the Engineering Department at the University of Southern California in Los Angeles had asked her to drive over to complete a follow-up study as part of her master's thesis. Realizing she'd pass right through all the places her father's dam had been built to protect while making her way back to Los Angeles, she'd phoned David to ask if he wanted to go on a road trip with her. He said he would if Mary would come along, and so the two of them had taken a train to Yuma, Arizona, and now here they were.

"Have you heard anything from Jim and Carol?" she asked.

"Just that Jim is going a little crazy his last year in residency," said Mary. "The hours are terrible and I know it bothers him to have to borrow so much money for his education, even though your father has helped as much as he can."

"We both appreciate the help you've given us. Does he know where he's going to practice when he finishes medical school in Seattle?"

"I think he wants to go to Portland so they can be closer to Carol's family."

"Lucky grandparents," said David.

Elizabeth slowed down as they approached the crown of a small rise. As they came to the top, she gasped. "What is that?"

"The Salton Sea." The midday sun was reflecting on the blue surface of the lake in a dazzling display of sparkling water. "If it weren't for our work on the river, that lake you see up ahead would be five times the size and we'd be under a couple of hundred feet of water."

She laughed at the thought then added in a more serious tone, "Instead, it's now covered with half a million acres of fruit and vegetables and feed crops." Elizabeth cast a quick glance at David. "I had no idea. Even after all I've seen up and down the river, I had no idea just how terrible it would have been if we hadn't taken control of the Colorado."

"That's what it means to be an engineer. You change the very course of nature if that's what people decide they want to do, and you reclaim the land for use by human beings."

Before she could reply, he said, "Turn left, right there."

As they turned into the country lane, they started kicking up a small cloud of dust behind them. "It's going to be okay. I'm sure the Capellis are going to be happy to see you."

"I hope so. I hope it doesn't just stir up a bunch of old emotions, like I'm feeling right now."

Elizabeth was going to ask him about Tony Capelli, but the strain in his voice suggested it would be better not to.

"Do you see all those palm trees?" asked Mary. "As an Idaho girl, I always thought palm trees were exotic.

David nodded. "When I called Paul to see if we could stop by, he said that we could find them because of the palm trees. They raise them to sell in Los Angeles."

"Sell palm trees?" Mary sounded even more astonished.

"To movie stars, I guess." David cast a quick glance around the farm. To the left was a field of asparagus, to the right a small citrus grove next to the stand of cultured and date palm trees. It really was like a tropical oasis in what otherwise would be a sandy desert. As they made their way farther down the lane they saw a small stand of young shade trees surrounding a rather stately adobe house with a red Latin tile roof.

"They've built a new house! This is several times larger than the one Pete and I came to after Tony died.

"Look, they're all coming out to see us."

David strained to see the family. "They're waving," he said with relief.

Elizabeth cast a sideward glance and was pleased to see the expression on her father's face.

"Tony would have been so proud of what Paul has done here." Elizabeth couldn't help but agree. It was easily one of the most impressive farms in a very impressive valley. "And look at how fit and grown-up Paul looks," he added.

As she pulled the car into the yard, she noticed the strikingly handsome young man standing next to an older woman, probably his mother. Somewhat shorter than her father, she was drawn to his eyes—dark, penetrating eyes set inside the fine features of his face. Elizabeth was surprised to feel herself blush when his eyes happened to meet hers. Of course, David didn't notice—he was a man—but Mary did. But she didn't say anything. It would only embarrass Elizabeth if she did.

"I'm so glad we came . . ." said David. "I can't wait to catch up on everything that's happened."

Elizabeth turned and smiled at David, now confident that this was going to turn out to be a great day for the father she loved. David got out of the car and held the door for his wife and then came around to let Elizabeth out as Paul Capelli came up to the car.

NOTES

Boulder Dam or Hoover Dam? The correct answer is two times for each name. The project started out as the Boulder Canyon Project, with the dam's intended name being Boulder Dam or Boulder Canyon Dam. Then it was changed to Hoover Dam by the secretary of the interior when the award was given to Six Companies. It was changed back to Boulder Dam when the Roosevelt Administration came into power, and then finally, by an act of Congress, to Hoover Dam, which is its official name today. Travel to Nevada and Southern California, however, and you'll meet a fair number of people who still call it the Boulder Dam. Such is the nature of politics.

There are a number of characters in this fictional account who were real-live human beings, including Frank Crowe, superintendent of construction; Walker Young, onsite engineer for the Bureau of Reclamation; Woody Williams, Frank Crowe's assistant; and Bud Bodell, who worked both for the Six Companies Consortium and as a law enforcement officer in Boulder City. While one should always be cautious in creating fictional words for historical characters, the story would be less authentic without at least some interaction between these people. The key is to keep their dialog to a minimum and to make every effort to keep it authentic according the written accounts of their temperament and historical roles.

Readers have asked about the historical authenticity of the book. To the best of my ability I've kept all the technical and historical details about the project correct, and I was fortunate to have them reviewed by David Boyd, a current engineer with the Bureau of Reclamation who has worked for decades in the lower Colorado region sited at Hoover Dam. The stories of the gas suits are authentic, right down to the entrapment Bud Bodell set up to lure Ed Kraus into betraying his sworn testimony of the debilitating effects he supposedly suffered while working in the tunnels. While Kraus was a scoundrel, the working conditions in the tunnels were atrocious, and the decision to use gasoline-powered vehicles really was the biggest stain on an otherwise monumental achievement in completing the Hoover Dam.

Unfortunately, the racism discussed in the book was real, with a mere handful of black, Hispanic, and Native Americans employed at the dam site. Those who did get a job suffered great inconvenience and indignity at the hands of the federal officials who were required by law to hire them.

Since I was a child I have been fascinated by technology and have taken advantage of that interest in my writing, using it as an excuse to learn about a variety of marvelous machines, from battleships and torpedo boats to steam locomotives, airplanes, and pipe organs. Luckily for me, hundreds of thousands of readers have shared my interest. The risk one runs in learning how things work is that sometimes as the mystery disappears, the sense of awe and wonder fade as well. That is not the case with the Hoover Dam.

In fact, I have to say that my sense of wonderment has actually increased as I have studied this great engineering project, and I went into it as a fervent admirer of Hoover Dam. After learning as much as I could from indirect research, I enjoyed the opportunity of a lifetime when David Boyd was kind enough to take me on a personal tour of the dam and the powerhouse. Because I was so immersed in the history of the place, I almost felt as if it were 1935. Walking through some of the tunnels inside the dam, standing inches from the massive stainless-steel shaft of the turbine as it rotated the powerful generator above it, and strolling along the five-hundred thousand-pound steel drums of the Nevada Spillway while David told of the great flood of 1983 that sent hundreds of millions of gallons of water cascading down through the spillway tunnels (the only time in the seventy-five-year history of the dam the spillways were needed) was one of the great thrills of my lifetime. As I felt the August heat of Nevada blast the skin on my face while we walked around the dam site, I could imagine the physical challenge it posed for those working without air conditioning in the 1930s sun.

A few months later I drove over to the Imperial Dam to see for myself how the completed project is able to take silt out of the river and send good, clear water out into the Imperial Valley. I then drove along the All-American Canal as it parallels the Mexican border while passing through nothing but sand dunes as it angles its way toward the fertile but otherwise arid farms of Southern California. The trip helped complete the picture in my mind of how this amazing project changed the life of the Southwest forever, and my regard for the people who thought all of this through with early twentieth century technology grew even greater. The dam is simply awesome, and if you've never taken the chance to visit it, you should.

Perhaps the best summary of the impact the Hoover Dam has had on America was actually prophetic in nature. President Franklin D. Roosevelt's dedicatory speech captured the moment perfectly for the people who worked to build the dam. Read his words below and see how well you think his predictions have turned out with regard to this great American icon. I think it's the perfect way to summarize the story.

Left: Walker Young and Frank Crowe in 1935. Crowe nicknamed Young "Slow-Down," and Young nicknamed Crowe "Hurry-Up." The names describe their respective roles as chief government engineer versus superintendent of construction for Six Companies. It was their genius and organizational skills that allowed the Hoover Dam to be completed nearly three years ahead of schedule and under budget.

Below: I had the chance to peer out of the Arizona Valve House while touring the Hoover Dam in 2008. The jet valves are seldom used now, since the diversion of water through seventeen high-capacity electric generators can almost always absorb the full flow of the Colorado River.

FRANKLIN D. ROOSEVELT
PRESIDENT OF THE UNITED STATES
DEDICATING THE
BOULDER DAM - SEPT. 30, 1935

President Franklin D. Roosevelt dedicates theHoover Dam on September 30, 1935.

Franklin D. Roosevelt's Dedication Day Speech

September 30, 1935

Senator Pittman, Secretary Ickes, Governors of the Colorado's States, and especially you who have built Boulder Dam, this morning I came, I saw and I was conquered, as everyone would be who sees for the first time this great feat of mankind.

Ten years ago the place where we are gathered was an unpeopled, forbidding desert. In the bottom of a gloomy canyon, whose precipitous walls rose to a height of more than a thousand feet, flowed a turbulent, dangerous river. The mountains on either side of the canyon were difficult of access with neither road nor trail, and their rocks were protected by neither trees nor grass from the blazing heat of the sun. The site of Boulder City was a cactus-covered waste. The transformation wrought here in these years is a twentieth-century marvel.

We are here to celebrate the completion of the greatest dam in the world, rising 726 feet above the bed-rock of the river and altering the geography of a whole region; we are here to see the creation of the largest artificial lake in the world—115 miles long, holding enough water, for example, to cover the state of Connecticut to a depth of ten feet; and we are here to see nearing completion a power house which will contain the largest generators and turbines yet installed in this country, machinery that can continuously supply nearly two million horsepower of electric energy.

All these dimensions are superlative. They represent and embody the accumulated engineering knowledge and experience of centuries; and when we behold them it is fitting that we pay tribute to the genius of their designers. We recognize also the energy, resourcefulness and zeal of the builders, who, under the greatest physical obstacles, have pushed this work forward to completion two years in advance of the contract requirements. But especially, we express our gratitude to the thousands of workers who gave brain and brawn to this great work of construction.

Beautiful and great as this structure is, it must also be considered in its relationship to the agricultural and industrial development and in its contribution to the health and comfort of the people of America who live in the southwest.

To divert and distribute the water of an arid region, so that there shall be security of rights and efficiency in service, is one of the greatest problems of law and of administration to be found in any Government. The farms, the cities, the people who live along the many thousands of miles of this river and its tributaries—all of them depend upon the conservation, the regulation, and the equitable division of its ever-changing water supply.

What has been accomplished on the Colorado in working out such a scheme of distribution is inspiring to the whole country. Through the cooperation of the States whose people depend upon this river, and of the Federal Government which is concerned in the general welfare, there is being constructed a system of distributive works and of laws and practices which will insure to the millions of people who now dwell in this basin, and the millions of others who will come to dwell here in future generations, a just, safe, and permanent system of water rights. In devising these policies and the means for putting them into practice, the Bureau of Reclamation of the Federal Government has taken, and is destined to take in the future, a leading and helpful part. The bureau has been the instrument which gave effect to the legislation introduced in Congress by Senator Hiram Johnson and Congressman Phil Swing.

As an unregulated river, the Colorado added little of value to the region this dam serves. When in flood the river was a threatening torrent. In the dry months of the years it shrank to a trickling stream. For a generation the people of the Imperial Valley had lived in the shadow of disaster from this river which provided their livelihood, and which is the foundation of their hopes for themselves and their children. Every spring they awaited with dread the coming of a flood, and at the end of nearly every summer they feared a shortage of water would destroy their crops.

The gates of these great diversion tunnels were closed here at Boulder Dam last February. In June a great flood came down the river. It came roaring down the canyons of the Colorado, was caught and safely held behind Boulder Dam.

Last year a drought of unprecedented severity was visited upon the West. The watershed of this Colorado River did not escape. In July the canals of the Imperial Valley went dry. Crop losses in that Valley alone totaled $10,000,000 that summer. Had Boulder Dam been completed one year earlier, this loss would have been prevented, because the spring flood would have been stored to furnish a steady water supply for the long dry summer and fall.

Across the San Jacinto Mountains southwest of Boulder Dam, the cities of southern California are constructing an aqueduct to cost $220,000,000, which they have raised, for the purpose of carrying the regulated waters of the Colorado River to the Pacific Coast 259 miles away.

Across the desert and mountains to the west and south run great electric transmission lines by which factory motors, street and household light and irrigation pumps will be operated in Southern Arizona and California. Part of this power will be used in pumping the water through the aqueduct to supplement the domestic supplies of Los Angeles and surrounding cities.

Navigation of the river from Boulder Dam to the Grand Canyon has been made possible, a 115-mile stretch that has been traversed less than half a dozen times in history. An immense new park has been created for the enjoyment of all our people.

At what cost was this done? Boulder Dam and the power houses together cost a total of $108,000,000, all of which will be repaid with interest in fifty years under the contracts for sale of the power. Under these contracts, already completed, not only will the cost be repaid, but the way is opened for the provision of needed light and power to the consumer at reduced rates. In the expenditure of the price of Boulder Dam during the depression years work was provided for 4,000 men, most of them heads of families, and many thousands more were enabled to earn a livelihood through manufacture of materials and machinery.

And this is true in regard to the thousands of projects undertaken by the Federal Government, by the states and by the countries and municipalities in recent years. The overwhelming majority of them are of definite and permanent usefulness.

Throughout our national history we have had a great program of public improvements, and in these past two years all that we have done has been to accelerate that program. We know, too, that the reason for this speeding up was the need of giving relief to several million men and women whose earning capacity had been destroyed by the complexities and lack of thought of the economic system of the past generation.

No sensible person is foolish enough to draw hard and fast classifications as to usefulness or need. Obviously, for instance, this great Boulder Dam, warrants universal approval because it will prevent floods and flood damage, because it will irrigate thousands of acres of tillable land and because it will generate electricity to turn the wheels of many factories and illuminate countless homes.

But can we say that a five foot brushwood dam across the head waters of an arroyo, and costing only a millionth part of Boulder Dam, is an undesirable project or a waste of money? Can we say that the great brick high school, costing $2,000,000, is a useful expenditure but that a little wooden school house project, costing five or ten thousand dollars, is a wasteful extravagance? Is it fair to approve a huge city boulevard and, at the same time, disapprove the improvement of a muddy farm-to-market road?

While we do all of this, we give actual work to the unemployed and at the same time we add to the wealth of the Nation. These efforts meet with the approval of the people of the Nation.

In a little over two years this work has accomplished much. We have helped mankind by the works themselves, and, at the same time, we have created the necessary purchasing power to throw in the clutch to start the wheels of what we call private industry. Such expenditures on all of these works, great and small, flow out to many beneficiaries. They revive other and more remote industries and businesses. Money is put in circulation. Credit is expanded and the financial and industrial mechanism of America is stimulated to more and more activity.

Labor makes wealth. The use of materials makes wealth. To employ workers and material when private employment has failed is to translate into great national possessions the energy that otherwise would be wasted. Boulder Dam is a splendid symbol of that principle. The mighty waters of the Colorado were running unused to the sea. Today we translate them into a great national possession.

I might go further and suggest to you that use begets use. Such works as this serve as a means of making useful other national possessions. Vast deposits of precious metals are scattered within a short distance of where we stand today. They await the development of cheap power.

These great government power projects will affect not only the development of agriculture and industry and mining in the sections that they serve, but they will also prove useful yardsticks to measure the cost of power throughout the United States. It is my belief that the government should proceed to lay down the first yardstick from this great power plant in the form of a state power line, assisted in its financing by the government, and tapping the wonderful natural resources of Southern Nevada. Doubtless the same policy of financial assistance to State authorities can be followed in the development of Nevada's sister State, Arizona, on the other side of the river.

With it all, with work proceeding in every one of the more than three thousand counties in the United States, and of a vastly greater number of local division of government, the actual credit of government agencies is on a stronger and safer basis than at any time in the past six years. Many States have actually improved their financial position in the past two years. Municipal tax receipts are being paid when the taxes fall due, and tax arrearages are steadily declining.

It is a simple fact that government spending is already beginning to show definite signs of its effect on consumer spending; that the putting of people to work by the government has put other people to work through private employment, and that in two years and a half we have come to the point today where private industry must bear the principal responsibility of keeping the processes of greater employment moving forward with accelerated speed.

The people of the United States are proud of Boulder Dam. With the exception of the few who are narrow visioned, people everywhere on the Atlantic Seaboard, people in the Middle West and the Northwest, people in the South, must surely recognize that the national benefits which will be derived from the completion of this project will make themselves felt in every one of the forty-eight states. They know that poverty or distress in a community two thousand miles away may affect them, and equally that prosperity and higher standards of living across a whole continent will help them back home.

Today marks the official completion and dedication of the Boulder Dam, the first of four great government regional units. This is an engineering victory of the first order—another great achievement of American resourcefulness, American skill and determination.

That is why I have the right once more to congratulate you who have built Boulder Dam and on behalf of the Nation say to you, "Well done."

About the Author

Jerry Borrowman is a best-selling, award winning, author of ten published books—four co-authored biographies from World War II and Vietnam, including *A Distant Prayer* with Joseph Banks; *Three Against Hitler* with Rudi Wobbe, and *Beyond the Call of Duty* with Colonel Bernard Fisher, USAF retired, and recipient of the Medal of Honor. He co-authored *Stories From the Life of Porter Rockwell* an icon of the old west, with John W. Rockwell. He has also written six novels from World Wars I and II and the Great Depression, including *One Last Chance*. To learn more, visit www.jerryborrowman.com